LETTERS OF A PERUVIAN WOMAN

FRANÇOISE DE GRAFFIGNY was born Françoise d'Issembourg
d'Happoncourt in Nancy on 11 February 1695, the daughter of a
prosperous military officer at the court of Duke Leopold of Lorraine.
In 1712, she married François Huguet de Graffigny, chamberlain to
the duke. He was a drunkard, and the marriage was brutal and brief;
the couple were separated six years later, and he died in 172⁵ M⁻
de Graffigny spent the following years at the c⁻⁻
Lunéville, leading an active social a⁻⁻
sionate relationship with Leopolc
Antoine Devaux who would becom
the court in 1738, and spent two m⁻
Mme Du Châtelet. Her stay ended

accused of copying a canto of Voltaire⁻⁻⁻⁻⁻⁻⁻⁻⁻⁻⁻⁻⁻⁻⁻⁻⁻.
Moving to Paris in February 1739, ⁻⁻⁻⁻⁻⁻⁻⁻⁻ous financial
hardship, particularly after the death in 1740 of her protectress, the
duchesse de Richelieu; she spent the next two years living in a convent as companion to the princesse de Ligne and others. In
November 1742, she bought her own house, and became close to
Jeanne Quinault, former actress and co-founder of a popular salon
which attracted many major figures. Following the end of her relationship with Desmarest in 1743, she began to write, publishing two
short stories; an unwise investment, however, increased her financial
difficulties. The publication in 1747 of her novel *Letters of a Peruvian
Woman* (*Lettres d'une Péruvienne*) made her famous throughout
Europe, a fame confirmed three years later when her sentimental
comedy *Cénie* was a triumph at the Comédie-Française. She
acquired new and influential protectors, and opened her own salon
which became one of the most distinguished of its day. In 1758 her
play *The Daughter of Aristide* (*La Fille d'Aristide*) failed unexpect-
edly, and was hastily withdrawn; she died later that year.

JONATHAN MALLINSON is a lecturer in French at the University
of Oxford, and a Fellow of Trinity College. He is General Editor of
the monograph series *SVEC*, published by the Voltaire Foundation,
and has written extensively on French theatre and prose fiction of
the seventeenth and eighteenth centuries.

OXFORD WORLD'S CLASSICS

*For over 100 years Oxford World's Classics have brought
readers closer to the world's great literature. Now with over 700
titles—from the 4,000-year-old myths of Mesopotamia to the
twentieth century's greatest novels—the series makes available
lesser-known as well as celebrated writing.*

*The pocket-sized hardbacks of the early years contained
introductions by Virginia Woolf, T. S. Eliot, Graham Greene,
and other literary figures which enriched the experience of reading.
Today the series is recognized for its fine scholarship and
reliability in texts that span world literature, drama and poetry,
religion, philosophy, and politics. Each edition includes perceptive
commentary and essential background information to meet the
changing needs of readers.*

OXFORD WORLD'S CLASSICS

FRANÇOISE DE GRAFFIGNY

Letters of a
Peruvian Woman

Translated with an Introduction and Notes by
JONATHAN MALLINSON

OXFORD
UNIVERSITY PRESS

OXFORD

UNIVERSITY PRESS

Great Clarendon Street, Oxford OX2 6DP

Oxford University Press is a department of the University of Oxford.
It furthers the University's objective of excellence in research, scholarship,
and education by publishing worldwide in

Oxford New York

Auckland Cape Town Dar es Salaam Hong Kong Karachi
Kuala Lumpur Madrid Melbourne Mexico City Nairobi
New Delhi Shanghai Taipei Toronto

With offices in

Argentina Austria Brazil Chile Czech Republic France Greece
Guatemala Hungary Italy Japan Poland Portugal Singapore
South Korea Switzerland Thailand Turkey Ukraine Vietnam

Oxford is a registered trade mark of Oxford University Press
in the UK and in certain other countries

Published in the United States
by Oxford University Press Inc., New York

© Jonathan Mallinson 2009

The moral rights of the author have been asserted
Database right Oxford University Press (maker)

First published as an Oxford World's Classics paperback 2009

All rights reserved. No part of this publication may be reproduced,
stored in a retrieval system, or transmitted, in any form or by any means,
without the prior permission in writing of Oxford University Press,
or as expressly permitted by law, or under terms agreed with the appropriate
reprographics rights organization. Enquiries concerning reproduction
outside the scope of the above should be sent to the Rights Department,
Oxford University Press, at the address above

You must not circulate this book in any other binding or cover
and you must impose the same condition on any acquirer

British Library Cataloguing in Publication Data

Data available

Library of Congress Cataloging-in-Publication Data

Data available

Typeset by Cepha Imaging Private Ltd., Bangalore, India
Printed in Great Britain by
Clays Ltd., Elcograf S.p.A.

ISBN 978–0–19–920817–3

10

CONTENTS

ACKNOWLEDGEMENTS

I am greatly indebted to Judith Luna for welcoming this novel into Oxford World's Classics, and for her astute and sympathetic editorial guidance. In preparing this volume, I have benefited much from conversations with a number of colleagues and friends: David Coward, Nathalie Ferrand, Russell Goulbourne, Christina Ionescu, Andrew Kahn, and Melissa Percival. I should like particularly to thank Nicholas Cronk and English Showalter for their many invaluable comments on the manuscript, and Lyn Roberts for her encouragement, advice, and numerous practical suggestions throughout the final stages. Finally, I express heart-felt gratitude to my wife Margaret, who has been with this project from the very beginning and whose help and support have been, as always, tireless, unconditional, and decisive. Any remaining errors or infelicities are mine, or Zilia's.

INTRODUCTION

Readers who do not wish to learn details of the plot may prefer to treat the Introduction as an Afterword.

The *Letters of a Peruvian Woman* (*Lettres d'une Péruvienne*) was one of the great European best-sellers of the eighteenth century. It made its author, Françoise de Graffigny, at the time of its publication in 1747 a relatively unknown and impecunious widow, one of the most celebrated writers, male or female, in Europe. There were at least fifty editions or reprints of the novel between its first publication and the end of the century, and forty editions or reprints of translations into English, German, Italian, Spanish, and Russian over the same period. Fréron, in his review of the novel published in 1749, exclaimed: 'Madame de G*** has added to the glory of her sex and of her nation with her *Letters of a Peruvian Woman*', and in 1751 the abbé Prévost dedicated his translation of Richardson's *Clarissa* to her, the 'illustrious author of the *Letters of a Peruvian Woman*'. For all this considerable fame, though, the text and the author disappeared from the canon and indeed from literary history for nearly 150 years. Sainte-Beuve, objecting in 1852 to what he perceived as the novel's dangerously socialist ideas, dismissed the text as not worth reading.

In the last thirty years of the twentieth century, however, the *Letters of a Peruvian Woman* enjoyed a renewal of attention almost as exceptional as its original celebration. Between 1975 and 2000 it inspired at least eighty journal articles, and four editions, and this popularity has continued to the present day. It has been translated again into different European languages, and is a prescribed text on many university courses in French, post-colonial, or women's studies. And with the rediscovery of the text has come the rediscovery of the author, as dramatist, salon hostess, and most particularly as letter writer; her surviving output of some 2,500 letters, currently being published by the Voltaire

Foundation in a projected edition of fifteen volumes, provides a special insight into the intellectual and cultural world of the mid-eighteenth century, besides being a unique, intimate record of the author's day-to-day life.

A Dramatic Life

The life of Françoise de Graffigny reads like the plot of a novel, or even of a fairy tale: born into a family of the minor provincial nobility, she was the victim of a brutal husband, lost three children in their infancy, came impoverished and vulnerable to Paris where she struggled to find financial security. Gradually establishing herself in the cultural life of the capital, she wrote two hugely successful works, a novel and a play, and for a while enjoyed a reputation in Europe second to none, only to sink again into obscurity after her death. Her life was in many ways the life of a single woman who struggled to survive by her pen.

She was born in 1695 to François d'Happoncourt, a military officer in the service of Duke Leopold of Lorraine, and Marguerite Callot, great-niece of the engraver Jacques Callot. Her marriage to François Huguet de Graffigny in 1712 was short and disastrous. Her husband, although he came from a prosperous and respectable family, was a drunkard and a spendthrift, and she was to obtain a legal separation from him on the grounds of brutality; he died in 1725. By 1733, she had lost both her father and mother, and had no obvious means of financial support. Living at the court of Lorraine at Lunéville, she led an active cultural life, first meeting Voltaire there who described her later as 'that delightful and beautiful widow'. She began a relationship with Léopold Desmarest, son of the court composer Henry Desmarest, and became a close friend of François-Antoine Devaux, a law student seventeen years her junior.

Following the dispersal of the court in the late 1730s, she moved to Paris, first staying for ten weeks with Voltaire and Mme Du Châtelet at their estate in Cirey. After a period of financial hardship following the unexpected death of her protectress, the duchesse de Richelieu, she began to play an increasingly active role in the cultural life of Paris and the literary salons. She had already become a keen and acute letter writer, establishing a correspondence with Devaux after she had left the Lorraine court which would continue until the end of her life. As a member of the informal salon presided over by the retired actress Jeanne Quinault and the comte de Caylus, she wrote two short stories for the group's collaborative volumes: the *Spanish Novella*, published in 1745 in the *Gentlemen's Collection* (*Recueil de ces Messieurs*), and, the following year, a fairy tale, *Princess Azerolle*. The success of these works reawakened her literary ambitions, and led her to try to profit from her talent.

The nature, education and social role of women had become a subject of widespread discussion and debate. Poullain de La Barre's treatise of 1673 *On the Equality of the Two Sexes* had argued for the fundamental equality of the two sexes, and Fénelon and the marquise de Lambert had published important reflections on the education of women.[1] Few, however, would credit women with the capacity for serious intellectual activity, in spite of the achievements of such as Mme Dacier, author of a ground-breaking translation of Homer, or Mme Du Châtelet, translator and author of a commentary on Newton's *Principia mathematica*. Women's writing was most commonly associated with, and limited to, letters, moral or educational works, or novels of love, widely seen to be their unique province; writing of a more critical kind largely remained the province of men.

One of the most prominent debates of the day concerned the popularity of luxury in the emerging consumer society, a phenomenon associated with what was frequently depicted as a cult of appearances. For some writers, not least Voltaire, luxury was a sign of social progress and prosperity, and could be defended on both cultural and economic grounds; for others, though, it suggested a greater moral danger, an attitude given powerful expression in Fénelon's moral novel *Télémaque*, and later, most famously, in Rousseau's *Discourse on the Sciences and the Arts*, which

---

[1] Extracts from the marquise de Lambert's *Advice from a Mother to her Daughter* are to be found in Appendix 4.

appeared shortly before the second edition of Graffigny's *Letters of a Peruvian Woman*.

The novel which would make her name displayed considerable thematic and aesthetic originality as she moved away from the kind of writing normally associated with women, and her success at the Comédie-Française in 1750 with her sentimental comedy *Cénie* was all the more remarkable as very few women dramatists succeeded even in having a play accepted by that theatre. But despite enjoying a Europe-wide reputation, her life was a constant struggle for independence and security. Marriage to a profligate husband, the death of her protectress, the relatively modest rewards of literary fame, and the expense of running her salon, all took their toll. She never truly found financial stability; at her death, she left 42,000 *livres* of debt which the assets in her estate barely covered.

A Tale of Exotic Love

What made this novel, appearing anonymously and with an ironic place of publication, *A Peine* (i.e. *with difficulty*), such an immediate success?

It appealed first on account of its exotic setting and subject matter: the Inca civilization of Peru. Works such as Galland's translation of the *Thousand and One Nights* (1704–16), Montesquieu's *Persian Letters* (*Lettres persanes*) (1721), or Prévost's *Tale of a Modern Greek Woman* (*Histoire d'une Grècque moderne*) (1740) had inspired and exploited an interest in the Middle East, while the western world, not least the Americas, had been successfully evoked in the final scenes of Prévost's popular novel *Manon Lescaut* (1732). Peru exerted a particular fascination on French readers. The *Royal Commentaries of the Incas* (*Comentarios reales de los incas*) of Garcilaso de la Vega were first published between 1609 and 1616, and still widely read over a century later. Garcilaso was of mixed Inca and Spanish descent; his mother was a granddaughter of the Inca Huayna Capac, who established Quito as a northern stronghold for the empire, and his father a conquistador. His *Royal Commentaries*, written in Spain, combined a detailed history of the Inca empire, an evocation of its culture and way of life, and an account of the Spanish conquest. It was first translated into French in 1633, and remained in print long into the eighteenth century, republished no fewer than five times in the forty years prior to the appearance of Graffigny's novel; a second French translation was published in 1744. This interest in Peru was exploited and sustained by two popular works of the 1730s: Rameau's *ballet héroïque The Gallant Indies* (*Les Indes galantes*) (1735), composed to a libretto by Louis Fuzelier, and whose most acclaimed interlude evoked Inca festivals and represented the Peruvian heroine's love for a Spanish officer; and one of Voltaire's most successful tragedies, *Alzire* (1736), a tale of cultural conflict which depicts the love of two Incas, threatened by the politically powerful, but morally inferior Spanish colonizers.

Unlike these works, though, which in different ways romanticized Inca culture, Graffigny provided a much more detailed evocation of the nation, drawing material from Garcilaso's work, and from other contemporary accounts.[2] Her text, both the novel itself and the *Historical Introduction* she added to the second edition of 1752, reveals a much closer reading of historical sources. She goes out of her way to use Inca terms such as *Cacique*, *Pallas*, *Amautas*, *Cucipata*, *Yalpor*, highlighted for her readers in italic; there are meticulous accounts of Inca artwork, clearly inspired by descriptions in Garcilaso, and of their beliefs and social customs; and most significant of all, she incorporates into the very conception of her narrative the use of *quipus*, knotted cords which were the Incas' nearest equivalent to writing. But like several contemporaries, not least Voltaire in *Alzire*, she attributes to the Incas values expressed in other writings of the Enlightenment, a morality based on reason and natural law which contrasts both with the savagery and greed of the Spanish at the time of the conquest, and with the hypocrisy and display of contemporary France.

In addition to this, the novel appealed to its first readers on account of its plot, a tale of love and separation narrated in a

[2] Extracts from a seventeenth-century English translation of the *Royal Commentaries* are to be found in Appendix 1.

sequence of letters. The epistolary laments of distressed heroines had a long tradition, from Ovid's *Heroïdes* extending through the letters of Abelard and Heloise to Guilleragues's *Portuguese Letters* (1669) and the *Letters of the Marquise de M**** (1732) of Crébillon fils. Such texts helped to establish a model for many fictional heroines, defined by their vulnerability to love, but also by their ability to give expression to their grief, longing, or disillusionment. Guilleragues's influential novel inaugurated and popularized a style which would long be associated with women's writing: the very opposite of controlled and measured rhetoric, it was characterized by its apparent randomness of composition and expression, uncontrolled by traditional syntax. So persuasive was this style of writing that the *Portuguese Letters* were long believed to be the translation of authentic letters written by a Portuguese nun to her faithless lover. Graffigny's novel clearly picks up several of these characteristics, and profits from the popularity of this tradition. Zilia is separated from her Inca lover, Aza, at the very start of the novel, a victim of the brutal conquest of her country; her letters frequently convey the feelings of lament, longing, and suicidal despair which had characterized many other heroines. This traditional identity is further confirmed in later letters, as she becomes the object of attention from a second lover, Déterville, the French officer who rescues her from her Spanish abductors and takes her back to France. Zilia's response to these two suitors is one of the central preoccupations of the text.

Exploring Cultural Difference

There is a third tradition to which Graffigny's text alludes, one which was particularly popular in the early decades of the eighteenth century: collections of critical observations in epistolary form, purportedly written by foreign visitors to France. Montesquieu's *Persian Letters* provided a model for such texts, and inspired many imitations, ostensibly involving travellers from different parts of the world (*Chinese Letters, Jewish Letters, Turkish Letters*). Such works juxtapose the familiar world of the reader and the unfamiliar perspective of the naive outsider. This can

lead to irony either at the expense of travellers who do not understand, or cannot adequately express, customs which seem evident
and natural to a French reader; or, conversely, at the expense of
the French, whose customs are scrutinized with fresh eyes, and
whose absurdity is unsparingly exposed. Graffigny's novel, both
in its form and subject matter, situates itself in this tradition, and
the heroine has many experiences and selects as targets numerous
aspects of French society similar to those highlighted by other
foreign travellers.

Zilia's innocence and inexperience are certainly at the forefront
of attention in the early letters. We follow her on a journey of
discovery, as she encounters new objects such as telescopes or
mirrors, carriages or ships, firearms, fountains, and fireworks.
Many such moments can only be conveyed through approximate
circumlocution, as the heroine struggles both to understand and
express the new world she is discovering, and the reader is invited
to translate her imperfect perceptions into his own language,
finding the familiar objects behind the elaborate descriptions we
are given. To identify the heroine as naive and ignorant is one of
the pleasures offered to the reader of the text.

In parallel with this, though, Graffigny, like Montesquieu and
other Enlightenment writers, subjects European customs to the
critical scrutiny of nature and reason. If the Spanish conquistadors are accused of being brutal in the opening letter, so too are
the French in their laws of primogeniture (letter 19); and Zilia
exposes the 'inconsistency' of several French customs: the way
girls are educated, the unjust and uneven distribution of wealth,
or the discrepancy between the morals they profess and the customs they follow. In this context, Graffigny's choice of Peru as the
origin of her foreign visitor is not without significance: this is not
just any critical outsider, but one whose nation was widely associated in the eighteenth century with moral superiority, as the
author reminds the reader in her Foreword. This allows for a
particularly stark and uncompromising opposition of Peruvian
authenticity to French pretence. The French obsession with
luxury (or its appearance) is seen to be all the more absurd, both
economically and morally, when contrasted with the genuine

abundance of the Incas; and French social behaviour seems even more empty when set against the principles of a nation where lying is unknown. The Inca is represented as one for whom words mean what they appear to mean, a moral and linguistic probity quite absent in France, where customs are based on a series of pointless rituals and meaningless language.

But Graffigny's novel is not simply the vehicle for outspoken criticism of the French. It also deals with problems of cultural difference, and the heroine's experience as an outsider in France is as significant as her comments on what she sees. Europeans are clearly seen to have difficulties dealing with otherness. The Spanish conquistadors represent one extreme form of this, and the indictment of their conquest of Peru exposes a greed and brutality which underlines their moral inferiority to the Incas they conquer. But Zilia's ordeals in the seemingly civilized France of the seemingly civilized eighteenth century are represented as not so very different; the reader witnesses in the French the same problems of understanding what is different, the same reduction of the outsider to a figure of curiosity, the same desire for appropriation. Such attitudes are sketched out in the Foreword, and represented at various moments in the text: the haughty treatment of the heroine at the social gathering (letter 11), the condescending attitude of Déterville's mother (letter 13), the imperious desire to convert her to Christianity (letter 22), but also, implicitly, in Déterville's own desire to transform the Inca heroine into a French lady of his own dreams, as he dictates words for her to learn and imitate (letter 9), or dresses her in the clothes of his own nation (letter 12).

Significantly, though, Graffigny does not simply idealize Peru or vilify France, and her exploration of these problems of difference extends further than a facile and reductive opposition of right and wrong. Zilia is given her own specific cultural identity which feeds into her attitudes; she is not just a disembodied critic. Indeed, like the French, she is seen to judge everything with reference to her own values, and she has the same kind of disparaging critical vocabulary, prompt to describe the French as savage, or barbarous, or superstitious. Like the French, too, her instinct is to see everything about her own culture as superior: she finds it inconceivable that the French might have more humanity than the Incas (letter 16), she considers their system of governance quite inadequate simply because it differs from that of the Incas (letter 20), and when she discusses education, difference is equated with ignorance (letter 34). For all its seemingly stark oppositions, the text also implies parallels between observer and observed; judgements cannot be seen as categorical, nor values as unequivocally absolute.

What is more, Zilia realizes in the course of the novel the limits of her own culture. In letter 12, she contrasts the restricted world of the Sun Temple with the beauties of nature which she only now discovers; in letter 18, she recognizes that her world is not the centre of the universe; and in letter 2, she observes in her own country a humiliating form of education not so different, it would seem, from what she condemns in France. Peru does not just serve to criticize France; her travels to France occasion a reassessment of Peru.

The novel brings together two very distinct structures: the opposition of naive foreigner and sophisticated European, and that of enlightened outsider and defective France. But there is no clear hierarchization of values, no overriding resolution of these two structures. Instead, Graffigny retains in a suggestive tension the oppositions of nature and society, the absolute and the relative, Peru and France.

A Feminist Novel?

What is particularly striking about this novel, and what has assured its popularity today, is its comments on women. In several places, and most notably in letter 34, Zilia reflects extensively and uncompromisingly on the inadequate education given to girls, on the reductive gender stereotyping which lies behind it, and on the duality of moral standards which distinguish men and women. Graffigny was not the first to make such criticisms of prevalent social practices, of course; the writings of the marquise de Lambert, for instance, cover much similar ground. But what is remarkable about this novel is not the fact that such observations are made, it is the way the author incorporates them into the very structure of her text.

The _Letters of a Peruvian Woman_ is significantly different from other collections of critical letters in that this text is the first where the observing character is a woman. But Graffigny has not simply undertaken an exercise in substitution, and if she rewrites, even 'feminizes' a tradition epitomized by the _Persian Letters_, this process is not limited to changing the gender of the central character, or grafting onto the stereotypical role of independent commentator traditional attributes of the fictional heroine: vulnerable captive and object of desire. Her transformation of pre-existing forms is more radical and more creative, both thematically and aesthetically.

In this novel, Graffigny brings together and transcends the two distinct literary traditions to which her text alludes: the tale of love and the critical anthology. Unlike the protagonists of the _Persian Letters_ and other similar works, Zilia is not a fully formed commentator from the outset; we witness, instead, her coming to maturity as a critic, a process which develops alongside her gradual mastery of the French language. Her letters deal less and less with her feelings, and more and more with her evaluation of the world around her. She begins the novel naive and uncertain, she will finish it experienced and confident; from an object of desire, she gradually evolves as an intellectual. At this level, what Zilia says is inseparable from her evolution as a character, and her criticisms reveal as much about her development as a new kind of heroine, intelligent and authoritative, as they do about the nation she observes. This new conception of the heroine is reflected too in Graffigny's innovations at the level of structure. Works written in the wake of the _Persian Letters_ were effectively anthologies, infinitely extensible; published over a long period, and often with an index, they implied a mode of reading driven as much by theme, or episode, as by linear progression. Montesquieu would suggest in his own preface that more letters could be added to his text, if it proved popular; a similar conception characterized Voltaire's _Letters Concerning the English Nation_, where each letter has its own thematic title in the manner of periodicals at this time. Graffigny's text, however, is a much more coherent fusion of narrative and reflection, harmonizing, in ways that Montesquieu and his imitators might never have imagined or intended, the satirical and the fictional, the observer and the character.

What is more, the text brings together in a quite unique way the heroine's double identity as foreigner and woman. The structuring narrative which depicts the experiences of a Peruvian abroad coincides with one of its principal thematic strands, the plight of the woman in French society. Zilia's painful experiences of European arrogance and aggression, be it the physical, colonizing savagery of the Spanish in Peru, or the more sophisticated, but no less manipulative and invasive treatment by the French in France, are set in parallel with the fate of women within French society as a whole. The heroine's ordeal as a foreigner abroad, regarded with a mixture of fascination and scorn, and struggling to find a means of expressing herself, enacts her observations on the plight of women, who are turned into decorative objects and denied the kind of education which enables them to be what they truly are. As a result, the text offers the reader the possibility of a double reading: the plight of Zilia the Peruvian echoes that of Zilia the woman, the one becomes a metaphor of the other. Her account of the treatment she receives on board the ship, where she is the object of both adoration and constraint, acts as a proleptic image of that paradoxical attitude of respect and contempt which she evokes in letter 34; her struggle to learn French dramatizes the struggle of women to find a voice; and if Graffigny notes in the Foreword that Europeans denigrate Peruvians to the point of denying that they have a soul, the same attitude is implicit in the male treatment of women as recorded in letter 34. Zilia does not simply observe from a detached standpoint what it is like to be a woman in France, she experiences it for herself. As the marquise de Lambert would suggest in her *Advice from a Mother to her Daughter*, women in society are treated very much as a 'species apart'. This double function is implicit in the French title of the work, but it has to be brought out more explicitly in an English translation: *Péruvienne* indicates both nationality and gender, the two are interdependent, inseparable. Graffigny's exploitation of this duality is one of the novel's most striking originalities.

But if Zilia is unique as a heroine because she appropriates a critical function traditionally associated only with heroes, who have the freedom to travel, the intelligence to observe, the means to express themselves, equally unique is Françoise de Graffigny herself who writes the kind of text which had never before been written by a woman. Her novel has more than just a sentimental plot, and she goes out of her way to present the reader with her credentials as a thinker. She claims for her work the intellectual seriousness of epistolary satires, reworking the model of Montesquieu's *Persian Letters* to which she alludes explicitly in her *Foreword*; the preface takes the form of a *Historical Introduction* which focuses not on the characters or the plot, but on the cultural background to the narrative, and underlines the author's thorough use of sources; and it is one of the rare eighteenth-century novels to have footnotes, a form of textual writing which allies the novel to the works of scholarship with which Graffigny seeks to be associated.

This is a novel, then, which is in the words of the *Foreword* a 'singular work'. It does not simply imitate different literary traditions, encroaching on the world of male writers, it goes beyond them. Indeed, Graffigny creates something truly original, a novel which brings together two forms of discourse, the sentimental and the critical, in ways which few writers, male or female, succeed in doing in the eighteenth century.

Challenging the Reader

Such innovations underlie a text which is as provocative, even shocking, as it is entertaining. It does not follow traditional patterns, but consciously questions and subverts the reader's expectations, both moral and aesthetic.

This challenging quality is particularly evident in the way the novel ends: Zilia does not marry either Aza who has converted to Christianity and become engaged to a Spanish lady, or Déterville who continues to love her. This absence of a marriage sets the

Letters of a Peruvian Woman apart from the traditional sentimental novel. What closes the text is not the consecration of the heroine as an object of love, but the realization of her sense of self.

This emotional autonomy is matched by an intellectual one, and extends crucially to her attitude to Christianity. Zilia is quite outspoken on this subject, not least in letter 19, where she comments on the mental stagnation of those who live in convents. And as she develops her own critical independence, she becomes even more daring; in letter 21, which appears to suggest her sympathy for Christianity, she comments nevertheless that its myths are not 'any more incredible' than those of her own culture. Later passages reflect her embittered view that this religion is the cause of her losing Aza because it does not permit the marriage of close relatives, unlike Inca beliefs. Her observations, however, are not simply those of a distressed lover. They have a more radical force and bring out the moral ambiguity of a religion whose principles authorize the transgression of secular, or natural, virtues, such as candour or integrity. Aza's infidelity is represented as not simply that of a lover but also that of a moral guide; his conversion is not an inspiration, but a betrayal.

The fact that Zilia does not ultimately convert provocatively undermines the motif which would have given the ending of this novel a more traditional harmony. The authority of Christianity would justify the 'infidelity' of the converted Aza, authorize Déterville's courtship of Zilia, and suggest the primacy of European moral values, enabling the heroine's complete integration into the French way of life. But a conversion would also have confirmed certain assumptions which Graffigny consciously draws into question: that fictional heroines (and women) are ultimately defined by their feelings, that female-authored novels are ultimately about love, and that European values have the ultimate authority. Instead of converting Zilia to Christianity, Graffigny gives her heroine an emphatic realization of her own identity, strikingly evident in her appreciation of the natural world which, significantly, does not focus on the Creator, but on the feeling of existence it inspires in the observer. The final letter sees Zilia in full control, with a sense of self no longer defined with respect to her emotions, or indeed to a man. Instead of being the object of Déterville's desire, it is she who controls his feelings, and then metaphorically, even literally, takes control of her own life, as she translates into French the *quipus*, which depict her at her most emotionally and intellectually dependent.

The impact of this ending is all the greater for its being quite unexpected. Graffigny exploits and subverts the reader's expectations about the kind of novel this is, and how it will end. Nothing could appear to be more traditional than the opening letters, which have all the hallmarks of a sentimental novel: a heroine defined by her love, lamenting her suffering. What is more, the novelist scatters her narrative with signs of a conventional ending in marriage, providing the reader with the possibility of two equally plausible (because precedented) partners for the heroine: Aza and Déterville. Aza is Zilia's one love, destined for her by their shared culture, referred to almost ritualistically as 'my dearest Aza', the source of her self-definition. The very structure of the novel seems to promise this outcome, as the tale of separation edges gradually towards the reunion which will take place at the end of letter 36. And it is an outcome authorized by recent precedent: Voltaire's *Alzire* had united two Peruvian lovers in its ending, and Graffigny explicitly, and approvingly, alludes to the tragedy in the *Foreword* to the novel. At the same time, though, the text encourages expectations that Déterville, the French suitor, will emerge as successful. He is gradually accorded the qualities of an Inca, and is seen to grow in stature, nobility, and devotion even as Aza loses his status as the perfect hero. We are encouraged to believe that we know Zilia better than she knows herself, to see her frequently expressed gratitude as no more than the provisional, and approximate, expression of a love which she does not yet recognize. Such an outcome was also authorized by recent precedent, not least by Rameau's *Gallant Indies* where Phani, the Inca heroine, loves and eventually marries a virtuous Spanish suitor rather than the brutal priest, Huascar. The fact that the seeds of two possible and equally traditional outcomes are sown in the text sustains the reader's suspense, but it also confirms his assumptions that one or other will be realized; the ending will reveal just how much he has been led astray.

The author's manipulation of the reader, though, is to be found not just in the outcome of the text, but also, significantly, at its start. Following the logic of the plot, the opening letters, those precisely which depict the vulnerable heroine, are actually the last to be written. The conclusion of the novel thus obliges us to return to the beginning, but to do so with new insights. Behind the insistent repetition of confidence in her lover's fidelity and integrity lies the irony of an enlightened and independent woman, behind the naive and love-struck Zilia is the controlling writer. At the moment of translating these *quipus*, the heroine's mastery of French is total. The linguistic awkwardness of these letters is revealed now to be quite deliberate, and there is an implicit detachment from her former identity, no more fulfilling or substantial than the language in which it is embodied. Her vision of Aza's suffering in letter 3 takes on in this context a particular significance, as Zilia enjoys the image of him scorched by the very sun he represents, and whose power is not invigorating but desiccating. The creative presence of the heroine is most evident in the opening letter which, strictly speaking, cannot be the translation of a surviving source; this is the only communication to which Aza sends a reply, and he does so, we are told in this very letter, by untying and reknotting the *quipu* he has received. The whole letter, therefore, is entirely constructed. Seen in this light, Zilia's opening lament that she calls in vain for Aza's help takes on in retrospect a more powerful force; she recognizes such language for what it is, an insubstantial mist which will soon dissipate into nothing. This act of rereading confronts the reader a second time with the fragility and emptiness of his assumptions. The very material which we might have taken as evidence of our superior cultural or aesthetic enlightenment is all shown to be an illusion. We are not reading the letters of a vulnerable heroine, whose nature is clear to us and whose fate we might confidently predict; we are being manipulated by an enlightened writer. We are made to experience as readers precisely what Zilia has experienced as a bemused outsider; we think we know where we stand, but our interpretations are shown to be quite mistaken. These first seventeen letters do not simply represent the naivety of the heroine, they enact the deception of the reader.

Contemporary Reception

A study of the novel's initial reception reveals much about the great popularity of this text, but also about its power to challenge and provoke. Readers of the mid-eighteenth century sought to accommodate, domesticate, or neutralize its effects. This was a text in need of translation.

In France, the novel was followed within a year of its publication by two rewritings, both of which attempted to give it a more conventional ending.[3] The first, an anonymous sequel, followed on quite literally from the last letter of Graffigny. Of the nine letters it contained, three were accorded to Déterville, and three, significantly, to Céline, who situates Zilia's discourse of freedom and independence in a quite different tradition. At the very centre of this text, she offers an explanation of the heroine's rejection of Déterville which replaces resolution with self-deception; Zilia is seen to have no more control of her self than she has of her language. Céline assumes an informed and confident stance, sketching out a route from the original novel to a much more traditional outcome, which she and, it is implied, many readers wish to see: that the friendship Zilia offers Déterville is merely an anticipation of the love to come. In so doing, the author of the sequel seeks to undermine Zilia's authority both as a writer and as a character who knows her own mind. Significantly, the sequel ends not with a letter from Zilia, but with Déterville's own vision of a happy future.

The second response to the novel, the *Letters of Aza* by Hugary de Lamarche-Courmont, rewrites the text from the perspective of Graffigny's other silent figure, Aza. It offers an explanation for the actions which are so problematic in Graffigny's text, and which threaten to undermine his heroic status: Aza's readiness to convert to Christianity and marry a Spaniard, and his coolness

---

[3] Extracts from both these works are to be found in Appendix 2.

when he sees Zilia in Paris. In this version of events, apparent infidelity is seen to be the result of misunderstandings: Aza believed Zilia to be dead when he arrived in Spain, and he believed her to be in love with Déterville when he came to Paris. At the end of this version, the misunderstandings have been clarified, and the prospect of reunion for the two Inca protagonists is very clear.

For all their great differences, what characterizes both these texts is the fact that they end with the promise of a marriage, and that neither seeks to develop Zilia's critical function. The independent heroine is recovered by tradition and redefined by her feelings. What is more, the titles of both works imply the same underlying objective: to complete a novel which seems, in the eyes of many readers, to be unfinished. The anonymous continuation is entitled *Sequel to the Peruvian Letters*, suggesting that the last word had not been said in Graffigny's text. Lamarche Courmont's version is more categorical still: *Letters of Aza, or of a Peruvian, Conclusion of the Peruvian Letters*. Significantly, these two works were very often published in subsequent editions of the novel itself, as if Graffigny's text were being literally, and irreversibly, colonized and perfected.

Similar responses are apparent, too, in some critical reviews of the work which reveal the discomfort of the reader: Graffigny's innovations are represented as aesthetic weaknesses, and what is challenging becomes simply defective. A number of critics pointed out elements of implausibility, or historical inaccuracy: in his review of the novel,[4] Élie-Catherine Fréron, one of Voltaire's most acerbic opponents, pointed out that Spain and France were not at war at the time of the Spanish conquest, that it does not take 200 years to cross from Peru to Europe by ship, and, most significantly of all, that *quipus* were not equipped to record and convey abstract ideas or emotional states. He acknowledged that such details are easily tolerated in a novel if it gives pleasure, but such criticisms imply nevertheless a more profound disquiet: unease about originality is hidden beneath criticism of clumsiness.

---

[4] Published in 1749 in his journal *Lettres sur quelques écrits de ce temps*.

Within this critical context, the representation of Zilia's ultimate autonomy is seen to reveal a novelist who does not know how to finish a novel, and several critics offer suggestions as to how this defect might have been corrected. The journalist and translator Pierre Clément, in a review of 1748 published in his *Cinq années littéraires*, proposes that Graffigny should have had her heroine die of love, the only way, he claims, to satisfy the reader's expectations. And even Fréron and La Porte,[5] who are both largely positive about the novel, confess to disappointment at its ending and attempt to discern signs of a more traditional conclusion, a marriage in the making with Déterville if not with Aza—signs, arguably, which are there precisely in order that they can be subverted. In all such cases, we witness attempts, undertaken in the name of the reader's satisfaction, to turn the disruptive into the reassuring. This aesthetic response imitates, ironically, the cultural response of characters to Zilia in the novel itself. The heroine's difference is seen as defective or threatening, and the aim is to neutralize it.

The different changes proposed for the novel restore the primacy of feeling as the defining characteristic of a heroine, but they imply too a desire to underplay her analytical qualities, by turning the novel largely into a novel of love. Raynal[6] describes Zilia's social commentary as 'superficial', and, more scathingly still, Clément will suggest that one of the chief implausibilities of the text is that the heroine is empowered to make critical observations. Some reviewers, however, do praise Zilia for her intellectual side. Both La Porte and Fréron see her double function very clearly, and situate the text in a tradition of writing which extends back to the *Persian Letters*. La Porte, though, remains uncomfortable with her judgements, and expresses the wish to see greater and more explicit authentication of French values. For one writer,

---

[5] The abbé Joseph de La Porte (1714–79), journalist and close collaborator of Fréron. His review appeared in 1749, in his periodical *Observations sur la littérature moderne*.

[6] The abbé Raynal (1713–96) was a regular at Graffigny's salon. He contributed to the *Encyclopédie*, and his polemical history of colonization in Asia and the Americas, the *History . . . of the Two Indies* (1770–80), on which he collaborated with Diderot and others, would make his name and his fortune. His review of Graffigny's novel first appeared in the manuscript periodical, *Nouvelles littéraires*.

however, Zilia has the status of an uncompromising outsider. Jaucourt cites this novel on six occasions in articles written by him for the *Encyclopédie*. The most revealing of these is doubtless the entry *Religieuse* (*Nun*) in volume xiv, which ironically quotes as an example of blind prejudice the comments made by Zilia in letter 19 about the inadequacies of a convent education. Jaucourt's article takes seriously, and implicitly celebrates, the subversive impact of the text; not insignificantly, in the same year, 1765, the novel was placed on the Index of banned books—the ultimate gesture of neutralization.

Many critical responses to the novel suggest to this extent a process of translation, that exercise of rewriting a text which is alien on account of its language (and, by extension, of its culture), and making it conform to the habits, tastes, or expectations of the public for which it is destined. That French writers and critics set out to do this with Graffigny's novel suggests just how clearly and keenly, even for her compatriots, its originality was to be felt; such originality is foreshadowed in the *Foreword*, behind which we might sense the author's own confident, provocative stance. This is an unusual, 'foreign' work not simply because it deals with an exotic subject, Peru, but because it deals with familiar subjects in an alienating way, challenging the reader to reassess his assumptions both as a member of society and as a reader of novels.

This desire to translate, both literally and figuratively, is replicated in several responses to the text in European countries. The novel itself was translated into English, for instance, no fewer than four times in the course of the century; of these, two were relatively literal, but two others embody more active adaptations.[7] The first, by Mrs Roberts, translates both the original text of 1747, and the *Sequel* of 1748; to this, she added letters of her own which culminate in the religious conversion of the heroine and her marriage to Déterville. The translator stressed her desire to make of this novel a religious inspiration for her readers, an ambition which Graffigny clearly did not share. She rewrites certain episodes in the original novel, not least Zilia's contemplation of

---

[7] Extracts from both these English continuations are to be found in Appendix 3.

nature, which in the French text underlines the observer's sense of self, but which in the English continuation is the first stage of her acceptance of Christianity.

The other rewritten translation, *Letters from Zilia to Aza*, is an adaptation in verse of the first few letters of the novel, followed by a number of scenes which reveal Zilia commenting on various aspects of contemporary life. Remarkably, we see the anonymous translator accepting and developing the role of Zilia as a critical observer of social manners; it was the first translation to do so. What is more, the text contains a fierce condemnation of Christianity in the wake of Aza's conversion. The heroine herself, however, does not emerge as an independent and original figure; she reverts instead to a different kind of traditional role, and dies of a broken heart.

For all their evident differences, these texts, both French and English, share the same ambition to remove Zilia's independence and originality; she is turned again into a conventional heroine, a lover who can be controlled and domesticated. With just rare and fleeting exceptions, she loses everything which singles her out— her intelligence and her autonomy. As Céline predicts in letter 5 of the *Sequel*, Zilia will inevitably realize that she is not complete as a person; but the process of 'completion' to which she is variously subjected is effectively one of neutralization, or neutering. Indeed, in a revealing parallel, the reception of the novel in the European literary world realizes what the 'editor' of the novel had anticipated in the *Foreword*. This novel does seem as strange to the readers of Europe as if it had come to them from another hemisphere; it is just too alien. For them, it can only be truly itself, if it stops being what it is: different.

Graffigny republished the novel in 1752, a sign of its great popularity, of course, but also of the author's defiant reaction to the responses it had aroused. In different ways this second edition (the text of which is the basis of this translation) demonstrates Graffigny's confidence in what she has written, and her refusal to change it. It proudly affirms that aesthetic innovations are not to be equated with inadequate technique; its originality is quite deliberate. It was for this second edition that she wrote two new letters, those numbered 29 and 34 in this translation, which emphasize the heroine's function as a critic of society, and bring out the thematic unity of the text. She added the *Historical Introduction* which brings to the forefront of attention the scholarly credentials of the work. And she included two illustrations, both of which focus on cultural opposition or tension—Zilia as she adopts French dress for the first time (letter 12), and as she is reunited with the ornaments from the Temple of the Sun (letter 27)—rather than on scenes of love. Such changes direct the way the reader might approach the text; they do not suggest a sentimental novel, but underline its intellectual content. Most significant of all, though, was what Graffigny did not change, most notably the ending itself; in spite of the critical comments or the familiarizing sequels, she maintains and implicitly celebrates the originality of her first version. In this context, the seemingly banal comment at the end of the text, added to the 1752 edition, affirms the finality of Zilia's decision, and the authority of the author: '*End of the second and last Part*'. There can be no more continuations. This is the last word.

Reading the Letters of a Peruvian Woman *Today*

Graffigny's novel has now become part of the literary canon, readily categorized and admired as a high point in eighteenth-century women's writing. It marks a welcome and quite justified return to the celebrity which it enjoyed in the fifty years following its publication. But this kind of acceptance does carry with it a risk of misappropriation, no different in principle from the rapturous but conditional reception it received at the time. Eighteenth-century readers wished to colonize Graffigny's text, to adapt it to their tastes and expectations; readers today may be tempted to do the same.

The fact that this novel was written by a woman has indisputable significance. It represents the positive and provocative statement of a woman writer, moving beyond a stereotypical conception of the fictional heroine, defined by love and lamenting her fate in letters, which is perpetuated in many male-authored texts; Graffigny gives her heroine a function and significance quite without precedent in novels before it. Her reflections on the status and treatment of women, their education, categorization, and reification, have a particular resonance in the context of the period, and are as compelling now as then. One might even see in the novel a reflection of the author's own life, aspirations, or beliefs. Graffigny, like Zilia, comes to Paris as an outsider, financially and socially insecure, and like Zilia, she uses letters to express herself and her view of this world. She is abandoned by the lover she adores, but is determined to create an identity for herself, ultimately finding some measure of emotional, intellectual, and financial independence. For all that, though, one has to be cautious about seeing the text simply as a defiant or optimistic allegory of self-discovery. If Zilia finds an identity for herself, it is on account of the most fabulous good fortune, and the house to which she retreats and realizes herself as a woman is described on more than one occasion as a fairy palace, the kind of domain associated with fantastical fiction, not with life.

To read the novel simply through the lens of gender, however, risks reducing its impact and originality. If the text has significance for us today, it is not just on account of this one theme; it explores other questions no less current now than they were in the mid-eighteenth century. In its juxtaposition of Peru and France, it dramatizes tensions created by cultural, racial, or philosophical difference, and traces the discourse of superiority which seeks to reduce what cannot be fully understood or what one fears to know better. In its representation of French manners, it uncovers the moral and economic dangers inherent in a society where display has become the new and only truth. And in its account of Zilia's gradual mastery of French, it examines the power of language as a means of understanding, criticizing, or manipulating others, and its limitations as a tool, always approximate and irreducibly subjective, for the representation of the self. In today's world of ideological imperialism, virtual realities, political 'spin', and marketing hype, the continued relevance of such themes is powerfully, even chillingly evident. That such questions are explored in this novel may well suggest Graffigny's modernity and that of her age, looking beneath the surface of its own reality to the means which constitute it; or it may just be a sign that certain problems are an indelible part of our culture, and that human history revolves as much as it evolves.

But the text is remarkable too for its bold and creative experimentation, blending in quite unprecedented ways completely different forms of writing. It is a novel which, like the most innovative narratives of the time, has the ability to unsettle. And this is not just because of the critical subject matter of some letters — about women, the Church, society — but also because of a structure which confronts the reader with the frailty of his assumptions that the familiar has a necessary primacy over the different. And this quality, which makes the *Letters of a Peruvian Woman* one of the most original novels (either female or male authored) in the century, can still involve readers today. The novel evades simple categorization either as a condemnation of French society or as a celebration of women's independence; its heroine can be as vulnerable as she is authoritative, as insular or manipulative as those she criticizes. Like many eighteenth-century works, it does not simply provide literary escapism, but intellectual engagement, turning the reader back on his own values as much as it expresses those of Graffigny herself. The *Letters of a Peruvian Woman* does not simply invite the reader of today to make the novel conform to our own contemporary preoccupations or paradigms; it invites us, above all, to respond to the moral and aesthetic challenges which it continues to pose.

NOTE ON THE TEXT AND TRANSLATION

As I have indicated in the Introduction, Graffigny's novel was translated four times into English in the eighteenth century. As was the custom at this period, the renderings were often quite literal, and at times incomprehensible to anyone unfamiliar with French.

The nineteenth century saw no new translations, but in the last thirty years there has been renewed interest in making the text available to readers, through both editions of the original text and translations. The first modern English version was produced by David Kornacker, *Letters from a Peruvian Woman* (New York, 1993); and in 1999 there appeared a new translation into German, *Briefe einer Peruanerin*, by Renate Kroll (Königstein, 1999).

A modern translator of the *Letters of a Peruvian Woman* inevitably finds himself in the same position as the fictional editor of Graffigny's text, aware that this is an unusual narrative whose foreignness risks appearing unpalatable or repellent; the modern English-speaking reader is not so very different from the original readers of the work.

This work has a stylistic remoteness typical of countless eighteenth-century texts. Many letters have a distinctive syntax and punctuation, not least those at the start of the novel; sentences proceed by the long accumulation of clauses separated by commas or semicolons, impressions cast out without an apparent organizing structure, creating the illusion of spontaneity. Elsewhere, the heroine has convoluted sentences, with long adverbial or adjectival clauses in apposition, introducing the main verb only after long delays. Similarly distinctive is Zilia's vocabulary, often elaborately metaphorical or poetic in her terms of endearment for Aza, or in her more abstract reflections. Such features are characteristic of many texts of this period which seek ways of conveying the shifting nature of human feeling with rigid and imprecise linguistic tools. But they are characteristic, too, of this Peruvian heroine, and it is such qualities which are singled out and disparaged in the editor's preface, implying a criticism not only of the foreign heroine's style but also of women's writing, widely held to be unpolished and imperfect. The parallels are very clear.

For the comfort of the modern reader, but at risk of appearing like the 'editor' of the original text, I have judged it necessary to modernize some of the punctuation, and to soften some of the more archaic, or abstruse, utterances. But much, too, has been retained. For these characteristics are not simply the symptoms of a foreign work, remote in time and culture from our own; they are part of the logic of the text which enacts the heroine's discovery of language, tracing a very clear development from naivety to confidence, inelegance to sophistication. To this extent, a certain measure of clumsiness has to be retained, particularly in the early letters, in order to provide the reader with a sense of development, of increasing assurance and fluency, as Zilia masters her own means of expression. This is all the more appropriate, given that the very awkwardness of the opening letters is, as we have seen earlier, a part of the heroine's narrative strategy. What is true of Zilia is true too, within reason, of the translator.

The text itself poses few editorial problems. The principal decision lies in which of the two editions to use, the original of 1747, or the revised and expanded version of 1752. The distinguished Graffigny scholar David Smith has put forward forceful arguments for preferring the 1747 text. It has been the custom among editors, however, to opt for the later edition, on the grounds that this represents the author's final thoughts on the novel and that it contains some of the heroine's most significant critical comments, not least in the letters numbered 29 and 34. For this translation, I use my edition of the novel, published by the Voltaire Foundation. This follows the 1752 text, but also incorporates a few corrections or changes made subsequently by Graffigny.

All the footnotes in the novel are Graffigny's own. Asterisks in the text refer the reader to editorial notes at the end of the book.

SELECT BIBLIOGRAPHY

The Text

The edition of the French text, *Lettres d'une Péruvienne*, edited by Jonathan Mallinson and published by the Voltaire Foundation in its *Vif* series, provides an authoritative text of the 1752 edition and a complete set of variants from the first (1747) edition; critical notes are in French, and there is an appendix containing extracts from contemporary reviews and rewritings. Other French editions, but with less reliable texts, include *Lettres portugaises, Lettres d'une Péruvienne et autres romans d'amour par lettres*, ed. B. Bray and I. Landy-Houillon (Paris, 1983), 237–363; *Lettres d'une Péruvienne* (1747), préface de Colette Piau-Gillot (Paris: Côté-femmes, 1990); *Romans de femmes au XVIIIe siècle*, ed. R. Trousson (Paris: Laffont, 1996), 59–164.

An alternative edition of the French text, with some brief annotation in English, is *Lettres d'une Péruvienne*, introduction by J. DeJean and Nancy K. Miller, MLA Texts and Translations Series 2 (New York: MLA, 1993).

Letters

The complete *Correspondance* of Françoise de Graffigny, edited by J. Alan Dainard and a team of specialists, is being published by the Voltaire Foundation; 11 volumes of a projected 15 have appeared to date. A very useful anthology of letters is Françoise de Graffigny, *Choix de lettres*, ed. E. Showalter, *Vif* (Oxford: Voltaire Foundation, 2001). The following articles are just some of the increasing number devoted to this fascinating collection of texts:

Cornand, Suzanne, 'La Lettre d'indignation ou l'éloquence dans la correspondance de Madame de Graffigny', *Revue d'histoire littéraire de la France*, 101/1 (2001), 37–50.

Dainard, J. Alan, et al., 'La Correspondance de Madame de Graffigny', *Dix-huitième siècle*, 10 (1978), 379–94.

Hayes, Julie Candler, 'Feedback: Françoise de Graffigny and François-Antoine Devaux', in *Reading the French Enlightenment: System and Subversion* (Cambridge, 1999), 79–85.

Landy-Houillon, Isabelle, 'Les Lettres de Mme de Graffigny entre Mme de Sévigné et Zilia: étude de style', in *La Lettre au XVIIIe siècle et ses avatars*, ed. Georges Bérubé and Marie-France Silver (Toronto, 1996), 67–81.

Roulston, Christine, 'No Simple Correspondence: Mme de Graffigny as "épistolière" and as Epistolary Novelist', *L'Esprit créateur*, 40/4 (2000), 31–7.

Showalter, English, 'Authorial Self-Consciousness in the Familiar Letter: The Case of Madame de Graffigny', *Yale French Studies*, 71 (1986), 113–30.

Studies in English

English Showalter's biography of Graffigny, *Françoise de Graffigny: Her Life and Works* (*SVEC* 2004:11), provides an excellent introduction to her life and times; a more concise account is Judith Curtis, 'Françoise d'Issembourg d'Happoncourt de Graffigny (1695–1758)', in *French Women Writers: A bio-bibliographical Source Book*, ed. Eva Martin Sartori and Dorothy Wynne Zimmerman (New York, 1991), 208–17.

The following works are very useful studies of French eighteenth-century women's writing:

DeJean, Joan, *Tender Geographies: Women and the Origins of the Novel in France* (New York, 1991).

Jensen, Katherine Ann, *Writing Love: Letters, Women and the Novel in France, 1605–1776* (Carbondale, Ill., 1995).

Miller, Nancy K., *French Dressing: Women, Men and Ancien Régime Fiction* (New York, 1995).

Wolfgang, Aurora, *Gender and Voice in the French Novel, 1730–1782* (Aldershot, 2004).

Woodward, Servanne (ed.), *Altered Narratives: Female Eighteenth-Century French Authors Reinterpreted* (London, Canada, 1997).

For a general overview of recent critical thinking on the novel, the following articles are particularly helpful:

Altman, Janet Gurkin, 'Interpreting Graffigny: Critical Debates in the 1990s', *SVEC* 2002:06, 37–48.

Davies, Simon, '*Lettres d'une Péruvienne*, 1977–1997: The Present State of Studies', *SVEC* 2000:05, 295–324.

Smith, David Warner, 'Graffigny *Rediviva*: Editions of the *Lettres d'une Péruvienne* (1967–1993)', *Eighteenth-Century Fiction*, 7/1 (1994), 71–8.

Among the many articles devoted to this novel, the following provide stimulating, if at times controversial, insights:

Adams, David J., 'The *Lettres d'une Péruvienne*: Nature and Propaganda', *Forum for Modern Language Studies*, 28 (1992), 121–9.

Altman, Janet Gurkin, 'A Woman's Place in the Enlightenment Sun: The Case of F. de Graffigny', *Romance Quarterly*, 38/3 (1991), 261–72.

Daniels, Charlotte, 'Françoise de Graffigny's *Lettres d'une Péruvienne* and the Privatization of the Family', in *Subverting the Family Romance: Women Writers, Kinship Structures, and the Early French Novel* (Lewisburg, Pa., 2000), 19–56.

Davies, Simon, 'The *Lettres d'une Péruvienne*: Mme de Graffigny's Novel of Translation and Transformation', in *Reading across the Lines*, ed. Christopher Shorley and Maeve McCusker (Dublin, 2000), 83–90.

Dobie, Madeleine, 'The Subject of Writing: Language, Epistemology, and Identity in the *Lettres d'une Péruvienne*', *Eighteenth Century: Theory and Interpretation*, 38/2 (1997), 99–117.

Douthwaite, Julia V., 'Relocating the Exotic Other in Graffigny's *Lettres d'une Péruvienne*', *Romanic Review* 82/4 (1991), 456–74.

Grayson, Vera L., 'The Genesis and Reception of Mme de Graffigny's *Lettres d'une Péruvienne* and *Cénie*', *SVEC* 336 (1996), 1–152.

Howells, Robin, 'The *Péruvienne* and Pathos', *French Studies*, 55 (2001), 453–66.

Kavanagh, Thomas M., 'Reading the Moment and the Moment of Reading in Graffigny's *Lettres d'une Péruvienne*', *Modern Language Quarterly*, 55/2 (1994), 125–47.

Mallinson, Jonathan, 'Re-conquering Peru: Eighteenth-Century Translations of Graffigny's *Lettres d'une Péruvienne*', *SVEC* 2007:06, 291–310.

Miller, Nancy K., 'The Knot, the Letter and the Book: Graffigny's *Peruvian Letters*', in *Subject to Change: Reading Feminist Writing* (New York, 1988), 125–61.

Piroux, Lorraine, 'The Encyclopedist and the Peruvian Princess: The Poetics of Illegibility in French Enlightenment Book Culture', *Publications of the Modern Language Association of America*, 121/1 (2006), 107–23.

Simon, Julia, 'On Collecting Culture in Graffigny: The Construction of an "Authentic" Péruvienne', *Eighteenth-Century: Theory and Interpretation*, 44/1 (2003), 25–44.

Undank, Jack, 'Grafigny's Room of her Own', *French Forum*, 13/3 (1988), 297–318.

Wolfgang, Aurora, 'Intertextual conversations: The Love-Letter and the Footnote in Madame de Graffigny's *Lettres d'une Péruvienne*', *Eighteenth-Century Fiction*, 10/1 (1997), 15–28.

Studies in French

The articles contained in *Françoise de Graffigny, femme de lettres: écriture et réception*, ed. Jonathan Mallinson (*SVEC* 2004:12) include a number of innovative studies of the novel, as well as providing a detailed overview of Graffigny's full range of writing. Another useful collection is *Vierge du soleil/Fille des Lumières: la 'Péruvienne' de Mme de Grafigny et ses suites*, Travaux du groupe d'étude du XVIIIe siècle, Université de Strasbourg II, 5 (1989), which includes some valuable work on the reception of the novel.

Among individual studies in French, the following articles are of particular interest:

Altman, Janet Gurkin, 'Lettres et le néant: l'invention de l'écriture postcoloniale chez Graffigny', *Sur la plume des vents: mélanges de littérature épistolaire offerts à Bernard Bray*, ed. Ulrike Michalowsky (Paris, 1996), 157–71.

Mall, Laurence, 'Langues étrangères et étrangeté du langage dans les *Lettres d'une Péruvienne* de Mme de Graffigny', *SVEC* 323 (1994), 323–43.

Mallinson, Jonathan, 'Re-présentant les *Lettres d'une Péruvienne* en 1752: illustration et illusion', *Eighteenth-Century Fiction*, 15/2 (2003), 227–39.

Rosset, François, 'Les Nœuds du langage dans les *Lettres d'une Péruvienne*', *Revue d'histoire littéraire de la France*, 96 (1996), 1106–27.

Further Reading in Oxford World's Classics

Montesquieu, *Persian Letters*, trans. Margaret Mauldon, ed. Andrew Kahn.

Prévost, Abbé, *Manon Lescaut*, trans. and ed. Angela Scholar.

Voltaire, *Letters concerning the English Nation*, ed. Nicholas Cronk.

A CHRONOLOGY OF
FRANÇOISE DE GRAFFIGNY

1695 11 February. Françoise d'Issembourg d'Happoncourt is born in Nancy, daughter of François d'Happoncourt, military officer, and Marguerite Callot, great-niece of the engraver Jacques Callot (1592–1635).

1699 Publication of Fénelon's *Télémaque*.

1712 19 January. Marriage to François Huguet de Graffigny, born around 1692, officer in the service of the duc de Lorraine. He is a violent drunkard and gambler.

1713 14 June. Christening of Charlotte-Antoinette; she dies in December 1716.

1715 March. Jean-Jacques born; he dies within a few days.

    Death of Louis XIV; accession of Louis XV, a minor.

1716 March. Marie-Thérèse born; she dies before her second birthday.

1721 Publication of Montesquieu's *Persian Letters* (*Lettres persanes*).

1723 She obtains a formal decree of separation from her husband.

1725 Widowed, her husband having died in mysterious circumstances. She subsequently moves to the court of Lorraine at Lunéville, under the protection of the duchesse de Lorraine.

    Publication of the *Selected Letters* (*Lettres choisies*) of Mme de Sévigné.

1727 17 May. Death of her mother; her father remarries within four months. She begins a relationship with Léopold Desmarest, cavalry officer and son of the composer Henry Desmarest, which will continue until 1743.

1728–33 Publication of Prévost, *Memoirs and Adventures of a Man of Quality* (*Mémoires et aventures d'un homme de qualité*), which includes *Manon Lescaut*.

1730 She is introduced to François Antoine Devaux, a lawyer, in the early 1730s. He will become her most faithful friend and correspondent, the recipient of nearly 2,500 letters.

1733 7 November. Death of her father.

    Publication of Voltaire's *Letters concerning the English Nation*.

1735 First performance of Rameau's *The Gallant Indies* (*Les Indes galantes*).

Departure of Bouguer, Godin, and La Condamine for Peru to measure the length of a degree at the Equator.

1736 First performance of Voltaire's *Alzire*; and publication of his *Man of Society* (*Le Mondain*), an outspoken defence of luxury.

Publication of d'Argens's *Jewish Letters* (*Lettres juives*).

1738 The Treaty of Vienna brings an end to the War of the Polish Succession, and to this happy period. The duke of Lorraine cedes his duchy to Stanislas Leszczynski, deposed king of Poland and father-in-law of Louis XV.

September. In debt and financially insecure because of the political upheaval, Graffigny leaves Lunéville for Paris, to become companion to the duchesse de Richelieu. She makes several stops on the way, ending with a ten-week stay (until February 1739) at Cirey, with Voltaire and Mme Du Châtelet. She is wrongfully accused of copying a canto of Voltaire's satirical epic *La Pucelle*, and sending it to Devaux.

1739 February. She arrives in Paris.

Publication of d'Argens's *Chinese Letters* (*Lettres chinoises*).

1740 August. Death of the duchesse de Richelieu, which makes Graffigny's financial position quite precarious. She spends two years as pensionnaire in Paris convents, serving as companion to the princesse de Ligne and other ladies she had met with the duchesse.

Publication of Prévost's *Tale of a Modern Greek Woman* (*Histoire d'une Grecque moderne*).

1742 November. She moves into her own house, rue Saint-Hyacinthe, close to the Jardin du Luxembourg. She establishes a new circle of friends, around the comte de Caylus and the actress Jeanne Quinault, to become known as the Bout-du-Banc; this brings together notable writers of the time, among whom are Claude Crébillon, Duclos, Nivelle de La Chaussée, Piron.

Publication of the French translation of Richardson's *Pamela*.

1743 Desmarest returns to Paris after the siege of Prague, and ends his affair with her. She becomes the mistress of Pierre Valleré, lawyer and lodger in her house; the affair is passionate but short-lived. But Valleré will remain her lodger and companion until her death.

Start of the personal reign of Louis XV.

1744   She hopes to make a good investment in a firm which will administer the fairs of Poissy and Sceaux. The investment fails, and her debts accumulate. She goes out little over the next two years, and spends much time writing.

1745   She publishes her first literary work, the short story *Spanish Novella* (*Nouvelle espagnole*), in the *Gentlemen's Collection* (*Recueil de ces Messieurs*).

1746   She publishes her fairy tale, *Princess Azerolle* (*La Princesse Azerolle*). In September, she welcomes Anne-Catherine de Ligniville, known as 'Minette', the daughter of her cousin. For five years, she will attempt to find a good match for her.

Publication of Diderot's *Philosophical Thoughts* (*Pensées philosophiques*).

1747   She publishes *Letters of a Peruvian Woman* (*Lettres d'une Péruvienne*), begun in 1745. It is an instant success. She opens her own salon, which will attract major writers (Casanova, Diderot, Duclos, Helvétius, Marivaux, Marmontel, Prévost, Rousseau), journalists (Fréron, Grimm), artists (Quentin de La Tour), scientists and mathematicians (d'Alembert, La Condamine, Maupertuis), and political figures (Choiseul, Maurepas, Turgot). She begins to write annual plays for performance by the Emperor's children in Vienna.

1748   The end of the War of the Austrian Succession places Maria-Theresa on the throne, and sees the election of her husband, François-Etienne former duke of Lorraine, as Emperor. Graffigny gains a larger pension, and her financial situation improves.

Publication of Richardson's *Clarissa*.

1750   June. Triumph of her sentimental comedy *Cénie* at the Comédie-Française, which confirms her status as one of the major literary figures in Europe. Her salon is very much in fashion.

Publication of Rousseau's *Discourse on the Sciences and the Arts* (*Discours sur les sciences et les arts*).

1751   Marriage of Minette to the philosopher, writer, and tax-farmer Claude-Adrien Helvetius. Graffigny moves to a new house, on the rue d'Enfer, overlooking the Jardin du Luxembourg. Prévost dedicates his translation of Richardson's *Clarissa* to her.

Publication of the first volume of the *Encyclopédie*; and of Duclos's *Considerations on the Manners of our Age* (*Considérations sur les mœurs de ce siècle*).

1752 Second edition of the *Letters of a Peruvian Woman*, published by the prestigious editor Duchesne, and including two engravings designed by the up-and-coming artist Charles Eisen.

Start of 'la querelle des Bouffons' which divides Paris on the respective merits of French and Italian opera. The first two volumes of the *Encyclopédie* are suppressed for attacks on the clergy.

1755 Publication of Rousseau's *Discourse on the Origin of Inequality among Men* (*Discours sur l'origine de l'inégalité parmi les hommes*).

Earthquake in Lisbon, with 30,000 victims. Death of Montesquieu.

1757 Publication of Mme Riccoboni's *Letters of Miss Fanni Butlerd* (*Lettres de Mistriss Fanni Butlerd*).

1758 April. First performance of *The Daughter of Aristide* (*La Fille d'Aristide*), a failure; Graffigny soon withdraws the play. She dies on 12 December.

She leaves her manuscripts to Devaux, with the instructions that her works, and a sample of her letters, be published. Devaux puts the papers in order, but publishes nothing. They are passed down to his relatives, who copy the Cirey letters around 1810, leading to their publication in 1820; also around 1820, they sell the manuscripts to the English bibliophile Sir Thomas Phillipps. They are sold at Sotheby's in 1965, and the bulk of the papers is given by the buyer, H. P. Kraus, to Yale University's Beinecke Rare Book and Manuscript Library, and the Pierpont Morgan Library, New York.

LETTERS OF A
PERUVIAN WOMAN

Illustration facing the title-page of Part One of
Lettres d'une Péruvienne (1752)

FOREWORD

If truth deviates from what is considered plausible, it normally loses its credibility in the eyes of reason, but this loss is not irreversible; but if it runs counter to prejudice however slightly, it is rarely granted leniency in that court.

With what trepidation, therefore, must the publisher of this work present to the public the letters of a young Peruvian woman, whose manner of writing and whose ideas are so different from the largely unfavourable image of her nation which unjust prejudice has caused us to fashion.

Enriched by the priceless spoils of Peru, we should at least consider the inhabitants of this part of the world to be a magnificent people, and a feeling of respect is not very far removed from the recognition of magnificence.

But prejudiced in our own favour as we invariably are, we recognize merit in other nations only insofar as their customs are similar to ours, and their language resembles our own way of speaking. *How can someone be Persian?*[1]*

We despise those from the Indies, we are scarcely willing to credit these wretched peoples with a thinking soul; and yet their history is available to us all, and we find recorded on every page of it the astuteness of their minds and the soundness of their philosophy.*

One of our finest poets has evoked these Indian customs in a verse drama which has surely helped to make them better known.[2]*

Since so much light has been shed on the character of these peoples, there might seem to be no reason to fear that these authentic letters will be taken for fiction; they simply develop what we already know of the Indians' lively and unspoiled mind. But does prejudice have eyes? Nothing can protect against its judgement, and we would certainly have taken care not to submit this work to it, if its dominion had no bounds.

[1] *Persian Letters.*   [2] *Alzire.*

It seems unnecessary to point out that Zilia herself translated her first letters; the reader will quickly realize that since they were composed in a language and recorded in a manner which are both equally unknown to us, the letters in this collection would never have come down to us if the same hand had not rewritten them in our language.*

We owe this translation to Zilia's leisure in her retreat, to her willingness to pass the letters on to the chevalier Déterville, and to her granting him permission to keep them.

The reader will soon see from the grammatical errors and stylistic lapses how much care we have taken to leave intact the spirit of innocence which predominates in this work.* We have simply removed many of the expressions foreign to our own written style, retaining just enough to show how necessary it was to prune them.

We also decided that we could, without making any changes to the substance of the ideas, express with greater clarity some of the more metaphysical remarks which might otherwise have seemed obscure. This is our only intervention in this singular work.

HISTORICAL INTRODUCTION
to the *Peruvian Letters*

No other people has such limited knowledge of their origins and antiquity as the Peruvians. Their annals cover barely four centuries of their history.

Mancocapac was, according to the tradition of these peoples, their law-giver and their first Inca. The Sun, whom they called their father and regarded as their God, troubled by the barbarity in which they had lived for a long time, sent down to them from Heaven two of his children, a son and a daughter, to bring them laws and to encourage them, by founding towns and cultivating the land, to become men of reason.

It is therefore to *Mancocapac* and to his wife *Coya-Mama-Oello-Huaco* that the Peruvians owe the principles, customs, and arts which had made them a happy people, until greed, coming from the depths of a world whose very existence they did not even suspect, cast tyrants onto their lands, whose barbarity brought shame on humanity and was the crime of their age.

The circumstances in which the Peruvians found themselves at the time of the Spaniards' invasion could not have been more advantageous to the latter. There had been talk for some time of an ancient oracle which foretold that *after a certain number of Kings, there would come to their country extraordinary men, such as had never been seen, who would invade their kingdom and destroy their religion.**

Although astronomy was one of the Peruvians' principal areas of knowledge, they were terrified by extraordinary natural events, as many other peoples are. Three circles which had been observed around the moon, and, above all, a number of comets, had spread terror among them; an eagle pursued by other birds, the sea overflowing its bounds, all such happenings made the oracle's prediction seem as inescapable as it was deadly.

The eldest son of the seventh Inca, whose name in the Peruvian language heralded the inevitable fate of his age,[3] had once seen a figure whose appearance was quite different from that of Peruvians. A long beard, a robe which covered the spectre down to his feet, an unknown animal which he led on a leash, all this had terrified the young prince whom the phantom had told that he was a son of the Sun, brother of *Mancocapac*, and that his name was Viracocha. This ridiculous fable had, unfortunately, been preserved by the Peruvians, and as soon as they saw the Spaniards with their full beards, their covered legs, and mounted on animals the likes of which they had never seen before, they believed that they saw before them the sons of this Viracocha who had called himself the son of the Sun. As a result, the usurper was named the descendant of the god these people worshipped, by the ambassadors he sent out to them: all bowed down before them; people are the same everywhere. The Spaniards were hailed by almost everyone as gods, but their wrath could not be calmed by even the most extravagant gifts or the most humiliating worship.*

Having noticed that the Spaniards' horses were champing at their bits, the Peruvians imagined that these tamed monsters, whom they also respected and perhaps even worshipped, fed on metal; so they went to find them all the gold and silver in their possession, and each day surrounded them with these offerings. We limit ourselves to this one example to demonstrate the gullibility of the Peruvian people, and the ease with which the Spaniards were able to enthral them.

Whatever homage the Peruvians might have paid to their oppressors, they had revealed too much of their immense wealth to be treated with any consideration.

An entire people, conquered and pleading for mercy, was put to the sword. Having violated all the rights of human kind, the Spaniards were left absolute masters of the treasures of one of the most beautiful parts of the world. *Mere commercial victories* (exclaims Montaigne,[4] recalling the base purpose of these

---

[3] He was called *Yahuarhuocac*, which meant literally, *Weeps-Blood*.
[4] Volume v, chapter 6, *On carriages.*

conquests), *never did ambition* (he adds), *never did public enmity drive men against one another to such dreadful acts of hostility or to such wretched disasters.**

So it was that the Peruvians became the pathetic victims of a greedy nation, having first shown them only good faith and even friendship. Their ignorance of our vices and the innocence of their customs, delivered them into the hands of their cowardly enemies. To no avail had vast distances kept apart the cities of the Sun and our world, they were to become its prey and its most precious realm.

What a sight for the Spaniards were the gardens of the Temple of the Sun, where trees, fruits and flowers were made of gold, and fashioned with a skill unknown in Europe!* The walls of the Temple decked in the same metal, countless statues covered with precious stones, and an abundance of other riches hitherto unseen, all this dazzled the conquerors of this unfortunate people. Giving free rein to their cruelty, they forgot that the Peruvians were also human beings.

An analysis of the customs of this ill-fated people, as brief as the account we have just given of their misfortunes, will conclude this introduction which we thought it necessary to add to the letters which are to follow.

These peoples were, in general, honest and humane; their commitment to their religion made them strict observers of the laws, which they considered to be the work of *Mancocapac*, son of the Sun, whom they worshipped.

Although this Star was the only god to whom they had built Temples, they acknowledged above it a God Creator whom they called *Pachacamac*; this was for them the *great name*. The word *Pachacamac* was spoken only rarely, and with displays of the utmost awe.* They also had great veneration for the Moon, which they considered as the wife and sister of the Sun. They regarded her to be the mother of all things; but they believed, as did all Indians, that she would bring about the end of the world by falling to the earth and destroying it by her fall.* They considered thunder, which they called *Yalpor*, and flashes of lightning, to be ministers of the Sun's justice, and this belief contributed in no small way to the feeling of sacred respect which the first Spaniards inspired in them, and whose firearms they took to be instruments of thunder.*

Belief in the immortality of the soul was well established among the Peruvians; they believed, like most Indians, that the soul moved on to unknown places where it would be rewarded or punished according to its deserts.

Gold and all their most precious possessions made up the offerings which they laid before the Sun. The *Raymi* was the principal festival of this god, to whom they presented, in a chalice, a kind of potent liquor called *maïs*, which the Peruvians knew how to extract from one of their plants, and which they consumed to the point of drunkenness after the sacrifices.

There were a hundred doors in the magnificent Temple of the Sun. The ruling Inca, called the *Capa-Inca*, alone had the right to have them opened; it was also his right alone to enter as far as the inner part of this Temple.

The Virgins dedicated to the Sun were brought up in this place almost from birth, and they kept their virginity for life, under the guidance of their *Mamas*, or governesses, unless the laws destined them for union with Incas, who were always required to marry their sisters, or, should there be none, the first Princess of the Blood, who was a Virgin of the Sun.* One of the principal occupations of these Virgins was to fashion the Incas' diadems, whose supreme richness lay in their fringe-like decoration.

The Temple was decorated with various Idols taken from the peoples conquered by the Incas and made to accept the cult of the Sun. The priceless value of the metals and precious stones with which it was decorated gave it a magnificence and splendour worthy of the God worshipped there.

The obedience and respect shown by Peruvians for their kings was based on their belief that the Sun was the father of these kings. But their attachment and love for them was the result of their own virtues, and of the Incas' justness.

They raised their children with all the care required by the serene simplicity of their moral values. They were not alarmed by the idea of subservience, because they were shown its necessity from an early age, and because neither tyranny nor pride had any part to play in it. Modesty and mutual respect were the very foundations of their children's education; taking care to correct shortcomings at their earliest stage, those responsible for their instruction halted the growth of incipient passions,[5]* or turned them to the benefit of society. Some virtues imply the presence of many others. To give an idea of those found in the Peruvians, it is enough to say that before the arrival of the Spaniards, it was taken for granted that a Peruvian never told a lie.

Amautas, the philosophers of this nation, taught the young of discoveries made in the sciences. The nation was still in its infancy in this respect, but it was at the peak of its happiness.

The Peruvians were less enlightened, less knowledgeable, and less skilled than we are, and yet they were sufficiently advanced not to lack any necessity. *Quapas* or *Quipos*[6] took the place of our art of writing. Cords of cotton or gut, to which were attached other cords of different colours, recorded through a system of knots placed at varying distances whatever they wished to remember. They served as Annals, Codes, Rituals, etc. They had public officials, called *Quipocamaios*, who were entrusted with the safe-keeping of the *Quipos*. Finances, accounts, the payment of tributes, all aspects of business and all calculations could be handled as easily with *Quipos* as they could have been using writing.*

The wise law-giver of Peru, *Mancocapac*, had made cultivation of the land a sacred act; it was undertaken as a community, and the days devoted to such work were days of rejoicing.* Canals of extraordinary length spread freshness and fertility throughout the country. But what is scarcely conceivable is that the Peruvians had been able, without a single tool of iron or steel, but with just the strength of their arms, to overturn rocks, to cross the highest mountains in order to construct their mighty aqueducts, or the roads which they built across their land.

The Peruvians knew as much geometry as was needed to measure or divide up their lands. Medicine was a science unknown to

---

[5] See *Religious Ceremonies and Customs. Dissertations on the Peoples of America.* Chapter 13.

[6] The *Quipos* of Peru were also in use among other peoples of Southern America.

them, although they used secret remedies for particular misfortunes. *Garcilaso* says that they had a sort of music, and even some kind of poetry. Their poets, whom they called *Hasavec*, composed works similar to tragedies and comedies which the sons of the *Caciques*,[7] or of *Curacas*,[8] performed at festivals for the Incas and the whole court.

Morality and the art of creating laws beneficial to society were thus the only things which the Peruvians had learned with any success. *It has to be admitted* (says one Historian[9]) *that they achieved such great things, and established such a well-ordered society, that few nations can claim to have bettered them in this respect.**

---

[7] *Caciques*, a kind of provincial governor.

[8] Rulers of a small region; they never appeared before Incas and their wives without bringing them an offering of the local produce from the province where they ruled.

[9] Puffendorf, *Introduction to Hist.*

PART ONE

LETTER ONE

Aza! my dearest Aza! the cries of your loving Zilia* rise and disperse like a morning mist before they can reach you; in vain I call out to you for help, in vain I wait for you to come and break the chains which enslave me; alas, perhaps the misfortunes which are as yet unknown to me are more dreadful still, perhaps your suffering is greater than mine!

The city of the Sun, delivered up to the fury of a barbarous nation, ought to be the reason for my tears; but my grief, my fears and my despair are for you alone.

What did you do in that frightful commotion, my life's dear soul? Did your courage prove fatal to you, or was it just of no use? What cruel alternatives! What dreadful anxiety! O my dearest Aza, may your life have been spared, and may I succumb, if it must be so, to the ills that overwhelm me.

Ever since that terrible moment (which should have been snatched from the chain of time and thrown back into the timeless depths of thought), ever since that moment of sheer horror when those godless savages tore me from my worship of the Sun, from myself, from your love, I have been kept in close confinement, denied all contact with our companions, ignorant of the very language of these brutal men whose chains I bear; I experience only the effects of my misery, but I cannot discover the cause of it. Plunged into the darkest abyss, my days are no different from the most terrifying nights.

Far from being touched by my laments, my abductors are not even moved by my tears; deaf to my words, they are just as indifferent to my cries of despair.

What people can be so brutal that they are not affected at all by signs of suffering? What barren desert could produce human beings insensitive to the voice of nature in distress? Barbarous masters of *Yalpor*,[10] proud of their power to destroy! cruelty alone inspires their actions. Aza! How will you escape their fury?

[10] Name of Thunder.

Where are you? What are you doing? If my life is dear to you, let me know your fate.

Alas! How mine has changed! How can it be that days which in themselves are so alike, should be so fatally different for us? Time continues to pass, day shades into night, no sudden changes have disrupted nature's cycle; and yet from supreme happiness, I find myself plunged into the horrors of despair, without any interval to prepare me for this dreadful change of state.

As you well know, my heart's delight, this awful day, this eternally dreadful day, was meant to shine on the triumph of our union. Dawn was scarce breaking when I ran to my *Quipos*,[11] impatient to carry out a plan which love had inspired in me during the night; taking advantage of the silence which still filled the Temple, I hastened to knot them, hoping with their assistance to immortalize the story of our love and of our happiness.

As I worked, I found the task less difficult; with every moment this mass of countless cords became, in my fingers, a faithful record of our actions and our feelings, just as in the past they had expressed our thoughts, during those long periods which we spent apart.

Completely absorbed in my work, I lost track of time, when the sound of commotion brought me down to earth and made my heart miss a beat.

I thought that the blessed moment had come and that the hundred doors[12] of the Temple were opening to give free passage to the Sun of my life; I swiftly hid my *Quipos* under a fold of my dress and I ran to greet you.

But what a terrible sight met my eyes! Never will the memory of that dreadful scene be wiped from my mind.

The floor of the Temple covered in blood, the image of the Sun trampled underfoot, raging soldiers pursuing our distraught Virgins and slaughtering whatever stood in their way; our *Mamas*[13]

---

[11] A large number of short strings of different colours which the Indians, who had no system of writing, used to calculate payments to their troops, or the number of their population. Some authors claim that they also used them to record for posterity the memorable deeds of their Incas.

[12] In the Temple of the Sun there were one hundred doors which only the Inca had the power to have opened.

[13] Something like Governesses of the Virgins of the Temple.

dying from their blows, their robes still burning in the fire cast by their weapons of thunder; the groans of terror, the frenzied cries filling the air with horror and dread robbed me of my very consciousness.

Returning to my senses, I found myself hiding behind the altar, clinging to it as if moved by a natural and almost involuntary instinct. There, paralysed with shock, I saw these barbarians go by; fear of discovery stopped my very breath.

I noticed however that their cruelty abated when they saw the precious ornaments which filled the Temple, that they were seizing those with the most striking brilliance, and that they were even tearing down the panels of gold which adorned the walls.* I concluded that plunder was the reason for their brutality, and that if I did not try to stop it, I might escape their blows. I devised a plan to leave the Temple, to have myself taken to your palace and to ask the *Capa Inca*[14] for assistance and refuge, for my companions and for myself; but as soon as I moved to slip away, I felt myself being stopped. Oh my dearest Aza, I still tremble at the thought; those heathens dared to lay their sacrilegious hands on a daughter of the Sun.*

Torn from my holy dwelling place, dragged ignominiously out of the Temple, I beheld for the first time the threshold of the Celestial Gate which I was only meant to cross in the trappings of Royalty;[15]* instead of flowers which should have been strewn beneath my feet, I saw the streets covered with blood and the dying; instead of sharing with you the honours of the throne as I was meant to do, I am the captive of tyrants, locked away in a dark prison; the space I occupy in the world extends no further than the confines of my own being. A mattress bathed in my tears is home to my body worn out by the torments of my soul; but such pain will be as nothing to me, my life's dear support, if I can but learn that you still live.

In the midst of this dreadful upheaval, I do not know by what happy chance I kept my *Quipos* with me. I have them still, my

---

[14] The generic name for the ruling Incas.

[15] Virgins dedicated to the Sun entered the Temple almost at birth and left only on the day of their marriage.

dearest Aza, they are this day the only treasure of my heart, as they will let us express both your love and mine; the same knots which will tell you of my existence, will tell me of your fate when they are retied in your hands.* But alas, by what means shall I be able to send them to you? By what cunning will they be returned to me? I do not yet know; but the same feelings which inspired us to put them to this use, will also show us how to deceive our oppressors. Whoever the faithful *Chaqui*[16] may be who brings you this precious gift, I shall forever envy his good fortune. He will see you, my dearest Aza; I would sacrifice every day which the Sun destines for me, just to be with you for a single moment. He will see you, my dearest Aza! The sound of your voice will inspire respect and fear in his soul. It would bring happiness and joy to mine. He will see you, and be assured that you live; he will give thanks for your life, as he stands before you, whereas I shall be in the grip of uncertainty, my blood frozen in my veins as I wait impatiently for his return. O my dearest Aza! Every torment known to loving souls is gathered in my heart; a single moment in your presence, and they would all just melt away; I would give my life for such a moment.

LETTER TWO

My dearest Aza, may the tree of virtue forever spread its shade over the family of that devoted subject who took from me at my window the secret fabric of my thoughts, and who delivered it into your hands! May *Pachacamac*[17] extend his years of life as a reward for so skilfully bringing me the joys of the blessed with your reply.

Love's store of treasures has been opened up to me; I draw from it a feeling of intense joy which intoxicates my soul. As I untie the secrets of your heart, my own bathes in a fragrant sea. You are alive, and the bonds which were to unite us have not been broken! Such happiness was the object of my desires, but I did not dare hope for it.

[16] Messenger.
[17] The God Creator, more powerful than the Sun.

Having abandoned all concern for myself, I feared only for your life; it is safe, there can be no more misfortune. You love me, and joy which had been reduced to nothing is born again in my heart. I taste the delight of knowing that I please the one I love; but this does not make me forget that I owe you everything you deign to approve in me. Just as the rose draws its brilliant colours from the rays of the Sun, the charms which please you in my mind and heart are simply the fruits of your own luminous inspiration; nothing is truly mine except my love.

If you were an ordinary man, I would have remained in that state of ignorance to which those of my sex are condemned. But your soul, rising above such customs, saw them as nothing more than abuses; you broke through their barriers to make me worthy of you. You could not allow that a being no different from you should be confined to the humiliating honour of giving life to your descendants.* You wished our holy *Amautas*[18] to adorn my mind with their sublime knowledge. But, oh light of my life, had it not been for my desire to please you, would I have had the resolve to give up my blissful ignorance in exchange for the painful activity of study? Without the desire to earn your esteem, your trust, your respect, with virtues which strengthen love, and which love turns to sheer delight, I would have been no more than the object of your gaze; absence would already have erased me from your memory.

Alas! if you still love me, why am I still captive? As I cast my eyes on the walls of my prison, my joy disappears, horror takes hold of me, and my fears are reawakened. You have not been robbed of your freedom, yet you do not come to my rescue; you know of my fate, yet it has not changed. No, my dearest Aza, these brutal people whom you call Spaniards do not leave you as free as you think. I can see as many signs of servitude in the honours they bestow on you, as I can in the captivity to which they subject me.

Your goodness deceives you. You believe the promises which these barbarians make you through their interpreters, because

[18] Philosophers of the Indies.

your own word cannot be broken; but I, who do not understand their language, I whom they do not consider worth deceiving, I can see what they are doing.

Your subjects take them for gods, they take sides with them: oh, my dearest Aza, woe betide a people ruled by fear! Free yourself of this illusion, beware the false kindness of these strangers. Surrender your empire, since *Viracocha* has foretold its downfall. Redeem your life and your freedom at the price of your power, your greatness, your treasures; you will be left with just what nature gave you. Our lives will be safe.

Rich in the possession of each other's heart, great through our virtues, powerful in our moderation, we shall retreat to the humblest shelter and take pleasure in the sky, the earth, and our love. You will be more a king ruling over my soul than you are now, doubting the affection of countless subjects: my submission to your wishes will enable you to enjoy, without need of tyranny, that glorious right to govern. As I obey you, I shall make your empire echo to the sound of my joyful songs; your diadem[19] shall be forever the work of my hands, and you will lose nothing of your sovereignty save its cares and travails.

How many times, my life's dear soul, have you complained of the responsibilities of your rank? How have the ceremonies which accompanied your every visit made you envy the lot of your subjects? You would once have wished to live for me alone; are you now afraid to cast off so many shackles? Am I no longer the same Zilia whom you would have preferred to your empire? No, I cannot believe it, my heart has not changed, why should there be any change in yours?

I still love, I can still see the same Aza who ruled over my soul from the first moment I saw him; I can recall that blessed day when your father, my sovereign Lord, first shared with you the right which was his alone to enter the inner part of the Temple;[20] I can picture still the lovely sight of our Virgins gathered together, their beauty given a new lustre by the

---

[19] The Diadem of the Incas was a type of fringe. It was the work of the Virgins of the Sun.

[20] The ruling Inca alone had the right to enter the Temple of the Sun.

enchanting order in which they were standing, just as the brightest flowers in a garden are given a new splendour by the symmetry of their beds.

You appeared among us like a rising Sun, whose gentle radiance heralds the serenity of a beautiful day; the burning light in your eyes brought blushes of modesty to our cheeks, innocent embarrassment held our gaze captive; radiant joy shone bright from yours, you had never before seen so many beauties in one place. Until then we had only ever seen the *Capa-Inca*; the silence of our astonishment reigned all around. I do not know what my fellow Virgins were thinking, but what feelings invaded my own heart! For the first time I experienced confusion, uneasiness, yet also pleasure. Troubled by the turmoil in my soul, I was about to flee from your sight; but you walked towards me, and respect held me still.

Oh, my dearest Aza, the memory of this first moment of my happiness will be ever dear to me! The sound of your voice, just like the sweet melodies of our hymns, filled every vein in my body with that sublime trembling and sacred awe which the presence of the Divinity inspires in us.

Quivering, overwhelmed, my timidity robbed me of the very power of speech; given courage at last by your kind words, I dared lift up my eyes to you, I met your gaze. No, not even death will wipe from my memory the tender feelings of our souls at this moment as they met and became one in a single instant.

If we had any doubts at all about our origins, my dearest Aza, this shaft of light would confound our uncertainty. What else but the principle of fire could have endowed us with that keen understanding of our hearts, which was imparted, absorbed, and experienced with inexplicable speed?

I was too ignorant of love's effects not to be deceived. My mind was full of the sublime theology of our *Cucipatas*,[21] and I took the fire which inspired me to be divine rapture; I thought the Sun was manifesting his will to me through you, that he was selecting me for his preferred wife:[22] I sighed at this thought, but once you had

---

[21] Priests of the Sun.
[22] One Virgin was chosen by the Sun, who should never be married.

gone, I looked inside my heart and found nothing there but the image of you.

My dearest Aza, what a transformation your presence had wrought in me! Everything around me took on a new aspect; I felt that I was seeing my companions for the first time. How beautiful they now seemed to me! I could not bear to be with them. Withdrawing to one side, I was giving way to the anxiety in my soul when one of them came to awaken me from my reverie, but gave me new reasons to lose myself in it again. She told me that, since I was your closest female relative,* I was destined to be your wife, as soon as my age permitted this union.

I knew nothing of the laws of your empire,[23]* but from the moment I first saw you, my heart was too enlightened not to sense happiness in the thought of being yours. However, far from grasping its full extent, and accustomed as I was to the sacred name of Wife of the Sun, I hoped for no more than to see you every day, to adore you, and to offer you my vows as I did to that Divinity.

It is you, my dearest Aza, it is you who later filled my soul with rapture when you told me that the noble rank of your wife would bind me to your heart, to your throne, to your glory, to your virtues; that I would enjoy without interruption those meetings which were too rare and too brief to satisfy our hearts, meetings which adorned my mind with the perfections of your soul, and which added to my happiness the delightful hope that I might one day be the cause of yours.

Oh, my dearest Aza, how flattering to my heart was your impatience at my extreme youth, which delayed our union! How long did these two years which have just passed seem to you, and yet how short their duration has actually been! Alas! that blessed moment had arrived. What fate has changed it to misery? What god persecutes innocence and virtue in this way? Or what infernal power has separated us from each other? Horror takes hold of me, my heart breaks, my tears soak the work of my hands. Aza! my dearest Aza!...

[23] The laws of the Indians obliged the Incas to marry their sisters, and, if they had none, to take for a wife the first Princess of the Blood of the Incas who was a Virgin of the Sun.

LETTER THREE

It is you, dear light of my days, you who call me back to life. Would I wish to preserve it, if I did not know for certain that death would reap, at a single stroke, both your life and mine! That moment had come when the spark of divine fire with which the Sun gives life to our being was about to be extinguished: nature, in its diligence, was already preparing to give another form to that material part of me which belongs to it. I was dying; you were about to lose for ever a half of your self, when my love returned me to life, and this I now offer up to you. But how shall I be able to tell you of the remarkable events which have befallen me? How can I recall thoughts which were already confused when they first came to me, and which have become even less intelligible with the passage of time?

No sooner had I entrusted the latest fabric of my thoughts to our faithful *Chaqui*, my dearest Aza, when I heard a great commotion in our dwelling: in the middle of the night, two of my abductors came to take me from my gloomy retreat, with no less violence than they had used to snatch me from the Temple of the Sun.

I do not know on what path I was taken; we walked only by night, and by day we halted in barren deserts, without seeking any shelter. Before long, overcome by exhaustion, I was carried by some kind of *Hamas* whose movements tired me almost as much as if I had continued to walk. Then one night, having finally arrived it seems at their destination, these barbarians picked me up and carried me to a house which, even though it was dark, I could tell was extremely difficult to reach. I was thrust into a place which was even more cramped and uncomfortable than ever my first prison had been. But, my dearest Aza! how could I convince you of what I cannot understand myself, if you did not know that a lie has never soiled the lips of a child of the Sun![24] This house, which I judged to be of great size given the number of people it contained, this house was not fixed to the ground, but seemed to be somehow suspended, in a state of perpetual rocking.

[24] It was regarded as axiomatic that a Peruvian had never lied.

Oh light of my mind, *Ticaiviracocha* would have needed to fill my soul like yours with his divine knowledge, if I were to understand this marvel. All I know for certain is that this dwelling has not been built by a friend of men: a few moments after I entered it, its constant motion, combined with a foul odour, caused me such violent sickness that I can scarce believe it did not finish me: and this was just the start of my troubles.

A considerable time had passed, I had almost recovered from my sickness, when I was torn from my sleep one morning by a noise more terrible than that of *Yalpor*. Our house was shaken as violently as the earth itself will be when the Moon falls upon it and reduces the universe to dust.[25] Cries, added to this uproar, made it even more dreadful; my senses, gripped by a secret horror, filled my soul with just a single thought: that the whole of nature was being destroyed. I believed this peril to be universal, and I trembled for your life. My terror finally reached the point where it could increase no more, when I saw a company of raging men, their faces and clothes all bloody, storm into my room. I could not bear this awful sight, my strength, my very consciousness forsook me: I still do not know what followed this dreadful incident. Restored to my senses, I found myself in a bed which was moderately clean, surrounded by several Savages who were different from those cruel Spaniards, but who were no less unfamiliar to me.

Can you imagine my surprise, finding myself in a new dwelling, among new men, yet unable to understand how this change had come about? I promptly closed my eyes again, so that I might collect my senses and then establish if I was still in this world, or if my soul had taken leave of my body and passed into the unknown regions.[26]

Shall I make a confession to you, my heart's dear Idol? Weary of this hateful life, sickened by all the different torments I had endured, crushed by the weight of my horrible fate, I was unmoved

---

[25] The Indians believed that the end of the world would be brought about by the Moon falling to the earth.

[26] The Indians believed that after death, the soul entered unknown regions where it would be rewarded or punished according to its deserts.

by the prospect of my life's end which I could feel drawing near. I obstinately refused all the help offered me; within a few days, I had reached the threshold of death, and I did so without regret.

The exhaustion of one's strength wipes out all feeling. Already, the images taken in by my enfeebled imagination were no clearer than the faintest of drawings, sketched by a trembling hand; already, objects which had once moved me the most now excited in me nothing more than that kind of vague sensation which we experience when we let our minds wander in aimless dreaming; I was almost gone. This state, my dearest Aza, is not as dreadful as we think. From afar it terrifies us, because we think about it with our strength intact; but when it comes, and we have been weakened by suffering, gradually increasing as we are brought nearer to it, that critical moment seems no more than a moment of repose. I discovered, however, that the natural instinct which impels us during our life to delve into the future, and even into the future which we shall not live to see, seems to acquire a new strength at the very point of death. We cease to live for ourselves; we want to know how we shall live on in the object of our love. It was during one of those hallucinations in my soul that I imagined myself transported inside your palace; I arrived there at the very moment you had been told of my death. I imagined so vividly what was sure to happen, that reality itself would not have been more convincing: I saw you, my dearest Aza, pale, disfigured, bereft of feeling, like a lily withered by the burning rays of the midday sun. Is love then sometimes brutal? I rejoiced in your grief, I inflamed it with sad farewells; I found comfort, even enjoyment, in pouring over your life the poison of regret; and this same love which made me cruel, wounded my heart at your horrible misery. Finally, awoken as if from a deep sleep, ravaged by your own suffering, trembling for your life, I called out for help, I beheld the light again.

Shall I ever see you again, you, dearest arbiter of my existence? Alas! who can promise me that? I no longer know where I am, perhaps it is far from you. But if we are to be kept apart by the vast spaces inhabited by the children of the Sun, the weightless cloud of my thoughts will never cease to hover about you.

LETTER FOUR

However great our love of life, my dearest Aza, suffering reduces
it, and despair snuffs it out. The scorn which nature seems to
have for our being by abandoning us to despair may appal us
at first; but then, our inability to free ourselves of it is such
humiliating proof of our inadequacy that we are driven to despise
ourselves.

I can no longer live in, or for myself; every breath I take is a
sacrifice made for love of you, and with each day it becomes more
painful; if time brings some relief to the violent anguish which
consumes me, it doubles the suffering in my mind. Far from
clarifying my fate, it seems to make it even more obscure.
Everything around me is unfamiliar, everything is new, everything stirs my curiosity, and nothing can satisfy it.* In vain I
concentrate and strive to understand, or to be understood; both
are equally beyond me. Weary from so much fruitless effort, I
thought I might stop such suffering at its source by concealing
from my eyes the very sight of the objects around me: I persisted
for a while in keeping them tight shut; what wasted effort! the
darkness to which I had freely condemned myself merely preserved my modesty from the constant offence of seeing men
whose attentions and help are nothing but torments to me; but it
did nothing to diminish the restlessness in my soul. Having
retreated into myself, my anxieties were all the more acute, and
the desire to express them more urgent. The impossibility of
making myself understood causes even now an agony in my very
body which is no less unbearable than pains which might seem
more real. Oh the cruelty of such a plight!

Alas! I thought I was beginning to understand some words of
those savage Spaniards, I was finding connections with our
own venerable tongue; I believed that in a little while I might be
able to communicate with them: I am far from imagining the
same possibility with these new tyrants, they express themselves
with such rapidity that I cannot even distinguish the inflections of
their voices. Everything leads me to believe that they are not of

the same nation; and judging by the difference in their manners and their outward character, it is easy to see that *Pachacamac* assigned them very different shares of those elements from which he formed human beings. The stern and fierce appearance of my first abductors shows that they were made from the same substance as the hardest metals; the men before me now seem to have slipped from the Creator's hands before he had done more than assemble for their composition just air and fire: the proud eyes, the dark, fixed look of the Spaniards clearly showed that they were cold-blooded in their cruelty; the inhumanity of their actions has proved this all too well. The smiling faces of these others, the kindness in their looks, a certain eagerness in all they do which seems to proceed from good will, all this argues in their favour; but I can see contradictions in their behaviour which leave me as yet undecided about them.

Two of these savages hardly ever leave my bedside: one, whom I take to be the *Cacique*,[27] judging by his noble air,* treats me I think with great respect, in his way; the other gives me some of the care which my illness requires, but his kindness is unfeeling, his assistance is cruel, and his familiarity overbearing.

From the moment I first recovered some strength and found myself in their power, this second one, much bolder than the others as I had clearly noticed, sought to take my hand, which I pulled back from him with indescribable alarm; he seemed surprised at my resistance, and with no regard at all for modesty, he instantly took it again. Frail, faint, and uttering only words which were not remotely understood, how could I stop him? He kept hold of it, my dearest Aza, for as long as he wished, and from that moment I have to give it to him myself several times a day, if I wish to avoid disputes which always turn to my disadvantage.

This kind of ceremony[28] seems to me to be a superstition of these peoples: I think they must find in it some insight into my illness; but one evidently needs to belong to their nation to feel its benefits, for I have experienced next to none. I still suffer from an inner burning which quite consumes me; I scarcely have enough

---

[27] *Cacique* is a kind of provincial Governor.
[28] The Indians had no knowledge of Medicine.

strength to knot my *Quipos*. I spend as much time doing this as my feeble state allows. These knots which touch my senses seem to make my thoughts more real; the kind of resemblance I imagine them to have with words creates an illusion which brings relief to my suffering. I fancy that I am speaking to you, telling you that I love you, assuring you of my devotion, of my affection; this sweet delusion is my sole possession and my life. If the burden of my suffering obliges me to put my work aside, I grieve at your absence; thus, devoted wholly to my affection, not a single moment of my life is not yours.

Alas! What other use could I put it to? Oh, my dearest Aza! even if you were not the master of my soul, even if the bonds of love did not tie me to you inseparably, how could I turn my thoughts away from the light of my life, plunged into the darkest abyss as I am? You are the Sun of my days, you illuminate them, you renew them, they are yours. You cherish me, I agree to live. What will you do for me? You will love me, that is my reward.

LETTER FIVE

How I have suffered, my dearest Aza, since the last knots I dedicated to you! The loss of my *Quipos* was the only misery I had left to endure; as soon as my interfering persecutors noticed that this occupation increased my dejection, they took them from me.

They have finally given me back this most precious part of my love, but it was at the price of many a tear. All I have left is this expression of my feelings, all I have left is the pitiful consolation of being able to paint my suffering for you; could I lose that and not despair?

Such is my strange destiny that I have been robbed even of that comfort which those in misfortune find in speaking of their troubles. We believe that we awaken pity when our troubles are heard, that some of our pain passes across the face of those who listen to us; whatever the reason, this seems to bring us solace. But I cannot make myself understood, and I am surrounded by nothing but jubilation.

I cannot even enjoy in peace the new kind of isolation to which I am reduced by my inability to communicate my thoughts. I am surrounded by importunate creatures whose attentive looks disturb the solitude of my soul, restrict the movements of my body, and inhibit my very thoughts. I often find that I have forgotten that delightful freedom given us by nature when it made our feelings impenetrable to others, and I sometimes worry that these inquisitive savages might detect the disapproving reflections which their strange behaviour inspires in me; I consciously strive to control my thoughts, as if they were able to read my mind, however much I might resist it.

A single moment can destroy the opinion which another moment might have given me of their character, and of what they think of me.

Leaving aside countless trivial refusals, they even deny me, my dearest Aza, the sustenance necessary to keep me alive, the very freedom to choose where I wish to be; they keep me, almost by force, in this bed which I can endure no longer. I can only conclude, therefore, that they regard me as their slave, and that their power is tyrannical.

On the other hand, if I consider their extreme concern to preserve my life, or the respect with which they perform the services they render me, I am tempted to think that they believe me to be of a species superior to human kind.

None of them appears before me without bending his body to a greater or lesser extent, just as we do when we worship the Sun. The *Cacique* seems to want to imitate our Inca ceremonies on the day of *Raymi*;[29] he kneels down very close to my bed, he stays for quite some time in this uncomfortable position; sometimes he remains silent, and with downcast eyes he seems lost in deep contemplation;* I can see on his face that respectful confusion which the *Great Name*[30] inspires in us when spoken aloud. If he finds an opportunity to take hold of my hand, he puts it to his lips with the

---

[29] The *Raymi*, principal festival of the Sun; the Inca and the Priests worshipped the Sun on their knees.

[30] The *Great Name* was *Pachacamac*, it was spoken only rarely, and with many signs of veneration.

same veneration we show for the sacred *Diadem*.[31] Sometimes he
utters a great many words which are quite unlike the ordinary
language of his nation. Their tone is gentler, clearer, more measured; he adds that look of concern which precedes tears, those
sighs which express the needs of the soul, that intonation which
is almost a moan, in short, everything associated with the desire
to obtain grace. Alas, my dearest Aza, if he knew me well, if he
were not somehow mistaken about what I am, what prayer would
he offer up to me?

Could it be that his nation worships idols? I have so far seen no
adoration of the Sun; perhaps women are the object of their devotion. Before the great *Manco-Capac* brought down to earth the
will of the Sun, our ancestors made gods of anything which struck
fear in them or brought them pleasure: perhaps these savages feel
those two emotions just for women.

But if they were worshipping me, would they add to my miser-
ies by keeping me in this dreadful confinement? No, they would
seek to please me, they would respond to any sign of my will; I
would be free, I would leave this hateful dwelling; I would go in
search of the master of my soul; just one look from him would
erase from my memory so many past misfortunes.

LETTER SIX

What a dreadful surprise, my dearest Aza! How our misfortunes
have increased! How we are to be pitied! There is no remedy for
our troubles; all I can do is tell you of them, and then die.

They finally allowed me to leave my bed. I eagerly took advantage of this freedom; I dragged myself to a small window, which
had long been the object of my impatient curiosity. I opened it
hurriedly: but what did I see! Dear love of my life! I shall not find
the words to convey the extent of my shock, and the mortal
despair which gripped me when I discovered that all around me
was nothing but that dreadful element, the very sight of which
makes me shudder.

---

[31] They kissed the Diadem of *Manco-Capac*, as we kiss the Relics of our Saints.

From my first glance, I understood only too well what caused that uncomfortable motion of our dwelling. I am in one of those floating houses which the Spaniards used to reach as far as our ill-starred lands and which had been described to me only very imperfectly.

Can you imagine, dearest Aza, what dreadful thoughts entered my soul at this appalling discovery? I am certain that they are taking me far from you, I no longer breathe the same air, I no longer live in the same element; you will never know where I am, whether I love you, if I exist; the extinction of my life will seem an event too insignificant even to be reported to you. Dear arbiter of my days, what value can my wretched life have for you from now on? Let me give back to our Divinity a gift which I can no longer bear, and no longer enjoy; I shall see you no more, I no longer wish to live.

I am losing what I love; the universe has been destroyed for me, it is no more than a vast desert which I fill with the cries of my love; hear them, dear object of my affection, feel for me, and let me die...

What illusion is leading me astray! No, my dearest Aza, no, it is not you who bids me live, it is my timid nature, shuddering in terror, which borrows your voice, more powerful than its own, to postpone a fate which never ceases to fill it with dread. But the time has come, and the readiest means will deliver me from nature's regrets...

Let the sea engulf in its depths for ever my wretched love, my life, and my despair.

Take these last feelings left in my heart, most wretched Aza, take them in. My heart admitted nothing but the thought of you, it wanted to live for you alone, it dies, filled with your love. I love you, I know it, I feel it still, I speak it for the last time...

LETTER SEVEN

Aza, you have not lost everything, you still reign over a heart; I am breathing yet. The vigilance of those who watched over me put a stop to my deadly scheme, leaving me only with the shame of having attempted it. I shall not tell you the details of a plan no sooner made than undone. Would I ever dare lift up my eyes to yours, if you had witnessed my loss of control?

My reason, ravaged by despair, could help me no more; my life seemed worthless; I had forgotten your love.

How cruel it is to regain our composure after a fit of madness! How different do the same objects seem to us! In the panic which springs from despair, we take rage for courage, and fear of suffering for firmness of resolve. When a word, a look, a shock returns us to our senses, we realize that weakness alone is the cause of our heroism; its outcome is just remorse, and contempt its sole reward.

The knowledge of my offence is the harshest punishment I can receive. Abandoned to bitter remorse, hiding beneath a veil of shame, I stand to one side; I am afraid that my body takes up too much space; I would like to hide it from the light; my tears flow in abundance, my grief is calm, no sound gives it voice; but I have surrendered to it entirely. Can I ever atone for my crime? It was a crime against you.

For the last two days, these well-meaning savages have tried in vain to make me share in the joy that delights them; I can only guess at its cause, but even if I knew what it was, I would not think myself worthy to join in their celebrations. Their dances, their cries of joy, a red liquor similar to Maïs[32] which they drink plentifully, their eagerness to gaze at the Sun from wherever they might catch sight of it, all this would have left me in no doubt that their rejoicing was in honour of the Divine Star, if the behaviour of the *Cacique* had been in keeping with that of the others.

But, ever since the offence I have committed, far from taking part in the general excitement, he shares only in my sorrow. His eagerness is more respectful, his concern more solicitous, his attentions more keen.

He has realized that the continual presence of the savages in his troupe added a feeling of constraint to my distress; he has

---

[32] Maïs is a plant from which the Indians make a potent, wholesome brew; they present it to the Sun on its festival days and they partake of it to the point of drunkenness after the sacrifice. See the *History of the Incas*, volume ii, page 151.

delivered me from their importunate looks; I now have scarcely more than his to endure.

Would you believe it, my dearest Aza? There are moments when I feel a kind of pleasure in these silent exchanges; the fervour in his eyes reminds me of the look I have seen in yours; the similarities I see there captivate my heart. Alas! How fleeting is this illusion, and how enduring the regrets which follow! They will end only with my life, since I live only for you.

LETTER EIGHT

When one object alone is the focus of all our thoughts, my dearest Aza, we take an interest in external events only to the extent that we can relate them to that object. If you were not the only motivation in my soul, would I have moved, as I have just done, from the torment of despair to the most flattering hope? The *Cacique* had already tried several times, without success, to draw me to that window which I can no longer contemplate without shuddering. At last, pressed to do so by renewed pleas, I let myself be taken there. Ah, my dearest Aza, how well was I rewarded for my consent!

By some miracle I cannot comprehend, by making me look through a kind of hollowed cane, he showed me land so distant that, without the help of this wonderful machine, my eyes could not have reached it.

At the same time, using signs which are now becoming more familiar to me, he gave me to understand that we are heading towards this land, and that the sight of it was the sole cause of the celebrations which I took to be a sacrifice to the Sun.

I immediately realized all the benefits of this discovery; hope, like a ray of light, has shone brightly to the very depths of my heart.

It is certain that they are taking me to this land they have shown me, it is clear that it is a part of your empire since the Sun sheds its beneficent rays upon it.[33] I am no longer a captive of the

---

[33] The Indians did not know our hemisphere, and believed that the Sun shone only on the land of its children.

cruel Spaniards. Who then could prevent me from returning to your rule?

Yes, dearest Aza, I am to be reunited with the one I love. My love, my reason, my desires, everything assures me that this is so. I fly into your arms, a flood of joy fills my soul, the past fades away, my troubles are no more; they are forgotten, the future alone concerns me, it is my sole treasure.

Aza, my dearest hope, I have not lost you, I shall see your face, your robes, your shadow; I shall love you, I shall tell you so myself. What torments would not be wiped away by such bliss?

LETTER NINE

How long the days seem, my dearest Aza, when we count them! Time, like space, is sensed only by its limits. Our thoughts and our sight both lose their bearings in the unchanging uniformity of the one and the other: if objects mark out the boundaries of space, it seems to me that our hopes mark out the limits of time; and that if hope abandons us, or if it is not clearly defined, we are no more aware of the passage of time than we are of the air which fills space.*

Ever since that fatal moment when we were separated, my soul and my heart, both equally withered by misfortune, were sunk in a state of total abandonment, one of nature's horrors, the very image of oblivion; the days went by without my taking notice of them, no hope focused my attention on their length. Now that hope marks out every instant of them, their duration seems infinite to me, and as I recover my peace of mind, I taste the delight of recovering the freedom to think.

Ever since my imagination has opened up to joy, countless thoughts spring up and occupy it until I am quite exhausted. Plans for pleasure and happiness succeed each other in turn; new ideas are readily admitted, even those which I had not been conscious of, take shape without any effort on my part.

Within the last two days, I have understood several words in the *Cacique*'s language which I did not realize I knew. They are still only terms applicable to objects, they can in no way express my thoughts, and do not help me at all to understand the thoughts of others; but they have already brought me some explanations which I needed.

I know that the name of the *Cacique* is *Déterville*, that of our floating house is *vessel*, and that of the land where we are going is *France*.

This last discovery alarmed me at first, I do not remember hearing of any province in your realm with such a name. But when I considered the countless lands in your empire whose names I cannot recall, this sudden fear soon passed; how could it survive for long beside the unshakeable confidence given me at every moment by the sight of the Sun? No, my dearest Aza, this Divine Star shines only on its children; to doubt that for a single moment would make me a criminal; I am returning to your dominion, I am on the point of seeing you. I hasten to my happiness.

Among my transports of joy, gratitude prepares me a sweet pleasure; you will heap honours and riches on the kindly *Cacique* who will return us to each other, he will carry the memory of Zilia back to his province. Rewarding his virtue will make him more virtuous still and his happiness will be to your glory.

Nothing can compare, my dearest Aza, to the kindness he shows me; far from treating me as his slave, he seems to be mine. He is as considerate to me now as he was disobliging during my illness; attentive to me, to my anxieties, to my pleasures, he seems to have no other concerns. I accept them with a little less embarrassment now that experience and reflection have clearly shown me that I was mistaken to suspect him of idolatry.

It is not that he does not often repeat more or less the same displays which I took to be signs of worship; but the tone, the look, and the manner which he adopts as he does so convince me that it is just a form of play widely practised in his country.

He begins by having me pronounce distinctly some words in his language. As soon as I have repeated after him, *yes, I love you*, or *I promise to be yours*, delight spreads over his face, he kisses my hands with great emotion and with a look of joy which is the very opposite of the gravity that accompanies divine worship.

But though I have no concerns about his religion, I am not so sure about the country from which he comes. His language and clothes are so different from ours that my confidence is often shaken by this. Anxious thoughts sometimes cast a shadow over my fondest hopes; I move in turn from fear to joy and from joy to anxiety.

Made weary by such confusion in my mind, sickened by the uncertainty which torments me, I had decided to stop thinking altogether; but how can one slow down the movement of a soul deprived of all communication with others, which acts only on itself and which is spurred to thought by such important concerns? I cannot do so, my dearest Aza, I seek enlightenment with an urgency which quite consumes me, yet I constantly find myself in the deepest darkness. I knew that the loss of one sense can sometimes lead us astray, but I find, to my surprise, that even with all my senses intact I merely drift from one error to another. Could it be that to understand a language is to understand the soul? O dearest Aza, how many distressing truths I am now glimpsing in my misfortune! But let me banish these sad thoughts; we are approaching land. The light of my life will disperse in an instant the shadows which surround me.

LETTER TEN

I have finally reached this land, the object of my desires, my dearest Aza, but I can as yet see no sign at all of the happiness I had expected: everything which passes before my eyes strikes me, surprises me, astonishes me, and leaves me with nothing but the vaguest impression, a sense of confused stupidity which I do not even try to shake off; my mistakes blunt my ability to judge, I remain uncertain, I almost doubt what I see.

No sooner had we left the floating house than we entered a town built on the bank of the sea. The people who crowded after us seem to me to be of the same nation as the *Cacique*, but the houses bear no resemblance to those in the cities of the Sun: if our cities have houses of greater beauty thanks to the richness of their ornaments, those here surpass ours by far in the marvels which fill them.

On entering the room which Déterville has made my dwelling, my heart leapt. I saw in a recess a young person dressed like a Virgin of the Sun; I ran towards her with open arms. What a surprise, my dearest Aza, what a great surprise it was to discover nothing but impenetrable resistance just where I could see a human figure moving about in the most extensive space!*

Astonishment stopped me in my tracks, my eyes fixed on this phantom, when Déterville showed me his own figure next to the one which held my attention; I was touching him, I was talking to him, and I could see him at once both very close and very far from me.

These marvels unsettle one's reason, they are an offence to one's judgement; what is one to think of those who live in this country? Are they to be feared, are they to be loved? I shall take care not to make up my mind just yet about that.

The *Cacique* explained to me that the figure I could see was my own; but what does that tell me? Does it make the marvel any less great? Am I less mortified to find nothing but error and ignorance in my mind? I realize to my distress, my dearest Aza, that the least knowledgeable in this country know more than do all our *Amautas*.

The *Cacique* has given me a *China*,[34] young and full of spirit; it is a great comfort for me to see women again and to be served by them; several others are eager to be of service to me, but I would prefer them not to do so, their presence reawakens my fears. Judging by the way they look at me, I can see clearly that they have never been to *Cuzco*.[35]* And yet I still cannot be sure of anything, my mind is still drifting on a sea of uncertainties; my heart, the one fixed point, desires, hopes for, and awaits just a single joy, without which there can be only sorrow.

[34] Servant or maid.
[35] Capital of Peru.

LETTER ELEVEN

Although I have made every effort in my power to shed some light on my fate, my dearest Aza, I know no more now than I did three days ago. All I have been able to observe is that the savages of this country seem as good, as humane as the *Cacique*; they sing and dance as if every day they had land to cultivate.[36] If I drew conclusions based on the differences between their customs and those of our nation, I would lose all hope; yet I remember that your venerable father conquered quite distant provinces whose peoples were no more similar to us than these are: why might not this be one of that number? The Sun seems content to shine on it, its rays are more beautiful, purer than I have ever seen, and I happily surrender myself to the confidence it inspires in me; my only remaining worry concerns the time it will take to discover all I need to know regarding our mutual interests; for, my dearest Aza, I am now certain beyond doubt that it is only by mastering the language of this country that I shall be able to learn the truth and put an end to my anxieties.

I do not miss a single opportunity to learn something of this language, I take advantage of every moment I am left alone by Déterville to take lessons from my *China*. But she is a poor resource; unable to make her understand my thoughts, I cannot have any kind of reasoned conversation with her. The *Cacique*'s signs are sometimes more useful to me. Habit has made them a kind of language between us, and this enables us at least to express our wishes. He took me yesterday to a house where, without this understanding, I would have behaved very badly.

We entered a room which was bigger and more richly decorated than my own; many people were gathered there. I disliked the widespread amazement which was shown when I appeared. The immoderate laughter which several young women attempted to stifle, and which began again when they looked at me, aroused such a painful feeling in my heart that I would have taken it for shame had I felt guilty of some offence. But feeling only great

[36] Land was cultivated by the whole community in Peru and the days of this work were days of rejoicing.

repugnance at remaining in their company, I was about to withdraw when a sign from Déterville stopped me in my tracks.

I understood that I would be committing an offence if I were to
leave, and I was very concerned to do nothing which might
deserve the blame they were already attaching to me, and without
cause; so I stayed where I was, and giving all my attention to these
women, I concluded that it was nothing more than the strange-
ness of my dress that caused the surprise of some and the offensive laughter of others. I felt pity for their weakness; my only
thought from that moment on was to persuade them by my bear-
ing that my soul was not quite as different from theirs as my
clothes were from their finery.

A man I would have taken for a *Curacas*,[37] had he not been
dressed in black, came and took me by the hand in a courteous
manner and led me over to a woman whose proud air led me to
believe she was the *Pallas*[38] of this country. He said some words
to her, which I recognized from having heard Déterville utter
them countless times: *How beautiful she is! What lovely eyes!*
Another man answered *Such grace, the figure of a Nymph!* Apart
from the women who said nothing, all the men repeated more or
less the same words; I do not yet know what they mean, but they
must surely express pleasant thoughts, because those who speak
them invariably have a beaming face.

The *Cacique* seemed extremely pleased with what people were
saying; he never left my side, or if he did move away to speak to
someone, he never lost sight of me, and using signs he advised me
of what I should do: for my part, I watched him very attentively
so as not to offend the customs of a nation which knew so little of
our own.

I do not know, my dearest Aza, if I shall be able to explain to
you just how extraordinary the behaviour of these savages has
seemed to me.

They have so lively and impatient a manner that words alone
are not enough for them to express themselves; they speak as

---

[37] The *Curacas* were the minor rulers of a Country; they had the privilege of wearing
the same robes as the Incas.

[38] The generic name for Princesses.

much through the movement of their bodies as they do by the sound of their voice. What I have seen of their continual gestures has quite convinced me that those displays of the *Cacique* which caused me such unease and about which I made so many false assumptions, actually meant very little.

Yesterday he kissed the hands of the *Pallas*, and those of all the other women; he even kissed them on the cheeks, which I had never seen before. Men came to embrace him, some took him by the hand, others pulled at his clothing, and all did so with a rapidity which we simply cannot conceive.

Judging their mind by the liveliness of their gestures, I am sure that our measured expressions, and the sublime comparisons which convey so naturally our tender feelings and our affectionate thoughts, would seem quite insipid to them; they would take our serious and modest look for stupidity, and our solemn manner for dullness. But would you believe it, my dearest Aza? Despite their failings, I would be quite happy to live among them if you were here. A certain cordiality in all they do makes them likeable, and if my soul were more at ease, I would take pleasure in the many different objects which constantly pass before my eyes. But as they have so little to do with you, their novelty loses its charm; you alone are the source of my well-being and of my pleasure.

LETTER TWELVE

It has been a long time, my dearest Aza, since I have been able to devote a single moment to my most cherished pastime, and yet I have many extraordinary things to tell you; I am taking advantage of some leisure to try to inform you of them.

The day after my visit to the home of the *Pallas*, Déterville brought me a most beautiful costume, such as is worn in his country. When my dear *China* had arranged it on me to her liking, she led me to that ingenious machine which reproduces objects: although I should have been accustomed to its effects, I still could not help feeling surprise at seeing myself, as if I were actually standing opposite myself.

My new apparel did not displease me; perhaps I would have missed rather more the one I am discarding if it had not made me the object of tiresome looks wherever I went.*

The *Cacique* came into my room at the very moment the young girl was adding just a few more small items to my dress; he stood in the doorway, and watched us for a long time without speaking. He was so lost in thought that he stood aside to let the *China* pass and then returned to his position without realizing it; his eyes fixed on me, he looked over my whole person with the closest attention, which made me feel uncomfortable without my knowing why.

However, in order to show him my gratitude for his latest acts of kindness, I offered him my hand and, unable to express my feelings, I thought that I could say nothing which would please him more than some of the phrases which he enjoys to have me repeat; I even tried to say them in the same tone of voice as he does.

I do not know what effect they had on him at that moment, but his eyes lit up, his cheeks reddened, he came towards me with an agitated look, he seemed to want to take me in his arms. Then, stopping suddenly, he took my hand and shook it firmly, saying with emotion in his voice, *No... respect... her virtue...* and several other words which I understand no better. And then he hastened to the other side of the room and threw himself onto his chair, where he remained, his head buried in his hands, and showing every sign of deep despair.

I was alarmed at his state of mind, quite certain that I was the cause of his distress. I went over to him to show my remorse; but he turned me away gently, without looking at me, and I dared say nothing more. I was in a state of extreme embarrassment when servants came in to bring us food. He stood up, we ate together in our customary manner, a hint of sadness being the only visible effect of his grief; for all that, he was neither less kind, nor less considerate than before. This all seems quite incomprehensible to me.

I did not dare raise my eyes to look at him, nor use the signs which commonly took the place of conversation between us;

however, we were eating at an hour which was so different from our usual time for meals that I could not conceal my surprise from him. All I could understand of his response was that we were about to change our dwelling. Indeed, after going out and coming in several times, the *Cacique* came and took me by the hand; I let myself be led, still reflecting on what had happened, and trying to determine if our change of place might be the result of it.

Scarcely had we gone through the last door in the house, than he helped me climb quite a steep step. I found myself in a room so low that one cannot stand upright without difficulty, where there is not enough room to walk about, but where we could sit in perfect comfort, the *Cacique*, the *China*, and me; this small space is agreeably furnished, a window on either side provides sufficient light.

As I looked about in surprise, trying to understand why Déterville was enclosing us in such a confined space,—oh, my dearest Aza! how commonplace are marvels in this country!— I felt this machine, or hut, I do not know what name to give it, I felt it move and change position. This movement made me think of the floating house; terror took hold of me. The *Cacique*, watching for the slightest sign of anxiety, put my mind at rest, showing me through the window that this machine, suspended just above the ground, was moving forward by a secret means I did not understand.

Déterville also showed me that several *Hamas*,[39] of a kind unknown in our land, were walking in front and pulled us behind them; oh, light of my life, it takes inspiration of a kind which is more than human to invent such useful and such singular things. But this nation must also have great defects which limit its power, otherwise it would rule over the whole world.

For four days we have been shut inside this wondrous machine, leaving it only at night to take rest in the first dwelling we come upon, and I never leave it without regret. I must tell you, my dearest Aza, despite the anxieties of my love, I have enjoyed pleasures on this journey which were unknown to me before. Shut away in the Temple since my most tender infancy,

---

[39] A generic term for animals.

I had not encountered the beauties of the universe; what treasures I had missed!

Oh my heart's friend, it must be that nature has endowed its creation with a secret charm which even the most skilled art cannot imitate. What I have seen of the marvels invented by man has not awakened in me anything like that sense of rapture I feel as I admire the universe. The limitless countryside, which seems to change and be constantly refreshed before our very eyes, transports my soul no less rapidly than we move across it.

Our eyes at once scan, embrace, and come to rest on an infinite number of objects, as varied as they are delightful. We believe that there are no limits to what we can see other than those of the world itself. This error flatters us; it gives us a comforting sense of our own stature, and seems to bring us close to the Creator of so many wonders.

At the end of a beautiful day, the sky offers us images whose splendour and majesty far surpass those of the earth.

On one side, transparent clouds gathered around the setting sun stand like mountains of light and shade before our eyes, their majestic disorder exciting our sense of wonder to the point that we lose ourselves in it. On the other, a paler star rises in the sky, absorbs and radiates a softer light on objects which, losing their vigour in the absence of the sun, now only stir our senses in a manner which is gentle, peaceful, and in perfect harmony with the silence which reigns on the earth. Then, as we return to our senses, a feeling of blissful tranquillity pervades our soul; we delight in the universe as if we were its sole possessor, we see nothing in it which is not ours. A feeling of sweet serenity inspires pleasant thoughts in us, and if some regrets come to disturb them, they arise only because we must tear ourselves from this delightful reverie and shut ourselves away once more in those prisons without sense or reason which men have constructed for themselves, and which all their efforts will never make anything other than worthless when compared with the works of nature.*

The *Cacique* was kind enough to let me out of the moving hut every day, so that I might contemplate at my leisure what he saw me admire with such satisfaction.

If the beauties of the sky and earth have such a powerful appeal for our soul, the beauties of the forest, simpler and more touching, have brought me no less pleasure and caused no less astonishment.

How delightful the woods are, my dearest Aza! as you enter them, their pervasive spell touches every one of our senses and seems to confuse their functions. You have the impression of actually seeing the cooling breeze before you feel it; the different shades of colour in the leaves soften the light that penetrates them, and seem to impress our feelings at the same time as our sight. A scent, pleasant but indistinct, scarcely allows us to tell whether we are tasting or smelling it; even the air, unperceived, brings to our entire being a feeling of the purest delight, which seems to give us an extra sense, without our being able to locate it in our body.

Oh, my dearest Aza! such perfect pleasures would be lovelier still if you were here! how I have longed to share them with you! As the witness of my loving thoughts, I would have you find in the feelings of my heart delights which are even more powerful than those bestowed by the beauties of the universe.

LETTER THIRTEEN

Here I am at last, my dearest Aza, in a town called Paris; this is the end of our journey, but, as things seem to me, it will not be the end of my troubles.

Since my arrival, I have been more attentive than ever to what is happening, but what I discover only causes me anguish, and bodes nothing but misfortune: I find that I am thinking of you in whatever awakens my curiosity, however trivial, yet I can find you in none of the objects I see before me.

As far as I can tell from the time it has taken us to cross this town, and by the large number of inhabitants who fill its streets, it contains more people than could be assembled in two or three of our provinces.

I remember the wonders I was told of *Quitu*;* I try to find here some traces of the picture I was painted of that great city; but, alas! what a difference there is!

This place contains bridges, rivers, trees, countryside; it seems more like an entire universe than a single settlement. I could not possibly give you a precise idea of how tall the houses are; they are so prodigiously high that it is easier to think that nature produced them as they are, than it is to imagine how men might have constructed them.

It is here that the family of the *Cacique* resides. Their house is almost as magnificent as that of the Sun; the furniture and some parts of the walls are made of gold, the rest is adorned with cloth in the most varied and lovely colours, which represent quite well the beauties of nature.

When we arrived, Déterville gave me to understand that he was taking me to his mother's room. We found her half reclined on a couch of almost the same form as that of the *Incas*, and made of the same metal.[40] After offering her hand to the *Cacique*, who kissed it, bowing down almost to the ground, she embraced him; but she did so with such cold affection, with such constrained joy, that if I had not been told who she was, I would not have recognized the natural feelings of a mother in these embraces.

When they had spoken to each other for a moment, the *Cacique* bade me step forward; she cast a scornful look at me, and without responding to what her son was saying, she solemnly continued to wind around her fingers a thread which hung from a small piece of gold.

Déterville left us to approach a tall man with a noble air who had moved towards him; he embraced both him and another woman who was similarly occupied to the *Pallas*.

As soon as the *Cacique* appeared in this room, a young maiden of about my age had run up; she followed him with a timid eagerness which was quite remarkable. Delight shone from her face, without entirely banishing an underlying sadness which was most affecting. Déterville embraced her the last, but with such

---

[40] The beds, chairs, and tables of the Incas were made of solid gold.

natural tenderness that it moved my heart. Alas! my dearest Aza, what joy would be ours, if fate were to reunite us after so many misfortunes!

Meanwhile, out of respect,[41] I had remained beside the *Pallas*; I dared not move away, nor lift my eyes to look at her. The stern glances which she cast upon me from time to time began to intimidate me, and made me feel under such constraint that it inhibited my very thoughts.

Finally, as if the young maiden had sensed my discomfort, she left Déterville, came over, took me by the hand and led me to a window where we sat down. Although I could understand nothing of what she said, her eyes, full of kindness, spoke in the universal language of sympathetic hearts; they inspired trust and friendship; I wanted to show her what I was feeling, but unable to express myself as I wished, I just repeated everything I knew of her language.

She smiled at this more than once, looking at Déterville with a sensitive and kind expression. I was enjoying this manner of conversation, when the *Pallas* uttered some words aloud, looking at the young maiden; she lowered her eyes, pushed away my hand which she had been holding in hers, and took no further notice of me.

Some time later, an old woman with a fierce countenance came in, went up to the *Pallas*, then came to take me by the arm and led me almost by force to a room at the very top of the house, where I was left, alone.

Although this was not to be the most wretched moment of my life, my dearest Aza, it was not one of the least distressing.* I was expecting that the end of my journey would bring some relief to my anxiety, I thought that I might at least find the same kindness in the *Cacique*'s family that he had shown me. The cold reception of the *Pallas*, the sudden change in the behaviour of the young maiden, the harshness of this woman who had forced me from a place where I would have rather stayed, the inattentiveness of Déterville who had done nothing to oppose the violence shown me; in short, all the circumstances which a wretched soul can

---

[41] Young girls, even those of royal blood, bore great respect for married women.

imagine to increase its suffering, presented themselves all at once, each in its most distressing guise. I thought I had been abandoned by everyone, I was bitterly lamenting my terrible fate, when I saw my *China* come into the room. In my present state, the sight of her seemed a real blessing; I ran up and embraced her tearfully; she was moved by this, her display of feeling touched me. When we think we have been reduced to self-pity, the pity of others is truly precious. The signs of affection from this young girl lessened my grief: I told her of my sorrows, as if she could understand me, I asked her countless questions, as if she could answer them; her tears spoke directly to my heart, my own continued to flow, but they were less bitter now.

I was still hoping to see Déterville again at dinner, but my food was brought to me and I saw nothing of him. Since losing you, my heart's dear idol, this *Cacique* is the only human being who has never ceased to show me kindness; the habit of seeing him has now become a need. His absence made my sadness twice as great, and after waiting in vain for him to come, I lay down. But sleep had not yet dried my tears, when I saw him come into my room, followed by the young person whose sudden disdain had hurt me so much.

She threw herself on my bed, and with countless embraces she seemed eager to make amends for her harsh treatment of me.

The *Cacique* sat next to the bed; he seemed as pleased to see me again as I was at not being abandoned by him; they spoke to each other, looking at me all the while, and overwhelming me with signs of the most tender affection.

Imperceptibly, their conversation grew more serious. Although I could not understand their words, I could easily tell that they were inspired by trust and friendship. I took care not to interrupt them; but as soon as they turned to me again, I tried to draw from the *Cacique* some explanation of the most extraordinary happenings since my arrival.

All I could understand of his replies was that the young woman I saw before me was called Céline, that she was his sister, that the tall man I had seen in the room of the *Pallas* was his elder brother, and that the other young woman was this brother's wife.

Céline became more dear to me when I learned that she was the *Cacique*'s sister; it gave me such pleasure to be with them both, that I simply did not notice that dawn had broken before they left.

Since their departure I have spent what time remained for rest in conversation with you; this is all I have, my only joy. It is to you alone, dear soul of my thoughts, that I open up my heart; you will always be the sole guardian of my secrets, of my tenderness, and of my feelings.

LETTER FOURTEEN

If I did not continue to take time from sleep to devote to you, my dearest Aza, I could no longer enjoy these delightful moments when I live for you alone. I have been made to dress again in my Virgin's clothes, and they require me to spend all day in a room filled with a crowd of people which seems to change and renew itself constantly, and scarcely ever diminishes in size.

This unwelcome waste of time often snatches me against my will from thoughts of love; but if I lose for a few moments my keen concentration which unceasingly unites my soul with yours, I soon think of you again when I compare you favourably with all that surrounds me.

Throughout the different regions I have crossed, I have not seen savages quite as proud or insolent in their manners as these. The women in particular seem to be disdainful in their civility, an attitude repellent to all that is human in us, and which might well inspire in me as much scorn for them as they show for others, if I were to know them better.

One of them caused an affront to me yesterday which still pains me today. At a time when the gathering was at its largest, this woman had already spoken to several people without noticing me. Then, either by chance or because somebody had pointed me out to her, she burst out laughing as she cast her eyes on me; she promptly moved from where she had been standing, came towards me, made me stand up, and, having turned me round and round as many times as she wished in her excited mood, and fingered every item of my clothing with fussy attention, she beckoned to a young man to come across and began to examine my person with him all over again.

Although I found the liberties which both of them were taking quite repugnant, the splendour of the woman's dress made me think she was a *Pallas*, and the magnificence of the young man's attire—all covered as it was with patches of gold—that he was an *Anqui*,[42] so I dared not oppose their wishes. But when this insolent savage, encouraged by the familiarity of the *Pallas*, and perhaps also by my reserve, had the audacity to lay a hand on my breast, I pushed him away with such indignant astonishment that he realized I knew more than he did about the rules of decency.

At my outburst, Déterville ran up: no sooner had he spoken some words to the young savage than he, leaning with one hand on his shoulder, laughed with such violence that his face was contorted.

The *Cacique* stepped back and, his face flushed, spoke to him with such coldness that the young man's mirth evaporated; and having, it seems, no reply to give, he moved away without a word, and did not return.

Oh, my dearest Aza, how the customs of these countries fill me with respect for those of the children of the Sun! How the insolence of this young *Anqui* makes me think fondly of your loving respect, your modest reserve, and that enchanting decency which reigned in our conversations! I noticed it when I first saw you, my soul's dear delight, and I shall remember it all my life. You alone combine every perfection which nature has scattered separately upon mankind, just as it has gathered together in my heart all the feelings of tenderness and admiration which bind me to you unto death.

LETTER FIFTEEN

The longer I live with the *Cacique* and his sister, my dearest Aza, the more difficult it is to believe that they are of this nation; they alone know and respect virtue.

[42] Prince of royal blood: permission was needed from the Inca to wear gold on one's clothes, and this was only given to Princes of royal blood.

Céline's artless manners, her unaffected kindness, her modest good humour would readily make one think that she has been brought up among our Virgins. The warm-hearted decency and compassionate thoughtfulness of her brother would easily persuade one that he was born of *Inca* blood. They both treat me with as much humanity as we would show them, if misfortune had cast them among us. I am now quite certain that the *Cacique* is one of those who pay tribute to you.[43]

He never comes into my room without bringing a gift for me of some of those marvellous objects which abound in this country: sometimes it is pieces of that device which duplicates objects, enclosed in small cases made of quite wonderful material. At other times, he brings stones, light in weight and of astonishing brilliance, with which people here decorate almost every part of their body; they attach them to the ears, wear them on the stomach, round the neck, on shoes, and it is all quite delightful to behold.

But what I find most pleasing are small tools made of a very hard metal, and quite remarkably useful. Some serve to fashion works which Céline is teaching me to make; others, designed for cutting, serve to divide all kinds of material, from which you can make as many pieces as you wish, without effort, and it is all most entertaining.*

I have been given countless other curiosities, more extraordinary still, but since they are not in use in our country, I can find no terms in our language to give you an idea of what they are.

I am carefully keeping all these gifts for you, my dearest Aza; apart from the pleasure I shall have to witness your surprise when you see them, I do so because such gifts are assuredly meant for you. If the *Cacique* were not subject to your rule, would he pay me such tributes which he knows are due only to your supreme rank? The marks of respect he has always shown me have made me think that he knows of my birth. The presents with which he honours

---

[43] *Caciques* and *Curacas* were obliged to provide the clothing and the provisions of the *Inca* and the queen. They never appeared before either one without offering them as tribute a gift of the produce particular to the province over which they ruled.

me convince me beyond doubt that he knows I am to become your spouse, since he treats me already as a *Mama-Oella*.[44]

This certainty reassures me and calms some of my anxieties. I realize that all I lack is the freedom to express myself in order to discover from the *Cacique* what obliges him to detain me in his home, and to persuade him to return me to your power; but until then, I shall have to endure more suffering yet.

The temperament of *Madame*, which is what they call Déterville's mother, is nowhere near as friendly as that of her children. Far from treating me with any degree of kindness, she shows me at all times a coldness and disdain which appal me, but I cannot discover the reason why; yet as a consequence of quite contradictory feelings which I understand even less, she requires me to be with her constantly.

I find this an unbearable ordeal; it is impossible not to feel the greatest constraint in her presence, and it is only by stealth that Céline and her brother can show me signs of friendship. Even they dare not speak freely to each other in front of her. As a result, they still spend a part of the night in my room; it is the only time we can enjoy in peace the pleasure of seeing each other. And although I can hardly take part in their conversations, I always find it a pleasure to be with them. It is not for want of concern from either of them that I am not happy. Alas! my dearest Aza, they do not know that I cannot be happy far from you, and that I only consider myself to be alive when thoughts of you, and my love, occupy me completely.

LETTER SIXTEEN

I have so few *Quipos* left, my dearest Aza, that I scarcely dare use them. When I wish to knot them, fear of seeing them come to an end stops me from doing so, as if by saving them I could somehow increase their number. I am going to lose my soul's pleasure, the nourishment of my life, nothing will lighten the heavy burden of your absence, I shall be crushed beneath it.

[44] This is the name taken by Queens on their ascent to the throne.

I took exquisite delight in recording the most secret stirrings of my heart and offering them to you in homage. I wanted to set down the principal customs of this singular nation to entertain you in your leisure when you know happier times. Alas! I have very little hope left of ever being able to accomplish these aims.

If I have such trouble even now putting my thoughts in order, how shall I be able to recall them in the future, without some help from outside? They offer me one way of doing so, it is true, but it is so difficult to put into practice that I think it is simply impossible.

The *Cacique* has brought me a savage of this region who comes every day to give me lessons in his language, and in the method they use here to give a manner of existence to their thoughts. This is done by tracing with a feather small shapes which they call *Letters* on a thin, white material which they call *Paper*; these shapes have names, these names, when put together, represent the sounds of words; but these names and sounds seem so very similar to each other that if I do one day succeed in understanding them, I am quite sure that it will not be without much toil. This poor savage takes unbelievable trouble to teach me, and I take even more to learn; and yet my progress is so slow that I would abandon the attempt if I thought some other means might bring me knowledge of your fate and mine.

But there is no other way, my dearest Aza! And so I shall take pleasure in nothing save this new and singular discipline. I wish I could live alone, so that I might devote myself to it without interruption; the requirement imposed on me to be forever in *Madame*'s room is becoming a torture.

At first, awakening the curiosity of others provided some satisfaction for my own; but when we have only our eyes to use, they are soon satisfied. All the women paint their face the same colour; their manners are alike, and I think that even their words are the same. Appearances are more varied among men. Some look as though they are thinking; but in general I suspect this nation is quite different from how it appears; affectation seems to me to be its ruling character.

If the displays of zeal and earnestness, with which the people here adorn even the most trivial of social duties, were natural, then, my dearest Aza, they would certainly have in their hearts more kindness, more humanity than we do in ours: how can that be possible?

If they had as much serenity in their souls as they do on their faces, if their inclination to cheerfulness which I see in all they do, were sincere, would they choose for their entertainment such spectacles as the one they have made me watch?

They took me to a place where they enact, rather like in your palace, the actions of men who are no more, but with this difference: where we evoke the memory of only the wisest and most virtuous, I think that here they celebrate only the insane and the wicked. Those who represent these figures rage and storm about like madmen; I have seen one take his fury so far that he killed himself. Beautiful women whom they seem to persecute weep unceasingly, and show such signs of despair that they have no need of the words they speak to convey the extremes of their suffering.

Is it credible, my dearest Aza, that an entire people, whose outward appearance is so humane, should take delight in the representation of misfortunes or crimes which once disgraced, or oppressed, their fellow man.*

But perhaps people here need to see the horror of vice in order to be led to virtue. This thought comes to me unbidden; if it were true, how I would pity this nation! Ours, more blessed by nature, cherishes goodness because it is attractive in itself; we require only models of virtue to make us virtuous,* just as one needs only to love you to become lovely.

LETTER SEVENTEEN

I no longer know what to think of the spirit of this nation, my dearest Aza. It moves to extremes with such rapidity that one would need to have more ability than I have to form a judgement about its character.

They have shown me a spectacle completely different from the one I saw before. The first one was cruel, terrifying, it repelled one's reason and was an affront to humanity. This one was entertaining, pleasurable, it imitated nature, and did honour to one's good sense. It involves many more men and women than the first. It likewise represents events in the life of man; but whether pain or pleasure, joy or sadness is being expressed, it is always through song or dance.

It must be the case, my dearest Aza, that sounds can be understood by everyone, because it was no more difficult for me to be moved by the representation of these different passions than if they had been expressed in our own language, and that seems quite natural to me.

Human language is doubtless an invention of man, since it varies from nation to nation. Nature, more powerful and alert to the needs and pleasures of its creatures, has given them general means of expression which are imitated very well by the songs I have heard.

If it is true that piercing sounds convey better the need for help at moments of intense fear or acute pain than words, which might be understood in one part of the world but which have no meaning in another, it is no less certain that tender laments touch our hearts with a more powerful feeling of compassion than words whose odd arrangement often has the opposite effect.

Do not light and lively sounds inevitably inspire in our souls a radiant joy, which the telling of an entertaining story, or a witty joke, can only ever produce in a more imperfect way?

Does any language have expressions which can convey innocent pleasure with as much success as the naive play of animals? It seems that dances seek to imitate these, or at least they inspire more or less the same feelings.

In short, my dearest Aza, everything in this spectacle conforms to nature and humanity. Oh! can anything be more beneficial to men than inspiring joy in them?

I too felt such joy, and I was transported by it almost in spite of myself, until it was shaken by an incident which befell Céline.

As we left, we had strayed a little from the crowd, and we were holding each other for fear of falling. Déterville was a few steps ahead of us, walking with his sister-in-law, when a young savage with a pleasant countenance came up to Céline, whispered a few words to her, gave her a piece of paper which she barely had the strength to take, and moved away.

Céline, who had been so alarmed at his approach that I could feel the trembling which took hold of her, turned languidly in his direction as he left us. She seemed so frail, that believing her to have been smitten by a sudden illness, I was about to call Déterville for help; but she stopped me and made me keep silent by putting a finger to my mouth. I preferred to feel anxious than to disobey her.

That same evening, when brother and sister came to my room, Céline showed the *Cacique* the paper she had received;* from the little I could make out from their conversation, I would have concluded that she loved the young man who had given it to her, if it were possible to be alarmed by the presence of the person one loves.

I could continue to share with you, my dearest Aza, many other observations I have made; but alas! I can see the end of my cottons, I am touching the last threads, I am tying the last knots. These knots, which seemed to me to be a chain linking your heart to mine, are now no more than the pitiful objects of my regret. Illusion deserts me, and dreadful truth takes its place; my aimless thoughts, lost in the immense void of absence, will henceforth be extinguished just as quickly as time itself. Dearest Aza, I feel that we are being separated once more, that I am being snatched a second time from your love. I am losing you, I am leaving you, I shall see you no more. Aza! my heart's dear hope, how far apart we are to be!

LETTER EIGHTEEN

How much time has been wiped from my life, my dearest Aza! The Sun has completed one half of its course since I last enjoyed the imaginary happiness I had created for myself of believing that

I was conversing with you. How long that double absence has seemed to me! How much courage I have needed to bear it! I lived only in the future, the present no longer seemed to merit being counted. All my thoughts were mere wishes, all my reflections mere projects, all my feelings mere hopes.

I can still barely form these shapes, but I am eager to make them the expression of my love.

I can feel myself coming back to life as I perform this cherished task. Restored to my self, I think I am beginning to live again. Aza, how dear you are to me, what joy it gives me to tell you so, to represent it, to give this feeling all possible forms of existence! I would like to inscribe it on the hardest metal, on the walls of my room, on my clothes, on everything around me, and to express it in every language.

Alas! how I have suffered for knowing the language I now use, how deceitful has been the hope which inspired me to learn it! As I have gained an understanding of it, a whole new world has opened up before my eyes. Objects have taken on another form, every new discovery has brought to light a new misfortune.

My mind, my heart, my eyes, everything has led me astray, even the Sun has deceived me. It shines on the whole world, of which your empire is but a part, just like many other realms which make it up. Do not think, my dearest Aza, that they have tricked me with these incredible facts: they have proven to me only too clearly that they are true.

Far from being among people who are subject to your rule, I am living not only under a foreign power, but one so distant from your empire that our nation would still be unknown to it, had not the greed of the Spaniards made them overcome appalling dangers to gain access to our land.

Can love not achieve what the thirst for riches has done? If you love me, if you desire me, if you still think of your wretched Zilia, I can expect everything of your love, or of your generosity. Let them show me the way which leads to you; the dangers to be overcome, the pains to be endured will then be so many pleasures for my heart.

LETTER NINETEEN

I am still so unskilled in the art of writing, my dearest Aza, that it takes me an eternity to form just a few lines. It often happens that after writing much, I myself cannot tell what I thought I was expressing. I am perplexed, my thoughts are muddled, and I forget what I had had such trouble recalling; I start again, I do no better, and yet I carry on.

I would find it much easier if it were only my love which I sought to put into words for you; the strength of my feelings would overcome every difficulty. But I also wish to give you an account of all that has happened during the interval of my silence. I would like you to know every one of my actions; and yet they have been so uninteresting for so long, and so alike, that I would find it impossible to distinguish one from another.

The most significant event in my life has been the departure of Déterville.

For a period of time which they call here *six months*, he has been away making war in the interests of his sovereign. When he left, I still knew nothing of his language; and yet, judging by his deep distress as he took leave of his sister and me, I could see that we were to lose him for a long time.

I shed many tears at this; my heart was filled with countless fears which Céline's acts of kindness could not dispel. Losing him was to lose my surest hope of seeing you again. To whom could I turn, if more misfortune were to befall me? Nobody could understand me.

I soon felt the effects of this absence. *Madame*, whose contempt had been all too clear, and who, it is said, had kept me in her room for so long only to indulge her vanity on account of my birth and the power she could exert over me, had me shut away with Céline in a House of Virgins where we still are.

This retreat would not displease me if, now that I am in a position to understand everything, it did not deprive me of the information I need for my plan to come and join you. The Virgins who live here are of such profound ignorance that they cannot answer my most trivial enquiry.

Their worship of the Divinity of this country requires them to renounce all his blessings, intelligence of the mind, feelings in the heart, and, I think, even reason itself; or at least, their conversation leads me to think so.*

Shut away just like our Virgins, they do have an advantage not enjoyed in the Temples of the Sun: here, the walls are open in some places, and secured only by crossed pieces of iron, set close to each other to prevent one from passing between them, but which give the freedom to see and converse with people from outside; it is what they call *parlours*.

It is thanks to these convenient places that I can continue to take writing lessons. I speak only to the teacher who instructs me; his ignorance of everything other than his art cannot help dispel my own. Céline does not seem to be any better informed; I notice in her answers to my questions a kind of perplexity which can only derive from a rather clumsy attempt to deceive, or from shameful ignorance. Whatever it is, her conversation is always limited to the concerns of her heart and to those of her family.

The young Frenchman who spoke to her that day as we were leaving the spectacle where there is singing, is her suitor, just as I thought. But Madame Déterville, who is opposed to their marriage, forbids her to see him, and to be doubly certain to prevent it, she does not allow her to speak to anybody at all.

It is not that her choice would be unworthy of her; it is rather that this vain and unnatural mother is taking advantage of a barbarous custom, established by the great in this land, to oblige Céline to take a Virgin's habit, so that her eldest son can become richer.* For the same reason, she has already forced Déterville to enter a certain religious order, which he will not be able to leave once he has pronounced the words they call *Vows*.

Céline, with great resolve, is resisting the sacrifice they demand. Her courage is strengthened by letters from her suitor, which I am given by my writing teacher and which I pass on to her; but her grief is bringing about such a change in her character that, far from showing me the same kindness she did before I could speak her language, she now brings a tone of bitterness to our conversations which makes my pain more acute.

As the permanent confidante of her troubles, I am quite happy to listen to her, I pity her readily, I comfort her as a friend; yet if my love, awakened by talk of her own, prompts me to seek relief from the burden of my heart merely by speaking your name, impatience and scorn appear on her face, she disputes your understanding, your virtues, and even your love.

Even my *China*—I know no other name for her, this one pleased so well it has continued—my *China*, who appeared to have affection for me, who obeys me in all other matters, has the audacity to tell me I must think of you no more, or, if I bid her be silent, she leaves the room. Céline then comes, and I must contain my grief. This oppressive constraint takes my suffering to its limit. All I have left is the painful pleasure of covering this paper with expressions of my love, since it is the only sympathetic witness of the feelings in my heart.

Alas! perhaps I am putting myself to such trouble for nothing, perhaps you will never know that I have lived only for you. This dreadful thought weakens my nerve without breaking my resolve to continue writing. I preserve my illusion in order to preserve my life for you, I banish cruel reason which seeks to enlighten me: if I had no hope of seeing you again, I would perish, my dearest Aza, I am quite sure of it; without you, my life is torture.

LETTER TWENTY

Until now, my dearest Aza, I have been concerned with the troubles in my heart, and have told you nothing of those in my mind; and yet they are scarcely less agonizing. I have sorrows of a kind unknown in our country, caused by the prevailing customs of this nation which are so different from ours that, unless I give you some idea of what they are like, you will not be able to sympathize with me in my anxiety.

The government of this empire, entirely different from yours, cannot fail to be imperfect. Whereas the *Capa-Inca* is obliged to provide for the sustenance of his people, sovereigns in Europe derive their own solely from the labours of their subjects; as a result, almost all crimes and misfortunes are the result of needs which have not been adequately satisfied.*

The unhappiness of the nobles derives in general from the difficulties they experience when they seek to reconcile their apparent prosperity with their actual poverty.

The common man only maintains his position through what they call commerce, or industry; dishonesty is the least of the crimes which result from this.

One section of the population is obliged to appeal to the humanity of others merely to survive; the results of this are so limited that these unfortunates scarcely have enough to keep themselves alive.*

Without gold, it is impossible to acquire a part of this earth which nature has given in common to all men. Without possessing what they call property, it is impossible to have gold, and by an inconsistency which is an outrage to natural common sense, and which exasperates one's reason, this haughty nation, following an empty code of honour entirely of its own invention, considers it a disgrace to receive from anybody other than the sovereign whatever is necessary to sustain one's life and position. This sovereign bestows his bounty on so few of his subjects, compared with the number of those in need, that it would be just as senseless to lay claim to a part of this as it would be ignominious to seek deliverance, by death, from the impossibility of living without shame.

The discovery of such dismal truths at first excited only pity in my heart for these wretched people, and indignation at these laws. But alas! the scornful way in which I heard people speak of those who are not rich inspired painful reflections on my own state! I have neither gold, nor lands, nor occupation, yet I must be one of the citizens of this town. Oh heavens! in what class should I place myself?

Although all feelings of shame are unknown to me which do not spring from a fault I have committed, although I can tell how foolish it is to have such feelings for reasons outside my will or control, I cannot help suffering at what others think of me. This pain would be unbearable if I had no hope that one day your generosity will enable me to reward those who humiliate me in spite of myself, through acts of kindness which I had thought to be to my honour.

It is not that Céline does not do all she can to ease my concerns in this respect, but what I see and what I learn of the people of this country tends to make me wary of their words; their virtues, my dearest Aza, have no more reality than their riches. Furniture which I thought to be made of gold, is gold only on the surface, its true substance is wood; in the same way, what they call politeness thinly covers their shortcomings with an outward show of virtue. But with a little attention, one can uncover its falseness just as easily as one can discern the emptiness of their displays of wealth.

I owe some of this knowledge to a kind of writing they call *books*; although I still have much trouble understanding what they contain, they are very useful to me. I learn basic notions from them, Céline explains to me what she knows of them, and I can then draw conclusions which I think are sound.

Some of these books teach what men have done, and others what they have thought. I cannot tell you, my dearest Aza, what incomparable pleasure it would give me to read them, if I could understand them better, nor how much I long to know some of the divine men who compose them. I can see that they are to the soul what the Sun is to the earth, and that I would find in their company all the enlightenment, all the help I need; but I can see no hope of ever having such satisfaction. Although Céline reads quite often, she is not sufficiently knowledgeable to satisfy me; she had barely considered that books were made by men, she doesn't know their names, or even if they are still alive.

I shall bring you, my dearest Aza, all that I can collect together of these wonderful works, I shall explain them to you in our language, I shall taste the supreme happiness of bringing a new pleasure to the one I love. Alas! shall I ever be able to do so?

LETTER TWENTY-ONE

I shall no longer lack things to tell you, my dearest Aza; they have made me speak with a *Cusipata*, known here as a *Man of Religion*.

Knowledgeable about everything, he has promised to leave me ignorant of nothing. As polite as one of grand Nobility, as wise as an *Amauta*, he knows the ways of the world just as well as he does the doctrines of his Religion. Conversation with him is more useful than reading a book, and it has given me a satisfaction I had not enjoyed since my misfortunes separated me from you.

He came to instruct me in the Religion of France, and to urge me to embrace it.*

From what he told me of the virtues it prescribes, they are drawn from natural law, and are, in truth, as pure as ours; but my mind is not subtle enough to see the relation which surely exists between these virtues and the nation's ways and customs. On the contrary, I see such striking inconsistencies between them that my reason flatly refuses to believe what my tutor tells me.

As for the origin and principles of this Religion, they did not seem to me any more incredible than the story of *Mancocapa*, and of the lake *Tisicaca*,[45]* and its morality is so noble that I would have listened to the *Cusipata* more willingly if he had not spoken scornfully of our own sacred worship of the Sun; all forms of partiality undermine one's trust. I could have countered his reasoning with the same objections he applied to mine, but if the laws of humanity forbid one to strike one's neighbour because of the hurt it causes, it is all the more important not to wound his soul by showing scorn for his opinions. I chose merely to explain my feelings to him without attacking his own.

What is more, a concern dearer to my heart impelled me to change the subject of our conversation; I interrupted him as soon as I could to question him about the distance separating the cities of Paris and *Cuzco*, and about the possibility of making the journey there. The *Cusipata* responded kindly, and although he represented the distance between these two towns in a disheartening way and made me see the journey as one of insurmountable difficulty, the knowledge that it could be done was enough to strengthen my nerve and to give me the confidence to share my plan with the kind *Man of Religion*.

[45] See the *History of the Incas*.

He seemed astonished at this, and made every effort to dissuade me from this undertaking with such gentle words that it moved me to think of the dangers to which I would be exposing myself. But my determination was in no way shaken, I begged the *Cusipata* most insistently to inform me how I might return to my homeland. He would not discuss this in any detail, telling me only that Déterville, through his high birth and personal merit, was held in great esteem, and that he could do whatever he wished; and that having an uncle with great influence at the court of Spain he was better able than anybody to bring me news of our ill-fated lands.

To persuade me once and for all to await Déterville's return, which he assured me was imminent, he added that given my obligation to this generous friend, I could not honourably decide my own fate without his consent. I agreed, and listened with pleasure to his praise of the exceptional qualities which distinguish Déterville from others of his rank. The burden of gratitude is very light, my dearest Aza, when one receives favours only from the hands of virtue.

The wise man also told me how chance had brought the Spaniards as far as your unfortunate Empire, and that thirst for gold was the sole cause of their cruelty. He then explained how the rights of war had put me in the hands of Déterville in a battle from which he had emerged victorious, having taken several Vessels from the Spaniards* among which was the one carrying me.

In short, my dearest Aza, if he has confirmed my misfortunes, he has at least delivered me from the painful ignorance in which I lived regarding so many dreadful events, and that is no small relief to my suffering. I await the rest from Déterville's return; he is humane, noble, virtuous, I must count on his generosity. If he returns me to you, what an act of kindness! What joy! What happiness!

LETTER TWENTY-TWO

I had counted, my dearest Aza, on making a friend of the wise *Cusipata*, but his second visit has destroyed the good opinion I had formed of him during the first.

If at first he had seemed gentle and sincere, this time I found only harshness and deceit in everything he said.

With my mind at rest concerning the interests of my love, I wanted to satisfy my curiosity about the marvellous men who make Books; I began by asking about their status in the world, about the respect in which they are held, in short about the honours or tributes which are bestowed on them for all the benefits they bring to the whole of society.

I do not know what the *Cusipata* found amusing in my questions, but he smiled at each one, and answered them with such ill-considered words that it was not difficult to see that I was being deceived.

Indeed, if I am to believe him, these men who are undeniably superior to others by the nobility and benefits of their work, are often left unrewarded; they are obliged to sell their thoughts in order to support themselves, just as the common people must sell the basest produce of the earth in order to survive. How can that be?

I find deceit hardly less displeasing, my dearest Aza, beneath the transparent mask of light-heartedness than when it is covered by the dark veil of seduction; the deceit of the Man of Religion outraged me, and I did not deign to respond.

Unable to find satisfaction, I turned the conversation back to my intended journey, but instead of dissuading me from it with the same gentleness as before, he opposed it with such strong and compelling reasons that I had only my love for you with which to combat them, and I did not hesitate to confess this to him.

At first he took on a cheerful expression, and, appearing to doubt that I meant what I was saying, merely mocked me in reply; however harmless his words were, this did not fail to offend me. I endeavoured to convince him of the truth, but the more I found expressions in my heart to demonstrate the sincerity of my feelings, the more his face and words grew stern; he had the audacity to tell me that my love for you was incompatible with virtue, that I must renounce either one or the other—in short that my love for you could only ever be a crime.*

At these senseless words my soul was gripped by the most furious rage. I forgot the moderation I had prescribed myself, heaped reproaches on him, told him what I thought of the falseness of his words, affirmed again and again that I would love you for ever, and, without waiting for his excuses, I left him, ran and shut myself away in my room where I was sure he could not follow me.

Oh, my dearest Aza, how strange is the reasoning of this nation! It acknowledges in general that the most important of all virtues is to do good, to be true to one's vows, but in particular it forbids one to respect those made by the purest of feelings. It requires us to be grateful, and seems to decree ingratitude.

I would be worthy of praise if I restored you to the Throne of your fathers, yet I am criminal because I keep safe for you a possession more precious than all the empires of the world.

They would applaud me if I rewarded your good deeds with the treasures of Peru. Deprived of everything, dependent for everything, all I possess is my love. They want me to rob you of it; to have virtue, it is necessary to be ungrateful. Oh, my dearest Aza! I would betray every virtue if I stopped loving you for a single moment. Remaining true to their laws, I shall also remain true to my love. I shall live for you alone.

LETTER TWENTY-THREE

I think, my dearest Aza, that only the joy of seeing you again could surpass the delight I felt at the return of Déterville; but as if I were no longer allowed to enjoy pleasures unalloyed, it was soon followed by a sorrow which still endures.

Yesterday morning Céline was in my room, when somebody came to fetch her, without explanation: she had not been gone long when she sent word for me to go to the parlour. I hurried there; imagine my surprise to find her brother with her!

I did not conceal my pleasure at seeing him, I owe him respect and friendship; these feelings are close to virtues, and I expressed them with all the sincerity in my heart.

I saw my saviour before me, the sole support of my hopes; I was going to talk freely about you, about my love, about my plans, my joy knew no bounds.

I could speak no French when Déterville left; how many things I had to tell him! how many questions to ask, how much gratitude to show! I wanted to say everything at once, I expressed myself badly, and yet I spoke on.

As I did so, I noticed that the sadness I had observed on Déterville's face when I entered was fading and giving way to joy. Congratulating myself on this change, I did all I could to increase his joy yet more. Alas! had I reason to fear bringing too much pleasure to a friend to whom I owe everything, and from whom I expect everything? however, my honesty plunged him into a misunderstanding which is now costing me many a tear.

Céline had left as I entered; perhaps if she had stayed, I would have been spared such a painful explanation of my feelings.

Déterville, attentive to what I was saying, seemed happy to listen without a thought of interrupting. Vague unease took hold of me when I sought to ask his advice about my journey, and to explain my reasons for undertaking it; I could not find the words, I struggled to express myself. He took advantage of a moment's silence, and, dropping on one knee in front of the grille which he was holding with both hands, said to me in a voice filled with emotion: To what feeling, divine Zilia, should I ascribe the pleasure I can see just as artlessly expressed in your beautiful eyes as in your words? Am I the happiest of men at the very moment my sister has led me to believe I am the most worthy of compassion? I do not know what sorrow Céline might have caused you, I replied; but I am quite certain that you will never be caused any by me. And yet, he answered, she has told me that I may never hope to be loved by you.

By me, I exclaimed, interrupting him, me, not love you! Oh, Déterville! how can your sister blacken my name with such a crime? Ingratitude is abhorrent to me, I would hate myself if I thought I could ever cease loving you.

As I spoke these few words it seemed from the earnestness of his gaze that he was seeking to read my very soul.

You love me, Zilia, he said to me, you love me, and your own lips tell me so! I would give my life to hear that charming avowal; but alas! now I do hear it, I cannot believe it. Zilia, my dearest Zilia, is it really true that you love me? are you not deceiving yourself? your tone, your eyes, my own heart, everything entrances me. But perhaps it is simply to plunge me back, all the more brutally, into the despair from which I am just escaping.

You shock me, I continued; what is the cause of your mistrust? Ever since I have known you, even if I could not make myself understood with words, have not all my actions shown that I love you? No, he rejoined, I still dare not believe it, you do not speak French well enough to dispel my well-founded fears. You are not trying to deceive me, I know, but explain to me what meaning you attach to these adorable words *I love you.* Let my fate be decided, let me die at your feet—of grief or of joy.

These words, I said to him, feeling rather daunted by the fervent way he uttered this last remark, these words should, I think, convince you that you are dear to me, that your future is of concern to me, that friendship and gratitude attach me to you; these feelings bring pleasure to my heart, and they should satisfy yours.

Oh, Zilia!, he answered, how your words lose their force, and your tone grows cold! Could it be that Céline has told me the truth after all? Is it not for Aza that you feel everything you are describing? No, I said to him, the feelings I have for Aza are quite different from those I have for you; it is what you call love... But how can that possibly hurt you? I continued, as I saw him grow pale, leave hold of the grille, and look up to the sky with distress in his eyes; I have love for Aza, because he has love for me, and because we were to be united. None of this concerns you in any way. You should have just those feelings for me, he exclaimed, which you see uniting you with him, for I have a thousand times more love than he ever felt.

How could that be? I returned, you are not of my nation; far from your having chosen me for your wife, chance alone has brought us together; and what is more, it is only since today that we have been able to express our thoughts freely to each other. What reason then could you have to entertain the feelings you describe?

Are other reasons needed, he retorted, beside your charms and my nature, to bind me to you unto death? Born sensitive, indolent, opposed to deceit, the trouble it would have given me to engage a woman's heart, and the fear of not finding the sincerity I sought, left me with just a vague or fleeting interest in women. I lived without passion until the moment I saw you. Your beauty struck me, but the impression it made might easily have been just as slight as that of many others, had not the sweetness and artlessness of your character made you the very being my imagination had so often fashioned. You know, Zilia, if I have shown respect for that object of my adoration! What did it not cost me to resist those enchanting opportunities offered me by the intimacy of a long voyage! How many times might your innocence have yielded to my passion, if I had heeded it? But far from dishonouring you, I took discretion to the point of silence; I even demanded of my sister that she should not speak to you of my love; I wanted to owe nothing to anyone save you. Oh Zilia! if you are not in the least moved by such loving respect, I shall flee your sight; but, I can feel it, my death will be the price of such a sacrifice.

Your death! I exclaimed, deeply touched by the genuine grief which I could see had overcome him, alas! what a sacrifice! I cannot tell if the loss of my own life would be any less dreadful.

Well, Zilia, he said, if my life is dear to you, then command me to live! What must I do? I said to him. Love me, he replied, as you loved Aza. I still love him in the same way, I replied, and I shall love him until death; I do not know, I added, if your laws permit you to love two people in the same manner, but both our customs and my heart forbid it. Be satisfied with the feelings I promise you, I can have no others; I value truth, and I give it you now, undisguised.

How calmly you end my life! he exclaimed. Oh Zilia! how I must love you, since I adore even your cruel honesty. So, he continued after a few moments silence, my love will be greater even than your cruelty. Your happiness is dearer to me than my own. Tell me with that sincerity which tears me apart without mercy: what do you hope for the love you still feel for Aza?

Alas! I said to him, all my hope rests with you alone. I then explained how I had learned that communication with the Indies was not impossible; I told him that I had imagined he might find me the means of returning there, or, at the very least, that he would be kind enough to have the knots delivered to you which would tell you of my fate, and to have your replies brought back to me, so that knowing your destiny, I might shape my own upon it.

I shall do whatever is necessary, he said with affected calm, to learn the fate of your beloved, you will be satisfied in that respect; however, you would be wrong to hope that you will see the fortunate Aza again—insuperable obstacles stand between you.

These words, my dearest Aza, dealt my heart a mortal blow. My tears flowed in abundance, and for a long time I could not answer Déterville, who for his part kept a melancholy silence. So, I said finally, I shall not see him again, but I shall live for him all the same; if your friendship is generous enough to find us some means of communication, this satisfaction will be enough to make my life less unbearable, and I shall die content, provided that you promise to let him know that I died loving him.

Oh, that is too much, he exclaimed, rising quickly to his feet. Yes, if it can be done, I shall be the only one to suffer. You will come to know this heart you spurn; you will see what efforts a love such as mine is capable of, and I shall at least oblige you to have pity for me. With these words he went out and left me in a state which I still do not understand. I remained where I stood, staring at the door through which Déterville had just left, lost in a confusion of thoughts which I could not even begin to make sense of; I would have stayed like that for a long time if Céline had not come into the parlour.

She asked me brusquely why Déterville had left so soon. I did not conceal what had happened between us. At first she was distressed at what she called her brother's misfortune. Then, moving from grief to anger, she heaped the severest reproaches on me, without my daring to say a single word in response. What could I have said? my unease scarcely left me the freedom to think; I went out, she did not follow. Having withdrawn to my room, I stayed there a whole day without daring to show myself, without news from anyone, and with my mind in such a state of confusion that I could not even write to you.

Céline's anger, her brother's despair, his parting words to which I wanted to give a favourable meaning, but dare not—each in turn delivered up my soul to anxieties of the cruellest kind.

I decided finally that the only way to relieve them was to put them into words for you, to share them with you, to seek the counsel I need in your love for me; this illusion has sustained me as I have been writing—but how fleeting it has been. My letter is finished, and the characters which make it have been formed for me alone.

You know nothing of my suffering, you do not even know if I exist, if I love you. Aza, my dearest Aza, will you ever know?

LETTER TWENTY-FOUR

I could once more call it an absence, my dearest Aza, the time which has passed since I last wrote to you.

A few days after my conversation with Déterville, I was struck down by an illness which they call a *fever*. If, as I believe, it was caused by the distressing passions which beset me at that time, I have no doubt that it was prolonged by the sad thoughts which possess me now, and by my regret at having lost Céline's friendship.

Although she has seemed concerned about my illness, and has taken all possible care of me, it has been with such coldness, she has had so little sympathy for my soul, that I cannot doubt that her feelings have changed. Her extreme friendship for her brother sets her against me, she never ceases to blame me for making him unhappy; the shame of appearing ungrateful intimidates me, Céline's strained kindness makes me uncomfortable, my embarrassment inhibits her, all sympathy and pleasure have been banished from our dealings with each other.

In spite of the upset and unhappiness caused by both brother and sister, I am not unmoved by the events which have changed their lives.

Déterville's mother has died. This unnatural mother has kept her character to the last, and has left all her wealth to her elder son. It is hoped that the men of law will prevent this injustice coming to pass. Déterville, indifferent about his own affairs, is taking infinite trouble to free Céline from such hardship. It seems that her misfortune is strengthening his friendship for her; not only does he come to see her every day, he writes to her morning and evening. His letters are full of such fond complaints about me, of such earnest concern for my health, that although Céline pretends as she reads them out that she wants only to tell me how their affairs are progressing, I can easily discern her real motive.

I have no doubt that Déterville is writing these letters so that they will be read to me; nevertheless, I am convinced that he would refrain from doing so, if he knew of the reproaches which follow Céline's reading of them, reproaches which are leaving their impression on my heart. Sadness is consuming me.

Until now, amid all the turmoil, I could still enjoy the meagre satisfaction of living at peace with myself; no stain soiled the purity of my soul, no remorse disturbed me; but now I can feel only a kind of scorn for myself when I think that I am making unhappy two people to whom I owe my life; that I am disturbing the serenity which would be theirs without me, and that I am causing them all the distress it is in my power to cause. And yet I cannot forswear my crime, nor do I wish to. My love for you is stronger than my remorse. Aza, how I love you!

LETTER TWENTY-FIVE

How harmful caution can sometimes be, my dearest Aza! I had long refused the insistent requests sent me by Déterville that I grant him a moment's conversation. Alas! I was avoiding my own happiness. Finally, and less out of kind-heartedness than weariness of quarrelling with Céline, I allowed myself to be taken to the parlour. When I saw the dreadful change in Déterville which makes him almost unrecognizable now, I was speechless; I was already regretting my decision, and awaited with trepidation the reproaches I felt he had every right to make me. Could I have guessed that he was going to fill my soul with delight?

Forgive me, Zilia, he said to me, for the violence I am doing you; I would not have obliged you to see me, if I were not bringing you as much joy as you cause me pain. Is it asking too much to see you just for a moment, in return for the cruel sacrifice I am making for you? And without giving me time to reply: Here, he continued, is a letter from the relative you have been told of. By informing you of Aza's fate, it will prove to you more surely than all my oaths, just how great is my love; whereupon he read me this letter. Ah! my dearest Aza, could I hear it without dying of joy? It tells me that your life has been spared, that you are free, that you are living in no danger at the court of Spain. What unexpected bliss!

This wonderful letter is written by a man who knows you, who sees you, who speaks to you; perhaps your eyes have looked for a moment on this precious paper? I could not tear my own from it; I could barely contain the cries of joy which were ready to escape my lips; tears of love streamed down my face.

If I had followed the instincts of my heart, I would have interrupted Déterville a hundred times to tell him everything my gratitude inspired in me; but I could not forget that my happiness would be sure to increase his suffering. I hid my excitement from him, he saw only my tears.

Well, Zilia, he said, when he had finished reading, I have kept my word, you know Aza's fate; if that is not enough, what else must I do? You may freely command it, there is nothing you have not the right to demand of my love, provided that it will add to your happiness.

Although I should have expected such extreme kindness, it took me by surprise and touched me.

For a few minutes I was lost for a reply, I feared I might increase the pain of so generous a man. I was looking for words to express what my heart truly felt, without wounding the sensitivity of his own. I could not find them, yet I had to say something.

My happiness, I said to him, will never be other than mixed, since I cannot reconcile the duties of love with those of friendship;

I would like to regain yours and Céline's, I would wish never to leave you, never to stop admiring your virtues, to pay every day of my life the tribute of gratitude which I owe you for your kindness. I just know that by taking my leave of two people who are so dear, I shall take with me everlasting regrets. But...

What! Zilia, he exclaimed, you want to leave us! Ah, I was quite unprepared for this deadly decision, I don't have the courage to bear it. I had summoned enough to see you here in the arms of my rival. The efforts of my reason and the tenderness of my love had given me the strength to withstand that mortal blow, which I would have brought about myself; but I cannot be separated from you, I cannot forgo seeing you; no, you will not leave, he continued passionately, do not think of it, you are abusing my affection, you are mercilessly tearing apart a heart lost to love. Zilia, cruel Zilia, see my despair, this is your doing. Alas! how do you repay the purest of loves?

It is you, I said to him, terrified at his resolve, it is you who are to blame. You are dishonouring my soul by forcing it to be ungrateful; you are torturing my heart with your fruitless love. In the name of friendship, do not tarnish a generosity beyond compare by giving in to despair which will poison my life and yet bring you no happiness. Do not condemn in me the very same feeling you cannot yourself overcome, do not oblige me to find fault with you, let me cherish your name, carry it with me to the ends of the earth, and let it be revered by peoples who worship virtue.*

I do not know how I uttered these words, but Déterville, his eyes fixed in my direction, seemed not to be looking at me; withdrawn into himself, he remained for a long time deep in thought. For my part, I dared not interrupt him. We were silent, both of us, when he spoke again and said with a show of composure: Yes, Zilia, I know, I can feel how unjust I am, but can one calmly give up the sight of so many charms! But it is your wish, you will be obeyed. What a sacrifice, oh Heavens. My joyless days will pass and come to an end without my seeing you. At least, if death... Let us speak of it no more, he added, interrupting himself; my weakness would betray me, give me two days to steady my resolve, I shall come back to see you, we must make preparations together for your journey. Farewell, Zilia. May the fortunate Aza realize just how blessed by fortune he is! And with those words, he left.

I must tell you, my dearest Aza, that although Déterville is dear to me, although I was deeply moved by his sorrow, I was too impatient to enjoy my happiness in peace not to be delighted that he had left.

How glorious it is, after so many troubles, to give oneself over to joy! I spent the rest of the day in the sweetest of raptures. I did not write to you at all, a letter could not contain what was in my heart, it would have reminded me of your absence. I could see you, I could talk to you, dearest Aza! What more could have been added to my bliss, if you had attached to the precious letter I received some marks of your love! Why did you not do so? They spoke to you about me, you know of my fate, and yet there is nothing to tell me of your love. But can I doubt your heart? My own answers for it. You love me, your joy is the equal of mine, you burn with the same passionate fire, the same impatience consumes you; may fear leave my soul, and joy reign supreme, unalloyed. And yet you have embraced the religion of this violent people. What religion is it? Does it require you to renounce my love, just as the religion of France wished me to renounce yours; no, you would never have submitted to that.

However it may be, my heart is ruled by your laws; following the light of your reason, I shall accept without question whatever can make us inseparable. What is there for me to fear? Soon to be reunited with my prince, my being, my all, I shall think only through you, I shall live for nothing but to love you.

LETTER TWENTY-SIX

It is here, my dearest Aza, that I shall see you again; my happiness grows greater each day by this very circumstance. I have just left the meeting which Déterville had granted me; whatever pleasures I might have promised myself in overcoming the hardships of the journey, telling you of my arrival, running to meet you, I gladly sacrifice them all for the joy of seeing you sooner.

Déterville has shown me so convincingly that you can be here in less time than it would take me to go to Spain, that, although he generously left me the choice, I did not hesitate about waiting for you, time is too precious to be wasted needlessly.

Perhaps, before making up my mind, I would have examined the advantages of this option more carefully, had I not discovered facts about my journey which made me secretly decide on the course I am taking, and this secret I can confide only to you.

I remembered that during the long journey which brought me to Paris, Déterville handed over pieces of silver and sometimes of gold in all the places we stopped. I enquired if this was out of obligation, or simply out of generosity. I learned that in France travellers must pay not only for their food, but for their lodging as well.[46] Alas! I do not have the smallest portion of what I would need to satisfy the greed of this selfish people; all would have to come from Déterville's hands. But could I willingly bring myself to contract a kind of obligation which is shameful almost to the point of being a disgrace? I cannot do it, my dearest Aza, and this reason alone would have been enough to persuade me to stay here; the pleasure of seeing you sooner merely strengthened my resolve.

Déterville has in my presence written to the Minister of Spain. He urges him to let you leave, with a generosity which fills me with gratitude and admiration.

What delightful moments I spent as Déterville was writing! What a pleasure it was to be busy with arrangements for your journey, to see preparations being made for my happiness, to doubt it no longer!

If at first I was reluctant to abandon my plan to travel to you, I must confess, my dearest Aza, I now find a thousand sources of pleasure in the decision, which I had not suspected to be there.

Several circumstances which seemed to me to have no value as reasons either to advance or delay my departure, I now find both

[46] The Incas had set up large houses on the roads, where they welcomed travellers without any charge.

interesting and pleasurable. I was blindly following the inclination of my heart, forgetting that I was going to meet you in the
land of those barbarous Spaniards, the very thought of whom fills
me with horror; it gives me infinite satisfaction to know for certain that I shall never see them again. The voice of love was sti-
fling the voice of friendship; I can now enjoy without remorse the
delight of combining them. On the other hand, Déterville assured
me that it was impossible for us ever to see again the city of the
Sun. Next to our own country, is there one where it is more pleasant to abide than France? You will like it, my dearest Aza, even
though sincerity has been banished from this country; so many
pleasures are to be found here that they make you forget the dangers of the society.

After what I have told you about gold, I do not need to advise
you to bring some quantity with you, you need no other virtue;
the smallest part of your treasure will be enough to win you admiration and to confound the pride of the haughty paupers in this
realm. Your virtues and your feelings will be appreciated only by
Déterville and me; he has promised that he will have my knots
and my letters delivered to you; he has assured me that you would
find interpreters to explain the letters to you. They have come to
collect the packet, I must leave you. Farewell, dear hope of my
life, I shall continue to write; if I can find no means of sending my
letters, I shall keep them for you.

How could I endure the length of your journey, if I denied
myself the only means I have to reflect on my joy, my rapture, my
happiness!

LETTER TWENTY-SEVEN

Ever since knowing that my letters are on their way to you, my
dearest Aza, I have enjoyed a feeling of calm which I had ceased to
know. I cannot stop thinking of the pleasure you will have in receiving them, I can see your delight, I share it with you; my soul is filled
from every side with nothing but pleasant thoughts, and, to make
my joy complete, peace has been restored to our little society.

The judges have returned to Céline the possessions denied her by her mother. She sees her suitor every day, her marriage has been delayed by no more than the time it will take to make the necessary arrangements. With all her wishes fulfilled, she no longer thinks of quarrelling with me, and I am no less obliged to her than I would be if it were to her friendship that I owed the kindness she once more begins to show me. Whatever their motives, we are always indebted to those who make us feel good.

This morning, she made me feel the full value of this with an act of kindness which took me from distressing unease to delightful peace of mind.

She was brought an enormous quantity of fabrics, clothes, trinkets of all kinds; she ran into my room, took me to hers and, after asking my opinion about the different charms of so much finery, she put together a pile of the items which had most attracted my attention, and she was already eagerly instructing our *Chinas* to take them to my room, when I objected as strongly as I could. At first, my pleas just amused her; but seeing her become more determined the more I resisted, I could no longer conceal my displeasure.

Why, I said to her, my eyes bathed in tears, why do you wish to humiliate me even more than I already am? I owe you my life, and everything I have, that is more than enough for me not to forget my misfortune. I know that, according to your laws, when gifts are of no use to those who receive them, the shame of receiving is wiped away. Wait then until I have no further need of your generosity before you practise it. It is with the utmost reluctance, I added, in a more measured tone, that I conform to attitudes so contrary to the law of nature. Our customs are more humane, to receive is just as honourable as to give; you have taught me to think differently, was it just so that you could give me offence?

This dear friend, moved by my tears more than angered by my reproaches, replied in an understanding tone: my dearest Zilia, my brother and I are both very far from wanting to offend your sense of decency, it would ill become us to be grand with you, you will soon understand what I mean. I simply wanted you to share with me the gifts of a generous brother; it was the surest way to show him my gratitude. In my present circumstances, custom allowed me to give them to you; but since you are offended, I shall not mention it again. Is that a promise, then? I said to her. Yes, she replied, smiling, but let me write a note to Déterville.

I let her do so, and good humour was restored between us. We began again to look more closely at her finery, until she was called to the parlour. She wanted to take me with her, but, my dearest Aza, could any pleasures be compared to that of writing to you! Far from seeking out others, I am quite anxious about those which Céline's marriage has in store for me.

She would like me to leave the Religious House, and to live in hers when she is married; but if I am to be believed...

Aza, my dearest Aza, what a delightful surprise interrupted my letter yesterday! Alas, I thought I had lost for ever those precious monuments of our former splendour, I no longer counted on recovering them, I no longer even thought of them, now I am surrounded by them. I can see them, I can touch them, and yet I can scarcely believe my eyes and my hands.

As I was writing to you, I saw Céline come in followed by four men, bending under the weight of the large chests they were carrying; they put them down and went out of the room; I thought they might be more gifts from Déterville. I was already grumbling to myself, when Céline said to me, handing me some keys: Open them, Zilia, open them and don't be upset, they come from Aza. I believed her. At the mention of your name, can anything stop my eagerness? I hastened to open them, and my error was confirmed when I saw before me, to my astonishment, the ornaments from the Temple of the Sun.

Confused feelings filled my heart, sadness and joy, pleasure and regret were mingled there. I threw myself down before these sacred relics of our religion and our altars; I covered them with respectful kisses, I bathed them with my tears, I could not tear myself away from them, I had even forgotten that Céline was still in the room; she roused me from my state of rapture, handing me a letter which she bade me read.

Still deceived, I thought the letter was from you, my delight was doubled; but although I could barely make it out, I soon realized that it was from Déterville.

It will be easier for me, my dearest Aza, to copy it for you than to give you an account of what it said.

DÉTERVILLE'S NOTE

These treasures are yours, fair Zilia, since I found them on the ship which was carrying you. Disputes among members of the crew have prevented me from disposing of them freely until now. I wanted to deliver them to you in person, but the concerns you expressed to my sister this morning no longer give me a choice as to when you should receive them. I cannot allay your fears too soon, I shall prefer your happiness to my own my whole life through.

I confess to my shame, my dearest Aza, that I was less sensitive at that moment to Déterville's generosity than I was to the pleasure of giving him proof of my own.

I promptly put on one side a vase, which chance rather than greed had caused to fall into the hands of the Spaniards. It is that same vase, and my heart recognized it, which your lips touched the day you wished to taste of the *Aca*[47] prepared by my hand. Wealthier with this cup than with all the other treasures being restored to me, I called the men who had carried them in; I wanted to have them take them back and give them to Déterville, but Céline was opposed to my plan.

How unjust you are, Zilia, she said. What! you wish my brother to accept immense riches, you who are offended by the gift of trifles; show justice in your own actions, if you wish to inspire it in others.

I was struck by these words. I was afraid that there might be more pride and vengeance in my action than generosity. How very close do virtues come to vices! I acknowledged my fault, I begged Céline's forgiveness; but I was suffering too much from the constraint she wished to impose on me not to look for some means of easing it. Do not punish me as much as I deserve, I said to her timidly, do not turn down some examples of the craftsmanship of

[47] A drink of the Indians.

our poor country; you have no need of them, my request should cause you no offence.

As I was speaking, I noticed that Céline was looking attentively at two finely wrought golden shrubs, with birds and insects on them; I hastened to offer them to her, with a small silver basket which I filled with shells, fish and flowers imitated to perfection: she accepted them graciously, which delighted me.

I then chose some idols taken from the nations conquered[48] by your ancestors, and a small statue[49] which represented a Virgin of the Sun; I added to these a tiger, a lion, and other beasts of prey, and I asked her to send them to Déterville. Write to him then, she said to me, smiling; without a letter from you, the presents would not be well received.

I was too happy to refuse anything, I wrote all that my gratitude dictated, and when Céline had gone out, I handed out small gifts to her *China*, and to mine, I set some on one side for my writing teacher. At last I could enjoy the delightful pleasure of being able to give.

This has not been without making careful choices, my dearest Aza; everything which comes from you, everything which has an intimate link with your memory, has not left my hands.

The golden chair[50] which was kept in the Temple for the days when the *Capa-Inca*, your revered father, would visit, stands on one side of my room in the manner of a throne, and represents for me your grandeur and exalted rank. The large figure of the Sun, which I myself saw torn from the Temple by the treacherous Spaniards, hangs above it, and inspires my devotion; I fall to my knees before it, my spirit adores it, and my heart is all yours. The two palm trees which you gave to the Sun as an offering and a pledge of the fidelity you had sworn me stand on either side of the throne, and remind me constantly of your loving vows.

[48] The Incas placed in the Temple of the Sun the idols of the peoples they conquered, having first made them accept the cult of the Sun. They also had idols themselves, since the Inca *Huayna* consulted the Idol of Rimace. *History of the Incas*, volume 1, page 350.

[49] The Incas decorated their houses with golden statues of all sizes, even gigantic ones.

[50] The Incas sat only on seats of solid gold.

Flowers,[51] birds arranged symmetrically in every corner of my room, represent in miniature those magnificent gardens where I so often filled my mind with thoughts of you. My delighted eyes can look nowhere without recalling your love, my joy, my happiness, in short everything which will forever be the life of my life.

End of Part One

[51] We have already said that the gardens of the Temple and those of the Royal Houses were filled with all kinds of imitations of nature in gold and silver. The Peruvians even made representations of the grass called *Maïs*, with which they would fill entire fields.

PART TWO

Illustration facing the title-page of Part Two of
Lettres d'une Péruvienne (1752)

LETTER TWENTY-EIGHT

I have not been able to withstand Céline's persistence, my dearest Aza; I have had to go with her, and for the last two days we have been at her country house where her marriage was celebrated on our arrival.

With what great difficulty, and with what regret, did I tear myself away from my solitude! Scarcely have I had time to enjoy the sight of those precious ornaments which made it so dear to me, than I have been obliged to leave them behind; and for how long? I cannot tell.

The joy and pleasures which seem to have intoxicated everybody else make me look back with all the more regret on those peaceful days I spent writing to you, or, at least, thinking of you. And yet I have never seen objects so unfamiliar to me, so marvellous, so liable to amuse me. Now that I have a reasonable knowledge of this country's language, I could make discoveries as pleasurable as they would be useful about everything I see happening around me, if only the noise and commotion left somebody with enough composure to answer my questions. But so far I have found nobody ready to do so, and I am scarcely less confused than I was when I first arrived in France.

The finery of both men and women is so dazzling, and it is covered with so many superfluous decorations; they all utter their words so rapidly that if I concentrate on listening to them, I do not see them, and if I make an effort to look at them, I cannot understand what they say. I am left in a kind of daze which would doubtless give them more to laugh at, if they had the time to notice it. But they are so absorbed in themselves that my astonishment escapes their attention. But it is all too well grounded, my dearest Aza, for I see marvels here whose workings I cannot begin to make sense of.

I shall say nothing about the beauty of this house, which is almost as large as a town, decorated like a Temple, and filled with countless pleasing trifles, which I see so little used that I cannot help thinking that the French have chosen luxury as the object of their worship. They dedicate their arts to it, which here they take far beyond the realm of nature; they appear to seek merely to imitate it, but they surpass it; and the way they make use of nature's creations often seems superior to that of nature itself. They bring together in gardens, in areas which one can view almost in a single glance, beauties which nature distributes sparingly across the surface of the earth; and it seems that the elements, which they have brought under their power, present difficulties for their schemes only to make their success in overcoming them more spectacular.

One is surprised to see the earth nourish and raise in its bosom plants from the furthest climes, without need, without any apparent necessity other than that of obeying the arts, and of adorning the idol of luxury. Water, so easy to divide, whose firmness derives solely from the vessels which contain it, and whose natural inclination is to follow slopes of whatever kind, is forced here to shoot into the air at great speed, without guidance or support, but by its own energy, and with no other purpose than to please the eye.

Fire, my dearest Aza, fire, that terrible element, I have seen it relinquish its destructive power and be tamely led by some superior force, taking all the forms required of it; sometimes drawing a vast picture of light across a sky made dark by the Sun's absence, and sometimes representing that divine Star, come down to earth with its fires, its life, and its dazzling light; in short, in a blaze which deceives both one's eyes and one's judgement. What art, my dearest Aza! What men! What genius! I forget everything I have heard, everything I have seen of their pettiness; I revert, in spite of myself, to my earlier state of wonder.

LETTER TWENTY-NINE*

It is not without genuine regret, my dearest Aza, that I move from wonder at the genius of the French to scorn of the use to which they put it. It truly gave me pleasure to appreciate the charms of this country, but I cannot ignore its evident shortcomings.

The excitement has at last died down, I have been able to ask questions, I have been given answers; no more is needed to find out even more than one wishes to know. It is with quite unbelievable honesty and light-heartedness that the French reveal the secrets of their perverse customs. However little one enquires, one needs neither subtlety nor insight to see that their unbridled passion for luxury has corrupted their reason, their heart, and their mind; that it has founded illusory riches on the ruins of what is essential; that it has substituted superficial politeness for good manners, and that it replaces common sense and reason with the empty brilliance of wit.

The overriding pretension of the French is to appear wealthy. Genius, the arts, and perhaps the sciences, all work in the service of extravagant display;* everything conspires to exhaust fortunes. And if the inventiveness of their own genius were not enough to increase the number of luxury objects, I know from their own mouths that they scorn the sound and attractive goods which France itself produces in abundance, and acquire at great expense, and from every corner of the world, insubstantial and purposeless furnishings to decorate their houses, dazzling finery with which to dress themselves, and even the food and drink which make up their meals.

It might be, my dearest Aza, that I would find nothing to condemn in such excess of luxury items if the French had riches enough to satisfy this taste, or if, to do so, they used only the wealth which remained once they had established their households on a foundation of honest comfort.

Our laws, the wisest ever given to men, permit certain adornments to each station in life, which distinguish levels of birth and wealth, and which, strictly speaking, one could call luxuries; this being so, the only luxury which seems criminal to me is that born of an imagination out of control, one which cannot be maintained without failing in one's duty to humanity or justice, in a word, it is the kind, precisely, which the French worship, and to which they sacrifice their peace of mind and their honour.

There is but one class of citizens among them who can take their worship of this idol to its highest level of magnificence, without failing in their duty to what is necessary. Those enjoying a high social position wanted to imitate them, but they are simply martyrs to this religion. What torment! What confusion! What toil to sustain their spending beyond their means! There are few nobles who do not apply more effort, ingenuity, and trickery to distinguish themselves by superficial pomp than their ancestors used prudence, courage, and talents useful to the state to bring lustre to their own name. And do not think, my dearest Aza, that I am deceiving you. I am enraged to hear every day young people disputing among themselves the honour of having used the most subtlety and skill in their schemes to acquire the luxury items with which they adorn themselves from the hands of those who work simply to avoid going without what is essential.

What contempt would such people inspire in me for their nation as a whole, if I did not also know that the French sin more frequently for lack of sound understanding than they do for lack of probity: their light-heartedness almost always prevents the use of reason. For them, nothing is serious, nothing has importance; it could be that none of them has ever considered the dishonour-ing consequences of his behaviour. One has to appear wealthy, it is a fashion, a custom, and they follow it. If an obstacle arises they overcome it with an act of injustice; they think they have simply triumphed over a difficulty. But this is not the end of their illusion.

In most houses, indigence and luxury are no more than one room apart. They both share the business of the day, but in quite different ways. In the morning, inside the study, the voice of poverty is heard from the lips of a man paid to find ways of reconcil-ing this with an image of opulence. Despondency and bad humour preside over such discussions, which usually conclude with the sacrifice of what is essential, a victim offered up to luxury. For the rest of the day, and now in other clothes, in another room, and one might almost say with another identity, dazzled by their own magnificence, they are cheerful, they call themselves happy; they even go so far as to believe themselves rich.

I have noticed, however, that some of those who parade their splendour with the most affectation do not always dare to believe that they impress. As a result they joke among themselves about their own poverty; they cheerfully insult the memory of their forebears who, in their prudent thrift, were satisfied with comfortable clothes, and decorations or furnishings befitting their income rather than their birth. Their family, they say, and their servants, enjoyed frugal and honest plenty. They gave dowries to their daughters, they established on solid foundations the fortune of the successor to their name, and they kept enough in reserve to relieve the misfortune of a friend, or of one in need.

Shall I tell you, my dearest Aza, in spite of the ridiculous light in which the manners of this bygone age were presented, they appealed to me so much, they seemed so close to the simplicity of our own that I was carried away by the illusion; my heart was so moved by each detail that by the end of their account, I might have been standing among our dear fellow countrymen. But as soon as I expressed approval of such wise customs, the outbursts of laughter which I provoked brought me back to the real world, and I found myself surrounded by none but the foolish French of the present age, who glory in the excesses of their imagination.

The same decadence which has turned the solid wealth of the French into empty trifles has made their social relations no less superficial. The wisest among them, who lament this decadence, have assured me that there was a time, as with us, when integrity was in their soul and humanity in their heart; that may be. But now, what they call politeness has taken the place of feeling; it consists of countless words without meaning, of marks of respect without esteem, and of concern without affection.*

In noble households, a servant has the task of fulfilling social duties. Each day he travels considerable distances to tell one person that there is concern about his health, another that there is distress at his suffering, or that there is joy at his happiness. When he returns, nobody listens to the replies he brings back. There is a mutual agreement to limit oneself to formality and to invest no feeling in it; and these gestures of courtesy take the place of friendship.

Shows of respect are enacted in person, and they are taken to childish extremes; I would be ashamed to tell you about some of them, if it were not important to know everything about such a strange nation. They would be lacking respect for their superiors, and even for their equals, if, after a meal which they might have taken together in all familiarity, they satisfied an urgent need to take a drink without first asking for forgiveness as earnestly as they sought permission. Nor can they let their clothing touch that of a person of high status; it would be an act of disrespect to look at such a person attentively, but it would be even worse to fail to notice him. I would need more intelligence and a better memory than I have to give you an account of all the empty gestures which are given and received as marks of consideration, which is almost the same as esteem.

As for the abundance of words, you will one day hear for yourself, my dearest Aza, how exaggeration, which is disclaimed as soon as it is spoken, is the inexhaustible stuff of conversation for the French. They rarely fail to add a superfluous compliment to one which was already unnecessary, just so they might give the impression that they are not complimenting at all. It is with excessive flattery that they protest the sincerity of the praise they lavish, and they intensify their declarations of love and friendship with so many superfluous terms that the feelings behind them are nowhere to be seen.*

Oh, my dearest Aza, how dreary must seem my lack of enthusiasm for conversation, or the plainness of my speech! I do not think that my wit inspires any more respect. To earn any kind of reputation in this regard, you need to have shown great ingenuity in grasping the various meanings of words and in using them quite differently. You have to capture the attention of your listeners by the subtlety or, as is often the case, the incomprehensibility of your thoughts, or else conceal their obscurity beneath an abundance of frivolous expressions. I have read in one of their best books that: *Wit in fashionable society consists in speaking agreeably but saying nothing at all, in forbearing to utter the slightest sensible remark, unless the elegance of its formulation makes it forgivable; finally in concealing reason, whenever one is obliged to pronounce it.*[52]*

---

[52] *Considerations on the Manners of this Century*, by M. Duclos.

What could I say to show you more convincingly that good sense and reason, regarded as essential to the mind, are despised in this country, as is everything that is useful? In short, my dearest Aza, you can be certain that luxury rules so majestically in France that anyone with just a modest fortune is poor, anyone with only virtues is dull, and anyone with mere good sense is a fool.

LETTER THIRTY

The natural propensity which the French have to extremes is so great, my dearest Aza, that Déterville, although he is exempt from most of his nation's failings, is nevertheless prone to this one. Not satisfied with keeping his promise to speak no more of his feelings, he quite deliberately avoids coming near to me. We are constantly obliged to see each other, but I have not yet found the opportunity to speak to him.

Although there is always a joyful atmosphere among the many people constantly present, sadness governs his looks. It is easy to see that it is not without a great struggle that he submits to the rule he has imposed on himself. I should perhaps be grateful to him for this, but I have so many questions to ask about matters close to my heart that I cannot forgive his pretence of avoiding me.

I would like to ask him about the letter he sent to Spain, and if it might have arrived yet; I would like to have a precise idea of when you might be leaving, of how long your journey will take, so that I can calculate the moment of my happiness. Hope that is well founded is a real blessing, but it is even more precious, my dearest Aza, when we can foresee the moment it will be realized.

None of the amusements which occupy the others affects me, they are too noisy for my soul. I no longer have the pleasure of conversation with Céline. She is completely absorbed in her new husband, and I can scarcely find a few moments to pay her the respects due from a friend. I enjoy the company of others only insofar as I can elicit information from them about the various objects of my curiosity. And I do not always find the opportunity to do so. As a result, I often find myself alone in the midst of other people, having no distractions but my own thoughts; these are all for you, my heart's dearest friend; you will forever be the only confidant of my soul, of my pleasures, and of my sorrows.

LETTER THIRTY-ONE

I was quite wrong, my dearest Aza, to desire a meeting with Déterville with such eagerness. Alas! he has now spoken to me all too much; although I may deny the unrest he has caused in my heart, it has not yet completely gone.

A vague feeling of impatience combined yesterday with the weariness I often endure. The social round and its noise irritated me more than usual; everything I saw, even the tender happiness of Céline and her husband, inspired in me an indignation bordering on contempt. Ashamed to find such unjust feelings in my heart, I went to hide the distress they caused me in the remotest part of the garden.

Scarcely had I sat down beneath a tree when tears began to flow freely from my eyes. My head buried in my hands, I was lost in such a deep reverie that Déterville was kneeling in front of me before I noticed him arrive.

Do not be offended, Zilia, he said, chance has brought me to your feet, I was not looking for you. Tired of all the noise inside, I came outside to give way to my sorrow in peace. I noticed you, I struggled with myself to move away, but I cannot endure such unhappiness without some respite; out of pity for myself, I approached you, I saw your tears flow and I was no longer master of my heart. Yet if you bid me leave you, I shall obey. Could you do so, Zilia? Am I hateful to you? No, I said, far from it. Sit down, I am very glad to have this chance to speak with you. Ever since your last acts of kindness... Say no more about them, he said, interrupting me hastily. Let me speak, I replied, interrupting him in my turn, to be truly generous, one must be prepared to accept gratitude. I have not spoken a word to you since you gave me back the precious ornaments of the Temple from which I was abducted. Perhaps, in my letter, I expressed badly the feelings which such extreme kindness inspired in me, I wish... Alas! he said, interrupting me again, how unwelcome gratitude is for an unhappy heart! The companion of indifference, it is all too often the ally of hatred.

How can you dare think this? I exclaimed: oh, Déterville! how I would reproach you, if you were not so deserving of pity! far from hating you, from the first moment I saw you I felt less repugnance at being in your power than in that of the Spaniards. From that moment, your gentleness and kindness made me wish to win your friendship. The more I came to know your character, the more certain I was that you merited all my friendship, and, leaving aside my extreme obligation to you, since my gratitude causes offence, how could I not have the feelings which you justly deserve?

You were the only one whose virtues, in their simplicity, I found to be the worthy equal of our own. A son of the Sun would be honoured to have your feelings; your reason seems to be guided by nature itself; how many reasons, then, for holding you dear! Right down to your noble appearance, everything about you pleases me; friendship has eyes to see, as well as love. There was a time when, after a brief absence, I would not see you return without feeling a kind of serenity in my heart; why have you changed these innocent pleasures into grief and tension?

It is now only after much effort that you display your reason. I am in constant fear of your lapses from it. The feelings you describe hinder me from expressing my own, they deny me the pleasure of telling you, quite openly, what delight I would take in your friendship, if you did not yourself sour its sweetness. You even deny me that exquisite feeling of bliss at beholding my benefactor, your eyes confuse mine, I can no longer see in them that enchanting serenity which at times would reach my very soul: I find there now just wretched sorrow, and a constant reproach for being the cause of it. Oh, Déterville! how unjust you are if you think that only you are suffering!

My dearest Zilia, he exclaimed, kissing my hand fervently, how your kindness and candour add to my regret! What a treasure it would be to possess a heart such as yours! But what despair you make me feel at such a loss! Mighty Zilia, he continued, how great is your power! Was it not enough to take me from complete indifference to boundless love, from indolence to distraction; must I now overcome these feelings you have aroused in me? Can I do so? Yes, I said to him, such an effort is worthy of you and of your heart. Such a generous action raises you above other men. But can I survive it? he continued, sorrowfully. Do not imagine that I shall live on here, the victim of your lover's success; I shall go far away, to worship the thought of you, this will be the bitter nourishment of my heart; I shall love you, and I shall never see you again! But at least do not forget...

Sobs stifled his words, he hastened to hide the tears which bathed his cheeks. I too was shedding tears; moved as much by his generosity as by his suffering, I took one of his hands which I clasped in mine. No, I said, you shall not leave us. Let me keep my friend; you must be content with the feelings I shall have for you all my life. I love you almost as much as I love Aza, but I can never love you in the same way.

Cruel Zilia!, he exclaimed with passion, must you always accompany your acts of kindness with the most painful blows? Must a deadly poison always destroy the charm which your words convey? How foolish I am to be enchanted by their sweetness! How I humiliate and debase myself! But it is done, he added resolutely, I am now returning to my senses; farewell, soon you shall see Aza. May he never make you feel the torments which now consume me, may you find him just as you wish him to be, and worthy of your heart.

What alarm was cast into my soul, my dearest Aza, by the manner in which he spoke these final words! I could not hold back the suspicions which came crowding into my mind. I did not doubt that Déterville knew more than he wished to admit, that he was concealing from me letters which he might have received from Spain. In a word, dare I utter the thought, I suspected that you were unfaithful.

I implored him to tell me the truth, yet all I could draw from him were vague conjectures, as likely to confirm my fears as to dispel them. However, his remarks about the inconstancy of men, the dangers of absence, and your readiness to change your religion, all cast anxiety into my soul.

Now, for the first time, my love brought me pain, for the first time I began to fear the loss of your heart. Aza, if it were true, if you no longer loved me, oh, may such a suspicion never tarnish the purity of my heart! No, I alone would be guilty if I dwelt for an instant on such a thought, unworthy of my honesty, of your virtue, of your constancy. No, despair has suggested these dreadful thoughts to Déterville. Should I not be reassured by the turmoil and distraction of his mind? Should I not suspect the self-interest which made him speak? And so it was, my dearest Aza, my resentment turned completely against him, I treated him harshly, he left me in despair. Aza! I love you so dearly! No, never could you forget me.

LETTER THIRTY-TWO

How long your journey is, my dearest Aza! How fervently I wish to see you here! The end of my wait now seems more uncertain to me than I had hitherto imagined, and I am very careful not to ask Déterville a single question about it. I cannot forgive him for having such a poor opinion of your heart. The opinion I now have of his greatly reduces the pity I once had for his suffering, and my regret at being in some sense distant from him.

We have been in Paris for two weeks; I am living with Céline in her husband's house, which is far enough from that of her brother that I am not obliged to see him all the time. He often comes here to take his meals; but we live such a hectic life, Céline and I, that he does not have the opportunity to speak to me alone.

Since our return, we spend a part of our day on the tiresome task of dressing, and the remainder on what they call 'paying visits'.

These two activities would seem to me as fruitless as they are wearisome, if the second did not provide me the means of learning in even greater detail about the customs of this country. When I arrived in France, having no knowledge of the language, I made judgements based only on appearances. When I began to use their language I was in the Religious House, and you know that I could find little help there with my learning; in the country, I encountered only a particular kind of company; it is now that I am moving in what they call high society that I can see the nation as a whole, and I can examine it unhindered.

The duty of paying visits consists of going in a single day to as many houses as possible, in order to give and receive tributes of mutual praise for the beauty of one's face or figure, for the excellence of one's taste and one's choice of jewels, and never for the qualities of one's soul.*

It did not take me long to see why they go to such lengths to obtain this empty homage; it is because one simply has to receive it in person, and even then it lasts but a moment. As soon as one is gone, it takes a quite different form. The charms which were found in the woman who is leaving now serve only for contemptuous comparison to establish the perfections of the next one to arrive.

Censure is the prevailing taste of the French, just as inconsistency is their national character. Their books are a criticism of customs in general, and their conversations that of any individual, provided that they are not present; they then freely express all the ill they think of these absent others, and sometimes more than they think. Even the most respectable people follow this custom; what distinguishes them is just the formal apology they make for their frankness and love of truth, which allows them to reveal without any qualms the failings, follies, and even the vices of their friends.

If the sincerity which the French use against each other is without exception, their mutual trust is equally limitless. One needs neither eloquence to be listened to, nor integrity to be believed. Everything is said, and everything is accepted as true, with the same unconcern.

But do not imagine for all that, my dearest Aza, that the French are in general born malicious; I would be more unjust than they are if I left you with that false impression.

Sensitive by nature and moved by virtue, I have met not one of them who was not touched by the account I am often compelled to give of the honesty of our hearts, the candour of our feelings, and the simplicity of our manners. If they lived among us, they would become virtuous; example and custom are the tyrants governing their behaviour.

Someone who thinks well of another who is not present will nevertheless speak ill of him, so as not to be scorned by those who listen. Another would be sincere, humane, humble, if he did not fear to be mocked, and another makes himself ridiculous, who would be a model of perfection if he dared to show his merit openly.

In short, my dearest Aza, their vices are in the majority of cases as affected as their virtues, and the shallowness of their character does not allow them to be perfectly either one thing or the other. They are rather like certain playthings from their childhood, imperfect replicas of thinking beings; they appear substantial to the eye, but are light to the touch, their surface is brightly coloured, but their inside unfinished, they have an apparent price but no intrinsic value. As a result, they are prized by other nations scarcely more than pretty trifles are valued in society. Common sense smiles at their airs, and then coldly puts them back in their place.

Happy the nation which has nature alone as its guide, truth as its principle, and virtue as its motivating force.

LETTER THIRTY-THREE

It is not surprising, my dearest Aza, that inconsistency should be a result of the superficial character of the French; but I cannot help being astonished that, with as much enlightenment as any other nation, if not more, they seem not to notice the shocking contradictions which those from the outside notice in them from the outset.

Among the many such contradictions which strike me every day, I see none which dishonours their mind more than their attitude to women. They respect them, my dearest Aza, and yet at the same time they despise them just as excessively.

The first principle of their politeness, or, if you prefer, of their virtue (for up to now I have scarce discovered any other virtue in them), relates to women. A man of the highest social rank owes respect to a woman of the lowest possible status; he would bring shame on himself, and what they call ridicule, if he subjected her to any kind of personal insult. And yet the least important man, the least regarded, may deceive and betray a woman of merit, blacken her reputation with slanders, all without fear of either blame or punishment.

If I did not know that you will soon see these things for yourself, I would not dare describe for you contradictions which the simplicity of our minds can barely conceive. Obedient to nature's principles, our spirit does not move beyond them; we have found that the strength and courage of one sex signified that it should support and defend the other, and our laws comply with this notion.[53] In this country, far from showing sympathy for the weakness of women, those among the common people who are weighed down by labour are given no relief either by the laws or by their husbands; and those of a more elevated rank who are prey to wanton or wicked men have no compensation for such perfidy beyond the outward show of illusory respect, which is invariably followed by the most scathing satire.

I soon noticed when I first entered this society that women were the principal target of the nation's customary censure, and that among themselves men showed only moderate scorn for each other: I sought the reason for this in their good qualities, but then an unexpected incident led me to discover it in their faults.

In all the houses we have visited these last two days, there has been talk of the death of a young man, killed by one of his friends, and this barbarous deed has met with approval for the simple reason that the dead man had spoken ill of the one who survived. This latest extravagance seemed to me sufficiently serious to merit

[53] Laws dispensed women of all hard physical work.

further investigation. I asked more about it, and I discovered, my dearest Aza, that a man is obliged to risk his own life in order to take that of another, if he discovers that this other man has spoken against him; or he must banish himself from society if he refuses to take such cruel vengeance.* No more information was needed to bring me the enlightenment I sought. It is clear that men, who are by nature cowardly, shameless, and without remorse, fear only physical punishment, and that if women were allowed to punish the offences committed against them in the same way that men are obliged to avenge the slightest insult, those men whom one sees warmly received in society would be no more; or they would have retreated to a social wilderness, where they would hide their shame and malice. Impudence and effrontery completely govern young men, above all when they risk nothing. The reason behind their behaviour towards women needs no further explanation. But what I still cannot understand is the basis of that underlying contempt for them which I detect in the mind of almost everyone; I shall do all I can to uncover what it is; it is in my own interest to do so. Oh, my dearest Aza! how I should suffer if, when you arrived, they were to speak to you about me in the same way as I hear them speak about others.

LETTER THIRTY-FOUR*

It has taken me a long time, my dearest Aza, to fathom the cause of that contempt in which women are held in this country, and by almost everyone. Now, at last, I think I have uncovered it in the discrepancy between what women actually are and what it is imagined they should be. It is desired, here as elsewhere, that women should have merit and virtue. But nature would have had to make them like this, because the education they are given is so much at odds with the desired result that it seems to me to be the very masterpiece of French inconsistency.

We know in Peru, my dearest Aza, that in order to prepare humans for the practice of virtue, they must be inspired from childhood with courage and a certain moral resolve which strengthens their character; this is not known in France. In their infancy, children seem destined to do no more than entertain their parents and those responsible for their upbringing. It seems that the French wish to take shameful advantage of children's inability to discover the truth for themselves. They deceive them about what they cannot see. They mislead them about the evidence of their senses, and they laugh heartlessly at their mistakes; they increase their sensitivity and natural weakness by showing infantile compassion at every little accident that befalls them: they forget that children must one day become men.

I do not know what education is subsequently given by a father to his son; I have not discovered this. But I do know that as soon as girls are of an age to receive instruction, they are shut away in a Religious House to be taught how to live in the world. And that the task of enlightening their mind is entrusted to those for whom it might be considered a crime to have one, and who are quite incapable of providing an education for their heart, of which they know nothing.

Principles of religion, the seed from which all virtues naturally spring, are learned only superficially and by rote. Reverence owed to the Divinity is not inspired by any better method; it consists of small rituals which merely simulate worship. They are imposed with such rigour, but practised with such indifference, that this is the first yoke to be shed when entering society; and if some of these customs are still retained, one might well conclude from the way they are carried out that they are nothing more than a kind of courtesy extended to the Divinity out of habit.

What is more, nothing replaces the first foundations of this misguided education. People in France hardly know that feeling of self-respect which we take such care to instil in the hearts of our young Virgins. That noble feeling which makes us the harshest judge of our own actions and thoughts, which can become a sound guiding principle when it is truly felt, is not a resource available to women here. Judging by the lack of concern shown for women's souls, it is tempting to think that the French have the same misconception as certain barbarous nations who do not even credit them with one.*

Regulating the movements of one's body, adjusting one's facial expression, composing one's outer appearance, this is the essence of their education. It is on the basis of their daughters' ability to comport themselves more or less awkwardly that parents take pride in having brought them up well. They instruct them to be stricken with embarrassment if they commit any offence against social decorum; they do not tell them that an honest countenance is mere hypocrisy if it does not spring from the honesty of one's soul. They constantly encourage in them that despicable feeling of self-love, which is concerned only with their outer appeal. They are not taught the kind which shapes one's sense of worth, and which is satisfied only by the esteem of others. The only notion of honour given to them is limited to that of not having lovers, and this is coupled with the repeated assurance that they will be found attractive as a reward for the discomfort and constraint which is imposed on them. The most precious time for forming the mind is used to acquire imperfect talents which are of little use in one's youth and which become sources of ridicule in one's later years.

But that is not all, my dearest Aza; the inconsistency of the French knows no bounds. Starting with such principles, they expect their women to practise virtues with which they neither acquaint them nor even give them a clear understanding of the terms used to designate them. Every day I am made more aware of this than I need be through conversations with young women whose ignorance causes me no less astonishment than anything I have witnessed up to now.

If I talk to them of feelings, they claim to have none because they know only love. They understand by the word 'goodness' only that instinctive sympathy one feels for those who suffer; and I have even noticed that they are moved more by the suffering of animals than that of humans. But that goodness which is caring and thoughtful, which leads to noble, discriminating acts of kindness, which inspires forbearance and compassion, is quite unknown to them. They consider that they have fulfilled all their obligations to discretion if they reveal to just a few friends the trivial secrets they have found out by chance, or which they have been told in confidence. But they have no conception at all of that more circumspect, unobtrusive discretion which is necessary if one is not to be importunate or cause hurt, and one is to maintain harmony in society.

If I try to explain to them what I understand by moderation, without which even virtues may almost be turned into vices, if I speak of decency in one's manners, of fairness in one's dealings with social inferiors, so little practised in France, and of the determination to spurn and shun vice in high places, I can tell by their confusion that they suspect I am speaking to them in Peruvian, and it is only out of politeness that they pretend to understand me.

They are no better educated in their knowledge of the world, of men, and of society. They are ignorant even in the use of their native language; rarely do they speak it correctly, and it is with the utmost surprise that I now find myself to be more knowledgeable than they are in this respect.*

It is in such ignorance that girls scarcely out of childhood are married. From then on it seems, judging by the little interest that parents take in their behaviour, that their daughters no longer belong to them. Most husbands have no more concern. There would still be time to put right the mistakes of their early education; but nobody takes the trouble.

A young woman, at liberty in her apartment, can receive visits from anybody she wishes, without restriction. Her pastimes are usually childish, always pointless, and perhaps even less than idle. People fill her mind with nothing but malicious or empty trivialities, more likely to make her worthy of scorn than if she were actually stupid. Having no confidence in her, her husband makes no attempt to teach her to look after his affairs, his family, or his household. Her role in all aspects of this little world is limited to appearance. She is an ornament, there to entertain the curious; as a result, it only takes an imperious nature to combine with a taste for dissipation, and she will slip into a moral decline, move quickly from independence to licentiousness, and soon arouse the scorn and indignation of men, even though men are inclined through self-interest to tolerate the vices of youth on account of its attractions.

Although I am telling you the truth in all sincerity, my dearest Aza, do not think that there are no women of merit here. There are those fortunate enough to be born with the means to give themselves what their education denies. Their attachment to their duties, the decency of their behaviour, and the honest charms of their mind earn the respect of everybody. But such women are so few in number compared with the multitude of others that they are known and revered in their own name. Do not think either that the misconduct of the others is the result of a base natural disposition. In general it seems to me that women here are born, more often than in our country, with all the qualities needed to equal men in merit and virtue. But it is as if men recognized this equality deep down in their hearts, but through pride could not accept it; they do all they can to make women worthy of scorn, either by showing no respect for their own wives, or by seducing those of others.

When I tell you that in this country authority is vested entirely in men, you will have no doubt, my dearest Aza, that they are the ones responsible for all the disorder in society. Men who through cowardly indifference let their wives follow the inclinations which lead to their ruin may not bear the most guilt, but they are not the least shameful. But too little attention is paid to those who, through their example of immoral and improper conduct, lead their wives into a life of dissipation, either out of resentment or revenge.

And indeed, my dearest Aza, how is it that women have not rebelled against the injustice of laws which tolerate the impunity of men and give them authority to the same excessive degree. A husband, without fear of any punishment at all, can treat his wife in the most odious ways; he can squander in wasteful spending that is as criminal as it is exorbitant not only his own wealth and that of his children, but even that of his victim, while obliging her to suffer near penury through that miserliness with regard to honest expense which very often accompanies prodigality. He has the authority to punish severely the merest appearance of a tiny infidelity, while he can shamelessly abandon himself to every perfidy inspired by a dissolute spirit. In a word, my dearest Aza, it seems that in France the ties of marriage are shared only at the moment of the ceremony, and that thereafter it is wives alone who are bound by them.*

I think and feel that it would indeed be honouring these women to believe them capable of retaining love for their husbands in the face of the indifference and disrespect with which most are burdened. But who can withstand contempt?

The first feeling which nature inspired in us is the pleasure of being, and we experience this more and more intensely as we recognize the esteem in which we are held.

The unthinking happiness of our infancy comes from being loved by our parents and welcomed by strangers. Happiness in the rest of our life comes from sensing the importance of our being, to the extent that it becomes essential for the happiness of another. It is you, my dearest Aza, it is your boundless love, it is the honesty of our hearts, the sincerity of our feelings, which have revealed to me the secrets of nature and of love. Friendship, that wise and tender bond, ought perhaps to fulfil all our desires, but it can share its affections among several objects without dishonour or scruple; love, which makes and requires an exclusive preference, gives us such an elevated and rewarding sense of our being that it alone can satisfy the avid desire for primacy with which we are born, which is apparent in us at all ages, at all times, and in all states, and our instinctive appetite for possession strengthens and completes our inclination to love.

If the possession of a piece of furniture, a jewel, or a plot of land brings one of the most pleasurable feelings we can experience, what must we feel when we know that we possess a heart, a soul, a being who is free and independent, and who willingly surrenders itself in exchange for the pleasure of possessing in us those same qualities!

If it is true, therefore, my dearest Aza, that the dominant desire in our hearts is to be respected by people in general, and to be cherished by one person in particular, can you conceive by what inconsistent thinking the French can expect that a young woman, crushed by the offensive indifference of her husband, will not try to escape from this kind of desolation to which she is subjected in all sorts of forms?* Can you imagine how one could possibly suggest that she be attached to nothing at an age when one always lays claim to more than one deserves? Can you understand on what basis they require her to practise virtues which men dispense with, when they deny her the enlightenment and the principles needed to do so? But what is even harder to comprehend is the way that parents and husbands complain to each other about the contempt with which their daughters and wives are treated, and yet they perpetuate its causes down the generations through ignorance, incompetence, and poor education.

O my dearest Aza, may the dazzling vices of a nation which is so enchanting in other respects not infect our taste for the natural simplicity of our own customs. May you never forget your obligation to be my example, my guide, my support on the path of virtue; and may I never forget mine, to retain your esteem and your love by imitating my model.

LETTER THIRTY-FIVE

Our exhausting visits, my dearest Aza, could not have ended more pleasurably. What an enchanting day I spent yesterday! How delightful are my latest obligations to Déterville and his sister! But how precious they will be to me when I can share them with you!

After two days of rest we set out from Paris yesterday morning— Céline, her brother, her husband, and I—to go, so she told me, to visit her best friend. The journey was not long, we arrived early in the day at a country house whose location and setting seemed quite wonderful; but what surprised me as we entered was that we found all the doors open, and yet we met nobody there.

This house, which was too beautiful to be uninhabited, but too small to conceal the people who should have been living in it, seemed enchanted. This thought amused me; I asked Céline if we were in the dwelling of one of those fairies about whom she had given me tales to read, in which the mistress of the house and her servants were all invisible.*

You will see her, she answered, but as important business has called her away for the whole day, she has asked me to request that you perform the duties of the hostess until she returns. But first of all, she added, you must sign your consent to this proposal, which I have no doubt you will. Oh, with pleasure, I said to her, entering into the charade.

No sooner had I spoken these words than I saw a man enter, dressed in black, carrying a writing case and paper already written upon; he presented it to me, and I put my name on it where they indicated.

At that same moment there appeared another man of quite noble countenance, who invited us, as is the custom, to follow him to the place where food is served. There we found a table, laid with no less neatness than elegance; scarcely had we taken our seats than we began to hear charming music played in the next room; nothing was lacking to make our meal delightful. Even Déterville seemed to have forgotten his sorrow, so as to encourage us to be joyful; he spoke in countless different ways of his feelings for me, but always in a pleasant tone of voice, unmixed with complaint or reproach.

The day was cloudless; we decided with one accord to go for a walk after leaving the table. We found the gardens much more extensive than the house had led us to expect. Their wonderful art and symmetry served only to make more affecting still the charms of unadorned nature.

We finished our walk in a wood which marked the end of this beautiful garden. Sitting, all four of us, on a delightful lawn, we saw a group of peasants approaching from one side, clad neatly in their traditional costume, and preceded by some musical instruments; and from the other side, a number of young maidens dressed in white, their heads decorated with wild flowers, singing in an untaught but melodious fashion songs in which, to my surprise, I often heard my own name repeated.

My astonishment was even greater when the two groups had joined us, and I saw the one who seemed to be their leader approach me, go down on one knee, and offer me several keys in a large bowl, adding a compliment which in my confusion I did not fully understand. All I could make out was that, being the chief of the villagers of the region, he came to pay me homage as their sovereign lady, and to present me with the keys of the house of which I was also the mistress.

As soon as he had finished his speech, he stood up to make room for the prettiest of the young girls. She came forward to give me a bunch of flowers, decorated with ribbons, which she also accompanied with a short speech in praise of me, delivered most graciously.

I was too confused, my dearest Aza, to reply to the compliments I deserved so little; moreover, everything seemed so true to life that I often caught myself believing what I nevertheless found incredible. This thought led to countless others, and my mind was so occupied that I was unable to utter a word. If my confusion was entertaining for the others, it was so embarrassing for me that Déterville was moved to pity. He made a sign to his sister, who stood up after giving some gold coins to the peasants and young girls, telling them that these were just the first fruits of my future kindness towards them. She suggested that we take a walk in the wood, I followed her gladly, fully intending to reproach her for the embarrassment she had caused me; but I did not have time to do so. We had scarcely taken a few steps than she stopped and looked at me, a radiant smile on her face: Admit it, Zilia, she said, you are very angry with us, and you will be still more so if I tell you that this land and this house do truly belong to you.

To me! I exclaimed, oh Céline! Is that what you had promised me? You take the affront too far, or the joke. Let me speak, she said more seriously; suppose my brother had used some of your treasures to acquire it, and, instead of the tiresome formalities which he has attended to, he reserved for you just the surprise, would you hate us so very much? Could you not forgive us for having procured you a dwelling which at all events you seem to like, and for ensuring a life of independence for you? This morning you signed the deed which puts them both in your possession. Scold us now as much as you like, she added, laughing, if none of that pleases you.

Oh, my dearest friend! I exclaimed, throwing myself into her arms, I am so deeply moved by your kindness and generosity that I cannot express my gratitude. I could utter no more than these few words; I had realized right away the significance of such a favour. Touched, moved, carried away with joy as I thought of the pleasure I would have to dedicate this charming dwelling to you, the very throng of my feelings prevented me from expressing them. I embraced Céline, she embraced me likewise, with equal fondness; and after a moment to compose myself, we returned to her brother and husband.

Anxiety took hold of me afresh as we approached Déterville, and plunged me into a state of renewed discomfort; I offered him my hand, he kissed it without uttering a word, and turned away to hide the tears he could no longer contain. I took these to be signs of his pleasure at seeing me so happy; I was so moved I shed some tears myself. Céline's husband, less involved than we were in what was happening, soon restored a more light-hearted tone to the conversation; he complimented me on my new standing, and urged us to return to the house, saying that we should inspect its defects and show Déterville that his taste was not as faultless as he liked to think.

I must admit, my dearest Aza, everything I saw before me as we walked seemed to take on a new form; the flowers seemed more beautiful, the trees greener, the symmetry of the gardens better laid out. I found the house more charming, the furnishings richer, the smallest trifle now captured my interest.

I ran through the different rooms, so overcome with joy that I could look at nothing closely; the only place I paused was in a quite spacious room surrounded by a grille of gold, finely worked, which enclosed countless books in all colours and sizes, and of such elegant appearance; I was so enchanted that I thought I could not leave until I had read them all. Céline tore me away from them, reminding me of a golden key which Déterville had given me. I used it hastily to open a door which they pointed out to me; and I stood motionless at the sight of the wonders it contained.

It was a chamber quite dazzling with its mirrors and paintings. The hangings had a green background and were decorated with extremely well-drawn figures; they depicted some of the sports and ceremonies of the city of the Sun, more or less as I had described them to Déterville.

Our Virgins were to be seen there, represented a thousand times over, wearing costumes such as I had worn when I arrived in France; I was even told that they resembled me.

The ornaments of the Temple, which I had left behind in the Religious House, were placed on golden Pyramids and adorned every corner of this magnificent chamber. The figure of the Sun, suspended from the middle of a ceiling painted in the heavens' most attractive colours, had a brilliance which put the final embellishing touches to this charming retreat; furnishings of equal elegance which complemented the paintings made it all quite enchanting.

Déterville, seeing me reduced to silence by a mixture of surprise, joy and wonder, came up to me and said: You will be sure to notice, fair Zilia, that the Throne of Gold is not to be found in this new Temple of the Sun; a magical power has transformed it into a house, a garden, and a piece of land. If I have not used my own skill to bring about this metamorphosis, it has not been without regret, but I had to respect your feelings. Here, he said, opening a small cupboard ingeniously sunk in the wall, here is what remains of this magical operation. Saying this, he showed me a casket filled with pieces of gold such as are used in France. This, as you know, he continued, is not one of the least necessary things among us, I thought I should keep some for you.

I was beginning to show him my deep gratitude and admiration at such thoughtful concern, when Céline interrupted and took me into a room next to the marvellous chamber. I want to show you that I also have some skill in magic, she said. We opened large cupboards filled with rich fabrics, linens, jewellery, in short everything which is worn by women, but in such abundance that I could not help laughing and asking Céline how many years she would have me live to make use of so many fine things. For as many as my brother and I shall live, she answered. And for my part, I replied, my wish is that you both live as long as I shall love you, which means you will not die before me.

As I finished these words we returned to the Temple of the Sun, which is the name they had given to the marvellous chamber. At last able to speak freely, I expressed just as I felt them all the emotions brimming over inside me. What kindness! What virtue in the actions of both brother and sister!

We spent the rest of the day enjoying the utmost trust and friendship; I entertained them at supper even more cheerfully than I had done at lunch. I freely gave orders to the servants I now knew to be mine; I joked about my authority and my wealth; I did everything in my power to provide pleasure for my benefactors from their own benefactions.

I could not help thinking, however, as time passed that Déterville was lapsing again into his melancholy state, and even that Céline could not hold back a tear from time to time; but they both recovered their look of serenity so swiftly that I thought I must be mistaken.

I did all I could to persuade them to stay with me for a few days, so that we might enjoy together the happiness they had procured me. I did not succeed; we came back tonight, promising ourselves that we would return very soon to my enchanted Palace.

Oh my dearest Aza, what bliss will be mine when I can live there with you!

LETTER THIRTY-SIX

Déterville's sadness, my dearest Aza, as well as that of his sister, has only increased since our return from my enchanted Palace: they are both too dear for me not to have hastened to ask them the reason; but as they persisted in keeping it from me, I was afraid that some new misfortune had befallen you on your journey, and soon my anxiety exceeded their sorrow. I made no secret of its cause, and my friends did not let it continue for long.

Déterville has admitted that he had decided to keep secret from me the day of your arrival, so as to surprise me, but that my anxiety made him abandon his plan. Indeed he has shown me a letter from the guide he had given you, and making a calculation based on the time and place it was written, he has told me that you might be here today, tomorrow, at this very instant, in short that the interval is too small to measure before the moment comes which will fulfil all my desires.

Having confided this first secret in me, Déterville no longer hesitated to tell me all the other arrangements he had made. He showed me the room he intends for you; you will dwell here until we have been united and propriety allows us to live in my delightful palace. I shall lose sight of you no more, nothing will keep us apart; Déterville has made provision for everything, and has convinced me more than ever of his boundless generosity.

After this explanation, I need look no further than your imminent arrival for the cause of the sadness which consumes him. I pity him; I sympathize with his suffering, I wish him a happiness which does not depend on my feelings, and which would be a reward worthy of his virtue.

I even conceal some of the joy which transports me lest I add to his distress. It is all I can do, but I am too full of my happiness to contain it entirely; therefore, although I believe you to be very near, although my heart leaps at the slightest noise, and I leave my letter after almost every word to run to the window, I cannot stop writing to you, my heart needs this release for its excitement. You are drawing near to me, it is true; but is your absence any less real than if entire oceans still separated us? I cannot see you, you cannot hear me, why then should I stop conversing with you in the only way I can? One moment more, and I shall see you; but this moment has no existence yet. Ah! can I put to better use what remains of your absence than by describing for you the strength of my love? Alas! you have only ever seen it in distress. How distant that time now is. Joy will wipe it from my memory! Aza, dearest Aza! how sweet is that name! Soon I shall no longer call out to you in vain, you will hear me, you will fly at the sound of my voice: the most loving expressions of my heart will reward your eagerness...

LETTER THIRTY-SEVEN

To the Chevalier Déterville

In Malta

Were you able, Sir, to foresee without remorse the extreme pain you were adding to the happiness you had prepared for me? How could you have had the cruelty to let such happy events, such pressing reasons to show you my gratitude, be concluded by your departure, unless it was to make me feel more keenly your despair and your absence? Two days ago I was filled with the sweet joys of friendship, today I experience its most bitter pains.

Céline, for all her great distress, followed your instructions only too well. She presented Aza to me with one hand, and with the other gave me your cruel letter. At the very moment all my desires were fulfilled, grief took hold of my soul; as I recovered the object of my love, I could in no way forget that I was losing the object of all my other feelings. Oh, Déterville! how cruel is your kindness this time! But do not think that you can carry out your heartless plans; no, the sea will not keep you apart for ever from everything you hold dear; you will hear my name spoken, you will receive my letters, you will heed my prayers; blood and friendship will reassert themselves in your heart; you will return to a family to whom I must answer for your loss.

What! in return for so many acts of kindness, I would poison your days and those of your sister! I would break so loving a bond! I would bring despair to your hearts, even as I enjoyed the fruits of your kindness! no, it shall not be, I see myself with nothing but loathing in a house I fill with mourning; I recognize your concern for me in the kind treatment I receive from Céline, just when I could forgive her for hating me. But however pleasing this kindness may be, I renounce it and shall leave for ever a place which is hateful to me unless you return to it. But how blind you are, Déterville! What error carries you away on a course which is the very opposite of what you desire? You wanted to make me happy, you only make me guilty; you wanted to dry my tears, you make them flow, and by distancing yourself you lose the reward for your sacrifice.

Alas! perhaps you would have enjoyed only too much that meeting which you so dreaded! Aza, the object of so much tenderness, is no longer the same Aza I described to you in such loving terms. The coldness of his greeting, his praise of the Spaniards with which he constantly interrupted the outpouring of love from my soul, the offensive indifference of his intention to spend just a short time in France, his curiosity which even now has taken him away from me: all this makes me fear misfortunes which make my heart shudder. Oh, Déterville! you may not be the most wretched one for long.

If concern for yourself can have no influence on you, may you be brought back by what you owe to friendship; that is the only sanctuary for ill-fated love. If the misfortunes I dread were to befall me, how you would then reproach yourself! If you forsake me, where shall I find a heart sympathetic to my suffering? Could generosity, up to now so powerful a force in your heart, finally give way to discontented love? No, I cannot believe it; such weakness would be unworthy of you; you are incapable of giving in to it. But come back and convince me that it is so, if you love your honour and my peace of mind.

LETTER THIRTY-EIGHT

To the Chevalier Déterville

In Malta

If you were not the noblest of men, Sir, I would be the most humiliated; if you did not have the most generous of souls, the most compassionate of hearts, would it be to you that I confess my disgrace and despair? But alas! what have I left to fear? what is there for me to worry about? All is lost.

It is no longer the loss of my liberty, of my position, of my homeland that I lament; it is no longer the anxieties of an innocent love which wring tears from my eyes; it is the violation of good faith, it is love despised which tears my soul apart. Aza is unfaithful.

Aza unfaithful! what power do these dreadful words have on my soul... my blood freezes... a flood of tears...

I first learned the meaning of misfortune from the Spaniards; but the last of their blows is the most painful. It is they who take Aza's heart from me; it is their cruel religion that sanctions the crime he is committing; it approves, it commands infidelity, betrayal, ingratitude; but it forbids the love of those closest to him. If I were a foreigner, unknown to him, Aza would be able to love me; but united as we are by the bonds of kinship, he must desert me, take my life without shame, without regret, without remorse.

Alas! however strange this religion is, if I could have recovered by embracing it the possession it snatches from me, I would have submitted to its illusions. With bitterness in my soul, I asked to be instructed in it; my tears were not heeded. I cannot be admitted into so righteous a society unless I give up the very motive which inspires me to join it, unless I forsake my love, in short, unless I change my very existence.

I must admit that such extreme austerity impresses me as much as I find it repellent, I cannot help feeling a kind of reverence for laws which in all other respects seem so pure and wise; but is it in my power to adopt them? And if I did so, what benefit would I gain? Aza loves me no more; oh, wretched soul that I am...

Cruel Aza has lost all the candour of our customs, except that respect for truth which he puts to such deadly use. Seduced by the charms of a young Spaniard, ready to be united with her, his only reason for coming to France was to release himself from the oath he had sworn me, to leave me in no doubt about his feelings, to give back my liberty which I detest, in a word, to take my very life.

Indeed, it serves no purpose to tell me that I am free, my heart is his, and it will be his unto death.

My life belongs to him, let him take it from me, and let him still love me...

You knew my misfortune, why then did you only tell me of it in part? Why did you just fill my mind with suspicions which made me think ill of you quite unjustly? But why do I accuse you of this as if it were a crime? I would not have believed you: I was blind, and even if I had been warned I would simply have brought forward my deadly fate, I would have appeared before him a victim to my rival, I would be at this moment... O gods! spare me that dreadful thought!...

Déterville, too generous friend! do I deserve to be heard? Forget my injustice; pity a wretched one whose respect for you rises above her weakness for a thankless man.

LETTER THIRTY-NINE

To the Chevalier Déterville

In Malta

Since you complain about me, Sir, you cannot know the state from which Céline's cruel attentions have just drawn me. How could I have written to you? I was not even capable of thought. If I had had any feelings left, trust in you would surely have been one of them; but surrounded by the shadows of death, my blood frozen in my veins, I was for a long time unaware of my very existence; I had forgotten everything, even my misfortune. Oh, gods! why, in bringing me back to life, have they also brought back that fearful memory!

He has gone! I shall see him no longer! he is fleeing from me, he no longer loves me, he told me so; everything is over for me. He is taking another for his wife, he is abandoning me, honour condemns him to do so; so, cruel Aza, since Europe's absurd notion of honour has such charms for you, why then did you not also imitate the deceit which goes with it!

How fortunate you are, women of France, you are betrayed; but you can long enjoy an illusion which would be a real comfort to me at this moment. Dissimulation prepares you for the fatal blow which is now killing me. Deadly sincerity of my nation, are you now a virtue no longer? Courage, resolve, are you now crimes when occasion requires it?

You saw me at your feet, brutal Aza, you saw them bathed in my tears, and yet you leave me... Dreadful moment! why does the thought of it not tear this life from me?

If my body had not succumbed to the agonies of grief, Aza would not be triumphing over my weakness... You would not have left alone. I would have followed you, traitor, I would see you, I would at least die before your eyes.

Déterville, what fatal weakness has separated you from me? You would have come to my aid; what I could not achieve in the chaos of my despair, your reason, all-powerful as it is, would have obtained; perhaps Aza would still be here. But, already now in Spain, his every desire fulfilled... Vain regrets, fruitless despair!... Grief, come and overwhelm me.

Do not seek, Sir, to overcome the obstacles which keep you in Malta in order to return. What would you do here? Flee a wretched woman who can no longer feel the kindness shown to her, for whom it is a torture, who wants only to die.

LETTER FORTY

Be not discouraged, too generous friend, I did not want to write to you until my life was out of danger and my mind was more at ease, so that I might then calm your anxieties. I live; destiny will have it so, I submit to its laws.

The care of your dear sister has restored my health, some recovery of my reason has sustained it. The certainty that my misfortune is past hope has done the rest. I know that Aza has reached Spain, that his crime has been consummated. My grief has not been extinguished, but its cause is no longer worthy of my regret. If some still remains in my heart, it is due solely to the suffering I have caused you, to my mistakes, to my distracted mind.

Alas! as reason brings me enlightenment, I discover how powerless it is, what can it do for an afflicted soul? An excess of grief takes us back to the weakness of our earliest years. Just as in infancy, objects alone have power over us; it seems that sight is the only one of our senses which can reach the secret depths of our soul. I have discovered this to my cost.

As I emerged from the long and devastating lethargy into which Aza's departure had plunged me, the first impulse which nature inspired in me was to withdraw to that retreat which I owe to your far-sighted kindness. It was not without difficulty that I obtained Céline's permission to be taken there; I can find in that place ways of combating despair which society and even friendship could never provide. In your sister's house, her consoling words had no effect on objects which constantly reminded me of Aza's perfidy.

The door through which Céline brought him into my room the day you left and he arrived; the chair on which he sat, the place where he announced my misery, where he returned my letters, even the memory of his shadow which has now faded on the panel where I had seen it take shape, all these things, every day, inflicted new wounds in my heart.

But in this place I can see nothing which does not recall the happy thoughts I had when I first saw it; all I find here is the image of your friendship, and that of your dear sister.

If the memory of Aza comes back to me, it is in the same guise as I imagined him at that time. I see myself awaiting his arrival. I yield to this illusion for as long as it gives pleasure to do so; when it fails, I turn to books. It is difficult to read at first, then, imperceptibly, new thoughts cloak the terrible truth hidden in the depths of my heart, and in the end bring some relief to my sorrow.

Shall I confess it? The sweet pleasures of freedom sometimes offer themselves to my imagination, and I give way to them; surrounded as I am by delightful objects, possessing them has a charm which I make an effort to enjoy; at one with myself, I do not rely much on my reason. I indulge my weaknesses, I can only combat those of my heart by giving in to those of my mind. Maladies of the soul will not submit to violent remedies.

It could be that your nation's grand sense of decency does not allow one of my age to live alone in this independent state; at least, whenever Céline comes to see me, she tries to persuade me so. But she has not yet provided sufficiently good reasons to convince me; true decency is in my heart. It is not to the image of virtue that I pay homage, it is to virtue itself. I shall always take that as the judge and guide of my actions. I dedicate my life to it, and my heart I give to friendship. Alas! when will it reign there alone, and for ever?

LETTER FORTY-ONE
And last

To the Chevalier Déterville

In Paris

I receive at almost the same moment, Sir, news of your departure from Malta, and of your arrival in Paris. Whatever pleasure I shall have in seeing you again, it cannot overcome the concern caused by the note you have written me on your return.

Can it be, Déterville, that having taken it upon yourself to conceal your feelings in all your letters, after giving me cause to hope that I would no longer have to contend with a passion which grieves me, you now abandon yourself more than ever to its violence?

What does it achieve to feign deference for me, when you contradict it at the same moment? You beg leave to see me, you assure me that you will submit without question to my wishes, and yet you endeavour to persuade me of feelings which are completely opposed to them, which offend me, in short, which I shall never approve.

But since you are deluded by false expectations, since you take advantage of my trust and the state of my soul, it is time that I informed you of my resolutions, which unlike yours will not be shaken.

You imagine in vain that you might persuade my heart to take on new chains. The betrayal of another does not release me from my vows; would to heaven that I might forget the traitor!

But even if I were to do so, I am true to myself, I shall not betray my oaths. Cruel Aza abandons one who was once dear to him, but his rights over me are no less sacred. I may be cured of my passion, but I shall only ever have passion for him. All the feelings inspired by friendship are yours, you will share them with nobody, I owe them to you. I pledge them to you, I shall keep my word. You will enjoy to the same degree my trust and my sincerity; they will both be limitless. All the strong and tender feelings which love inspired in my heart will now be turned to the benefit of friendship. I shall confess to you with equal honesty my regret that I was not born in France, and my unwavering fondness for Aza; my wish that I might have owed to you the advantage of knowing how to think, and my eternal gratitude to the one who gave it to me. We shall read each other's souls; trust, no less than love, can make time pass quickly. There are countless ways of making friendship absorbing, and of preventing it from ever becoming dull.

You will teach me to know some of your sciences and arts, and taste the pleasure of being superior; I shall regain that pleasure by nurturing virtues in your heart which you do not know are there. You will adorn my mind with what can make it entertaining, you will enjoy the fruit of your work; I shall try to help you appreciate the innocent charms of simple friendship, and I shall take delight in my success.

Céline, by dividing her love between us, will bring to our conversations a cheerfulness which they might otherwise lack—what more could we wish for?

You are wrong to fear that solitude might impair my health. Believe me, Déterville, solitude is only ever dangerous when it is idle. Always occupied, I shall be able to create new pleasures for myself from everything which habit makes dull.

Without delving into the secrets of nature, the mere examination of its wonders is surely sufficient to bring infinite variety and freshness to occupations which are always a pleasure. Is one lifetime enough to acquire even a slight, if engaging knowledge of the universe, of what surrounds me, of my own existence?

The pleasure of being, this pleasure which has been forgotten, is not even known by so many people in their blindness; this thought which is so sweet, this delight so pure at saying to one-self, *I am, I live, I exist*, is alone enough to bring happiness, if we were to remember it, if we were to enjoy it, if we knew its true worth.

Come, Déterville, come and learn from me how to use wisely the resources of our soul, and the gifts of nature. Have done with tempestuous feelings, which imperceptibly destroy our being; come and learn to appreciate innocent and lasting pleasures, come and enjoy them with me—you will find in my heart, in my friend-ship, in my feelings, everything which can compensate you for the loss of love.

End of the second and last Part

APPENDIX 1

CULTURAL BACKGROUND

THE ROYAL COMMENTARIES OF PERU, in two parts; the first part, treating of the origins of their Incas or kings, of their idolatry, of their laws and government both in peace and war . . .; the second part, describing the manner by which that new world was conquered by the Spaniards . . ., written originally in Spanish by the Inca Garcilaso de la Vega; and rendered into English by Sir Paul Rycaut, Kt., London: Printed by Miles Flesher, for Samuel Heyrick, 1688

The *Royal Commentaries* of Garcilaso de la Vega (1539–1616) were published between 1609 and 1616, and provided a uniquely detailed account of Inca customs and history. Translated into French in 1633 and again in 1744, the work was widely read in the eighteenth century; an English version, used below, appeared in 1688.

(a) QUIPUS (Book VI, chapter 8)

Incas had no form of writing. Garcilaso describes their *quipus* (the Inca term for 'knot'), sets of coloured threads which were knotted in elaborate systems for accounting purposes. According to Garcilaso, though, they did not have the capacity of a written language.

That they made their Reckonings and Accounts by Threads and Knots; and that the Accountants were Men of great faith and integrity.

Quipu signifies as much as Knots, and sometimes Accounts; in ordering of which, the *Indians* dyed their Threads with divers colours; some were of one colour only, some of two, others of three, or more; which, with the mixed colours, were of divers and various significations. These strings were twisted of three or four Threads, and about three quarters of a Yard in length; all which they filed on another string in fashion of a Fringe. And by these colours they understood the number and meaning of every particular: By the yellow they signified Gold, by the white Silver, by the red Soldiers and Armies, and so of other things distinguished by their colours.

But as for other things which could not be so distinguished by Colours, they described them by their order and degrees of quality and goodness: For as we in *Spain* take every thing in their degrees of comparison, so they having occasion to mention Corn, do first nominate Wheat, then Barley, then Pease and Pulse, *&c.* So when they gave an account of Arms, the first mentioned were the most Noble, such as Lances, next Darts, then Bows and Arrows, Pole-axes and Hatchets, and so forward. So when they had occasion to number the people and several Families: The first were Aged Men of seventy years and upwards, then Men of fifty and so to seventy, then of forty; and so from ten to ten, until they came to sucking Children: the which Order also was kept in numbering their Women.

Then amongst these grosser strings, there were others which were more short, and slender adjoining to them; and these were Exceptions to the other more general Rules; for in the account made of Men and Women married, there was another string annexed to it, which signified Widows, and Widowers of such an age; all which accounts served only for one Year.

These Knots expressed numbers in their several orders, as by units, tens, hundreds, thousands, tens of thousands, but seldom went so far as to hundreds of thousands; but in case they should have had occasion to have arisen to so great a number, no doubt but their Language, which is full and copious, would have found words sufficient to express that sum, and the greatest number to which Arithmetic could arrive. All which Accounts were made by Knots on strings, one underneath the other, and knit on a cord, as the knots are on the Girdle of St. *Francis.*

At the top of the cord the greatest number was placed, as the tens of thousands, under that stood the thousands, and last of all was the place of the units; all which were placed directly with exactness one under the other, as our good Accountants, well skilled in the Art of Cyphering, are used to set and place their figures.

The *Indians* who kept the *Quipus*, or to whose charge the keeping of Accounts was committed, were called *Quipucamayu*, and were esteemed Men of good reputation, and chosen for that Service, on good assurance and proof of their fidelity and honesty; and though the simplicity of those people in that Age was without any mixture of malice, and that the strictness of the government admitted no cheats, or frauds on any score whatsoever; yet notwithstanding great care was taken to choose Men for this work of approved Ability, and of a tried and experienced Faithfulness and Probity. For indeed Offices were never amongst them chosen for favour, nor bought, or sold, because that Money was not

current amongst them; but it was Virtue and Merit only which purchased a Trust and Office: And though buying and selling was not
known to them, yet it was ordinary for them to truck or barter their
provisions of Food one for the other; but nothing else either of
Garments, Houses, or Inheritance.

The *Quipucamayus*, or Accountants, being honest and faithful, (as
we have said) served in the nature of Registers, of which there were
four at least appointed for every Lineage, or People, how little soever
it were; and in case the Country was great, they entertained twenty or
thirty; for though one Accountant might have served the turn, yet to
avoid all mistakes and frauds, they judged it requisite to constitute
many in an Office of such importance.

All the Tribute that was yearly payable to the *Inca*, was passed to
account, as also what every Family, according to their degrees, and
qualities, were to pay. The people likewise which went to the War
were numbered; and Bills of Mortality were kept of as many as died,
and were born, or miscarried by any accident; which were all noted in
the months wherein they happened. In short, they noted every thing
that could fall under Numeration, as how many Battles or Skirmishes
were fought, how many Ambassadors had been sent to the *Inca*, and
how many Answers the King had been pleased to return thereunto.
But what the substance of those Embassies was, or what were the par-
ticulars of the King's Discourse, or what occurrences passed in way of
History, were too various to be expressed by the barrenness of their
Knots, which served only for numbers, but not for words . . .

(b) INCA ART (Book VI, chapter 1)

The Incas were much admired for their craftsmanship, both in architecture
and metalwork. Graffigny draws heavily on Garcilaso's descriptions which
appealed to contemporary taste for luxury.

Of the Buildings, Ornament and Furniture of the Royal Palaces

The Services and Ornaments of the Royal Palaces belonging to the
Kings of *Peru*, were agreeable to the Greatness, Riches and Majesty of
their Empire, with which also corresponded the Magnificence of their
Court and Attendance; which, if well considered, might equal, if not
exceed the State and Grandeur of all the Kings and Emperors of the
Universe. As to their Houses and Temples, Gardens and Baths, they
were all built of Free Stone, rarely well polished, and so well joined

together, and so close laid, that they admitted no kind of Cement; the truth is, if any were used, it was of that sort of coloured Mortar which in their Language they call *Llancac Allpa*, which is a sort of slimy Cement, made up like a Cream, which so united and closed the Stones together, that no seam or crevice appeared between them; for which reason the *Spaniards* were of opinion, that they worked without Mortar; others said, that they used Lime, but both are mistakes; for the *Indians* of *Peru* neither knew the manner or use of Lime, Mortar, Tile or Brick.

In many of the Royal Palaces, and Temples of the Sun, they closed up the Seams of their Building with melted Gold, or Silver, or Lead. *Pedro de Cieça*, a *Spanish* Historian, saith, That for greater Magnificence they filled the joints between the Stones with Gold or Silver, which was afterwards the cause of the total destruction of those Buildings; for the *Spaniards* having found these exterior appearances of Gold, and some other heaps of Metal within, have for farther Discovery subverted the very Foundations of those Edifices, in hopes of finding greater Treasure, which otherwise were so firmly built, as might have continued for many Ages. *Pedro de Cieça* confirms the same at large, and saith farther, That the Temples of the Sun were plated with Gold, as also all the Royal Apartments. They also framed many Figures of Men and Women, of Birds of the Air, and Fishes of the Sea; likewise of fierce Animals, such as Tigers, and Lions, and Bears, Foxes, Dogs and Cats, in short, all Creatures whatsoever known amongst them, they cast and moulded into true and natural Figures, of the same shape and form of those Creatures which they represented, placing them in corners or cones of the Walls, purposely made and fitted for them. They counterfeited the Plants and Wall-flowers so well, that being on the Walls, they seemed to be Natural: The Creatures which were shaped on the Walls, such as Lizards, Butterflies, Snakes and Serpents, some crawling up, and some down, were so artificially done, that they seemed Natural, and wanted nothing but Motion. The *Inca* commonly sat on a Stool of Massive Gold, which they called *Tiana*, being about three quarters of a Yard high, without Arms or Back, and the seat something hollow in the middle; this was set on a large square Plate of Gold, which served for a Pedestal to raise it. All the Vessels which were for the service of the *Inca*, both of the Kitchen, and of the Buttery, were all made of Gold or Silver; and these were in such quantities, that every House, or Palace, belonging to the *Inca*, was furnished in that manner with them, that there was no occasion, when he Travelled, to remove them from one place to the other. In these Palaces also there were Magazines, or Granaries, made of Gold and Silver, which were fit to receive Corn, or Grain, but they were rather places of State and Magnificence, than of use.

. . . All the Royal Palaces had their Gardens, and Orchards, and places of Pleasure, wherein the *Inca* might delight, and divertise himself; and these Gardens were planted with Fruit-trees of the greatest beauty, with Flowers, and Odoriferous Herbs, of all sorts and kinds which that Climate did produce. In resemblance of these they made Trees, and Flowers of Gold and Silver, and so imitated them to the life, that they seemed to be natural: some Trees appeared with their Fruit in the blossom, others full-grown, others ripe according to the several seasons of the year; they counterfeited also the Mayz, or Stalk, of the *Indian* Wheat, with all its Grain and Spikes: Also the Flax with its Leaves and Roots as it grows in the Fields; and every Herb and Flower was a Copy to them, to frame the like in Gold and Silver.

They fashioned likewise all sorts of Beasts and Birds in Gold and Silver; namely, Conies, Rats, Lizards, Serpents, Butterflies, Foxes, Mountain Cats, for they had no tame Cats in their Houses; and then they made Sparrows, and all sorts of lesser Birds, some flying, others perching on the Trees; in short, no Creature, that was either Wild, or Domestic, but was made and represented by them according to its exact and natural shape.

(c) FOUNDATION OF CUZCO AND BIRTH OF THE INCA EMPIRE (Book I, chapters 7 and 8)

Garcilaso's account of the origins of the Inca Empire provides a powerful narrative of divine intervention and moral instruction. Graffigny evokes this in her Historical Introduction, and Zilia will make a bold comparison with Christian teaching in letter 21.

Our Father the Sun, (*for this is the language of the* Incas, *which is a title of Reverence and Respect, which they always adjoin, so often as they name the Sun; for they avail themselves much of the Honour of being descended from him; and his Name is so precious, that it is blasphemy for any, and by Law he is to be stoned, who dares to take this Name into his mouth, who is not an* Inca, *or descended from that Lineage*.) Our Father the Sun (*said the* Inca) beholding Men such as before related, took compassion of them, and sent a Son and a Daughter of his own from Heaven to Earth, to instruct our people in the knowledge of Our Father the Sun, that so they might worship and adore him, and esteem him for their God: giving them Laws and Precepts, whereunto they might conform their Lives, like Men of Reason and Civility; that they might live in Houses and Society, learn to sow the Land, cultivate Trees, and Plants, feed their Flocks, and enjoy them, and other Fruits of the Earth, as rational Men, and not as brute Beasts. With these Orders and Instructions Our Father the Sun placed his two Children in the Lake *Titicaca*, which is about eighty Leagues from hence, giving them liberty to go, and travel which way they pleased, and that in what place soever they staid to eat, or sleep, they should strike a little wedge of Gold into the ground, (which he had given them), being about half a yard long, and two fingers thick, and where with one stroke this wedge should sink into the Earth, there should be the place of their Habitation, and the Court unto which all People should resort. Lastly, he ordered them, that when they should have reduced People to these Rules and Obedience, that then they should conserve and maintain them with Reason, Justice, Piety, Clemency and Gentleness, performing all the good Offices of a pious Father towards those Children which he loves with tenderness; and that in imitation of him, and by his example, who doeth good to all the World, affording them light to perform their business, and the actions of Life, warming them when they are cold, making their pastures, and their seeds to grow, their trees to fructify, and their flocks to increase, watering their Lands with dew from above, and in its season bestowing cheerful and favourable weather: and to manifest his care of all things, said, I every day take a turn round the World, to see and discover the necessities and wants of all things, that so as the true Fomenter and Parent of them, I may apply my self to their succour and redress. Thus after my example, and as my Children, sent upon the Earth, I would have you to imitate me, and to instil such Doctrine into this People, as may convert them from Beasts unto Men: and from henceforth I constitute and ordain you Lords and Princes over this People, that by your Instructions, Reason and Government, they may be conserved. Thus Our Father the Sun, having declared his pleasure to these his two Children, he dispatched them from him; and they taking their journey from *Titicaca* Northward, at every place where they came to repose, they tried with their wedge to strike it in the ground, but it took no place, nor would it enter; at length they came to a poor Inn, or place to rest in, about seven or eight Leagues southward from this City, which to this day is called *Pacarec Tampu*, which is as much as to say, *the Shining or Enlightened Dormitory*. This is one of those Colonies which this Prince planted, the Inhabitants whereof boast of this Name and Title which our *Inca* bestowed upon it; from whence he and his Queen descended to the Valley of *Cozco*, which was then only a wild and barren Mountain.

. . . The first stop (*proceeded the* Inca) which they made in this Valley, was in the Desert called *Huanacauti*, which is to the southward of this City, and there they again struck their wedge of Gold into the Earth, which received it with great facility, and which sucked it in with so much ease, that they saw it no more. Then said the *Inca* to his Sister, and Wife, in this Valley Our Father the Sun hath commanded that we should stay, and make our abode, and in so doing we shall perform his Pleasure; in pursuance whereof it is necessary that we now separate each from the other, and take different ways, that so we may assemble and draw the People to us, in such manner as we may be able to preach and propagate the doctrine amongst them, which he hath committed to us. Accordingly our first Governors proceeded by divers ways from the Desert of *Huanacauti* to convocate the People, which being the first place, of which we had knowledge, that they had hallowed by their Feet, and from whence they went to do good unto Men, we have deservedly (as is manifest) erected a Temple, wherein to adore and worship our Father the Sun, and remember this good and benefit he hath done unto the World. Our *Inca* the Prince took his way northward, and the Princess to the southward, and to all the Men and Women which they met in the wild thickets, and uncultivated places, they declared to them, that their Father the Sun had sent them to be Teachers and Benefactors to those . . . habitants, and to draw them from that rude and savage Life, and to another method of living, more agreeable to Reason and humane Society; and in farther pursuance of the Commands of their Father the Sun, they came to gather them from those Mountains, and rude places, to more convenient Habitations, where they might live in humane Society, and to assign them such food, as was appropriated to Men, and not to Beasts. These, and such like matters, these Princes declared to those savages, whom they found in Deserts and Mountains, who beholding these two persons clothed, and adorned with such Habit as Our Father the Sun had vested them in, and observing that their Ears were bored through, for wearing Jewels, and more large and open than usual, that they might hear and receive the Complaints of the oppressed; (in which we also are like them, who are of their Offspring and Family), and that by the gentle-ness of their words, and grace of their Countenance, they manifested themselves to be Children of the Sun, and such as were employed to assemble People into societies, and political ways of living, and to administer such sorts of food as were wholesome and appropriated to humane Sustenance, they were struck with such admiration of their figure and Persons, and allured with the promises they made them, that they gave entire credence to their words, adored them as Children of the Sun, and obeyed them as their Princes: And these poor wretches relating these matters one to the other, the fame thereof so increased, that great numbers, both of Men and Women, flocked together, being willing to follow to what place soever they should guide them.

APPENDIX 2

FRENCH CONTINUATIONS

1. *Letters written by a Peruvian princess. Translated from the French. The second edition. Revised and corrected by the translator. To which is now first added,* The Sequel of the Peruvian Letters. *Printed for J. Brindley, 1749*

The first continuation in French was published anonymously; Graffigny attributed it to the chevalier de Mouhy (1701–84), a prolific but impecunious novelist. She exclaimed scornfully in a letter of 21 September 1748, 'Ah, poor chevalier de Mouhy, you have not disguised yourself well enough. You will not be mistaken for me.' The work was soon translated into English.

LETTER XLIII

Celina to Deterville

[*Celina re-examines Zilia's offer of friendship to her brother, and encourages Deterville to hope for love*]

I am not ignorant, that being master of this fair Indian, by the laws of war, you have respected her beauty, her sentiments, and her misfortunes: I know it was not your fault, that the only good, which could render her happy, was not restored to her, and that even at the expense of your wealth. I admired you as a prodigy, when I saw you call out of the heart of *Spain* the happy *Aza*, in order to return to him, with his other treasures, the only jewel which you could not be happy without. This was the very height of generosity.

In the mean time, by an unexampled turn of fortune, when the infidelity of *Aza* rendered your benefits useless, and you had more right than ever to hope, the unforeseen constancy of *Zilia* for an ungrateful man, adds the last and severest stroke to your misfortunes.

But, my dear brother, while I indulge your grief, and lament the fatality of your stars, suffer me to inform you, that you make your case worse than it really is. The anxiety of your heart, doubtless, prevents your seeing the least glimpse of hope: but perhaps the indifference, in which you formerly lived, keeps you ignorant of the resources which are still left by fortune. As a woman, I should be tempted still to leave you partly in ignorance; but as a sister, I cannot take such an unkind resolution. Hear me then, my dear *Deterville*. *Aza* was naturally the only object that Zilia could be attached to. A prince, tender, young, and charming, and Zilia in all the force and sweetness of her first fires, united by taste and by duty, and by the virtue which ennobled both. A hideous mishap, a cruel revolution separates them, and enlivens the image of that felicity of which they see themselves fatally deprived. Represent to yourself how much force even despair must add to a passion before so warm and so legitimate. It was a heart new in love, full of fire, given up for the first time, and which did not know a more sensible pleasure, than that of adhering to the object it had chosen; in short, it was a heart amorous to excess, inflamed by difficulty, and which, at the very brink of felicity, saw itself in that instant snatched from the expected enjoyment. My dear brother, put yourself for a moment in the place of Zilia: is it possible that any other lover could make her so soon forget a bridegroom that was so dear to her, and restore her tranquillity? Reflect on the nobleness of her soul, and you will conceive that a heart so generous, may be capable of carrying her attachment beyond the bounds of ordinary sensibility, and of continuing to love an object which it is sure never to possess. This is such a musical string, as sounds a long time after it has been once briskly touched.

But do you not see, my dear Deterville, that this sentiment is too contrary to nature to be durable? Do you doubt whether Zilia, when she comes to reflect more quietly, will perceive the injustice of Aza, the weight of his indifference, and the inutility of loving without return? Maintained hitherto in her tenderness, by a kind of sorcery, the illusion she puts on herself will soon dissipate, the image of Aza will in a short time become burdensome, and then her heart, void of interest and employment, will with difficulty support itself in such a state of inaction. A tiresome state of languor is an insupportable burden for an active soul. Zilia will wish for some pretence to get rid of it, and what pretence will be more happy for you both, than that of gratitude? Zilia professes her acknowledgements to you, and is fully sensible how much she owes to your generous proceedings.

I come now to the friendship which she offers you. By your refusing this friendship, it should seem to be offensive, or at least unpleasant to you. You look upon it as a sentiment too weak to answer to the vivacity of your love. It seems like a payment in counterfeit coin; and you reject it because it is not absolute and complete love. But pray dear brother, is it the name only that you would obtain? For my part, I cannot help thinking so: for the friendship of Zilia ought to inspire you with less repugnance. Let me tell you, even this ought to charm you. Why do you oblige me here to disclose the great secrets of the fair sex? Know, that this sentiment of friendship, so sweet among men, so rare among women, is always the most lively betwixt persons of different sexes. Men love one another with cordiality, women love each other with diffidence; but two persons of the two sexes add to the taste of friendship a spark of that fire which nature never fails to inspire. A sprout of passion will attend the very birth of this friendship, so pure in appearance; as such sort of friends are fully enough sensible. Let them both keep mutually upon their guard, it matters not: all their precautions will make no change in the imperceptible progress of nature, and they will soon be surprised, that they are fallen in love with each other without perceiving it.

The friendship offered you then, my dear *Deterville*, is, in my opinion, the first act of that interesting play, of which you so much desire to see the unravelling; it is the first discovery of the heart, and since that is favourable to you, have you any room to complain?

It is true, that the name of friendship spreads a veil, which hides a part from your sight: but it is a veil wrought by the hands of love, made only to deceive jealous eyes, but which hides nothing from eyes that can penetrate, nor long conceals the truth from him who is the object of it. Do you not now confess, my dear brother, that I had room to be surprised, when I heard you complain so bitterly of the only part that *Zilia* ought to have taken? Reflect upon it well, and you will be of my sentiment. Can there be a more happy method, a method better adapted to the delicacy of you both?

Would you not always have the better opinion of a lady, who chooses to be the more reserved, to make your happiness the more complete? Who, by giving your passion a reasonable character, intends to refine and increase your pleasure?

Indeed, my brother, you are obliged to *Zilia*, who in the way of friendship is preparing for you pleasures more ecstatic than you proposed for yourself: She neither dared, nor ought to make you a return of passion in the manner that you desired. You must consult the fair sex for sentiments of this nature; and be not ashamed that the women are here beforehand with you; since without them, the men would perhaps be ignorant in the finesses of the art of love. Women are allowed, as a natural consequence of the temper of their hearts, to have more suppleness of genius than men. I do not suppose any artifice to enter into this art of love, of which I am speaking; these two characters, as much as they resemble one another, ought to be distinguished. All the women of wit love with art, but not all with artifice. As to your dear *Zilia*, her heart is honest, noble, and elevated; but she is ingenuous in the most fine and subtle manner of any woman I know. That heart of hers, which is at present wholly taken up with the most tender and virtuous passion, but a passion cruelly deceived, you will at last find to be reserved for you. Allow only a reasonable term to *Zilia* for grief, and, without complaining, leave time to destroy in her that idea of glory which flatters her hitherto.

That singular honour of remaining faithful to her first ties, even when they are broken without possibility of a reunion, is a sentiment which certainly she has not learned among us: she will therefore at last give way to our example. Being then free, fearing liberty through a habitude of not enjoying it, and sensible at the same time of your generous cares; the friendship, which she now regards only as a sweet sympathy, will want but one advance farther to become love; and that miracle will be accomplished without her perceiving it.

My dear *Deterville*, what a charming prospect lies here before you! I think you must see enough of it to engage you, without the least difficulty, to accept the party which Zilia proposes to you with so good a grace. From your solicitudes, disinterested in appearance, and more still from the nature of a female heart, expect the felicity of which you began to despair.

2. Lamarche-Courmont, *Letters of Aza, a Peruvian. Being the conclusion of the Letters wrote by a Peruvian princess*. Dublin, 1751.

Ignace Hugary de Lamarche-Courmont (1728–68) served in the households of the duc de Chartres and the duc d'Orléans, but wrote relatively little.

LETTER XXXIV
To Zilia

[*Aza gives an account of his own experiences following the arrival of the Spanish in Peru; he explains his apparent infidelity to Zilia.*]

The dread of displeasing you still keeps in my trembling hands the knots which I form. Those knots which were once consolation and joy to you, *Zilia*, are now twined by grief and despair.

Do not imagine that I would conceal my crime from your eyes. Distracted with anxiety for having believed you unfaithful, how should I presume to justify it? But am I not sufficiently punished? What remorse!... The remorse of a lover who adores you. Ah! You would hate me! Have I not rather merited your contempt than your hatred?

Reflect for a moment on all my misfortunes. Barbarians snatched thee from my love, at the moment it should have been crowned with success. Armed for thy defence, I fell, and was loaded with their base fetters. Carried to their country, the waves on which we floated, supported for a time, it is true, all my hopes. I lived only by them. My heart went with you. Thy ravishers being swallowed up by the sea, plunged me into the most cruel error. That which I thought had destroyed thee, could not destroy my love. Grief augmented my passion. I would have died to follow thee. I only lived to avenge thee. All things I essayed. Even my very oaths I would have sacrificed, and have united myself, in defiance of a thousand remorses, with a *Spanish* woman, and have purchased at that price, my liberty and my vengeance. When on a sudden, O unhoped for felicity! I learned that you lived, and that you still loved me. O too pleasing remembrance! I flew to thee; to happiness the most pure, the most ecstatic... Ah! vain hope: cruel reverse! Scarce had I enjoyed the first transports with which thy sight inspired me, than a fatal poison, of which thy heart is too pure to know the pangs, jealousy seized my soul: his most rancorous serpents have devoured my heart; that heart which was only formed for the love of thee.

The most amiable of virtues, gratitude, was the object of my suspicions. That which you owed to *Deterville*, I thought he had obtained: that your virtue had been confounded with your duty. I thought... It was these fatal ideas that troubled our first transports. You were unable, even in the bosom of love, to forget friendship. I forgot virtue. The eulogies of *Deterville*, his letter, the sentiments it expressed, the concern it gave you, the grief you showed for the loss of your deliverer; all these I attributed to the sentiment that I felt, and that I still feel, to love.

I concealed in my bosom the fires that consumed it. What was the consequence? From suspicion I soon passed to a certainty of your perfidy. I meditated even a punishment for it. I would not employ reproaches: I did not think you worthy of them. I will not endeavour to conceal my crimes from you: truth is even as dear to me as my love.

I would return to *Spain*, to perform a promise to which my former oath had engaged me. Repentance soon followed that rage which had declared to you my crime. I vainly endeavoured to undeceive you, with regard to a resolution that love had destroyed almost as soon as it was formed. Thy determination not to see me relumined my fury. Again given up to jealousy; I fled from you: but far from going to *Madrid* to consummate a crime that my soul detested, though you were induced to believe it, sinking under the weight of my misfortunes, I sought in solitude, in an estrangement with mankind, that peace which tranquillity of mind alone can afford. Overcome by my distress, the powers of life forsook me. A long time absent from thee, shall I, in spite of myself, avow it to thee, *Zilia*? All my faculties were exerted in reviling thee. I thought I saw you, pleased with my flight, recall my rival. I thought I saw... Alas! You know my offence; but you do not know my punishment; it even surpasses my crime. Ah *Zilia*, if the excess of love could effect it: no, I can no more be guilty. Do not imagine that I intend to move thy pity; that were too little for my tenderness. *Zilia*, give me back your love, or give me nothing.

LETTER XXXV AND LAST

To Kanhuiscap

[*Writing to his friend, Kanhuiscap, he describes his joyful reconciliation with Zilia*]

Would that by striking thy mind with surprise, I could communicate to thy heart that joy with which mine now pants. O happiness! O transport! Kanhuiscap, Zilia has given me up her heart. She loves me. Roving in the ravishments of my love, I shed at her feet the most tender tears. Her looks, her sighs, her transports, are the only interpreters of our love and our felicity.

Imagine, if you can, our joys: that moment constantly presents to my sight; that moment... No, such love, anguish, and delight, are not to be expressed by words.

Her eyes, her animated countenance, told me her love, her anger, my shame... She turned pale. Faint, and speechless, she sunk into my arms. But as the flames excited by the winds, so my heart, agitated by fear, burnt with greater violence. My head reclining on her bosom, I breathed that fire of love which animated her life, and united it with mine. She died and instantly revived... Zilia, my beloved Zilia! Into what intoxicating pleasure hast thou plunged the happy Aza! No, Kanhuiscap, you can never conceive our happiness; come and bear witness to it. Nothing should be wanting to my felicity. The Frenchman who delivers you this letter will bring you hither. You will then behold my Zilia. My felicity will every moment increase.

The story of our present happiness, as well as that of our past misfortunes (far be they removed from us) has reached even to the throne. The generous monarch of the French nation has ordered certain ships that are going to encounter with the Spaniards in our seas, to carry us to Quitto. We soon again shall see our native land, that mournful country so dear to our desires: those abodes, O Zilia! where sprang our first delights, thy sighs and mine. May they be witnesses! may they celebrate! may they augment! if it be possible, our present felicity... But I go to Zilia.

My dear friend, love cannot make me forget friendship, but friendship keeps me too long from love. Those delightful transports that ravish my soul, it is in thy enjoyments that I have again found life... I am lost in the excess of happiness; in ecstatic bliss! Zilia is again my own; she waits my coming, I fly to her arms!

APPENDIX 3

ENGLISH ADAPTATIONS

1. *Letters from Zilia to Aza, taken from the French* (Dublin: Henry Saunders, 1753) [attributed to 'Colonel Beaver']

This anonymous English text offers a unique verse abridgement of Zilia's opening letters, before using Graffigny's novel as the pretext for extended social and religious satire.

To Her Grace, the Duchess of Dorset

The following Poem, which I now have the Honour to present to Your Grace, was published at the Desire of several of my Friends, who I fear were too Partial to the Merit of it: It is taken from a *French* Novel, which I have adhered to, only to preserve the thread of the History 'til our Heroine's arrival in *Paris*; where I have endeavoured to heighten all the Descriptions I met with, and added others, where occasion offered.

I have quitted the Original in the Middle of my sixth Letter, as not consisting with my Purpose: The rest is entirely my own.

LETTER VI

[*Deterville introduces Zilia to the world of gaming*]

> The *Cazique* pointed to my wond'ring View,
> Small, square, thin Leaves, array'd in milk-white Hue,
> On one Side this; on the reverse appears,
> Large deep-stain'd Spots, and mystic Characters,
> These are the Ministers that Fortune gives,
> With these, her misled Votary's deceives,
> 'Tis from their Aspect, each his Fate attends,
> On these, their short-liv'd Happiness depends,
> Or lasting Mis'ry; and the shining Oar
> That decks the Board, must yield to Fortune's Pow'r;
> Precarious Chance! now each his Soul betrays,
> And various Fortunes various Passion's raise,
> Here Indignation eyes his parting Hoard,

While calm Contentment sweeps the shining Board;
Here the pale Wretch, to Desperation driv'n,
Gnashes his Teeth, and seems to rail at Heav'n;
The Females too perform their diff'rent Parts,
While their Eyes tell th'Emotion of their Hearts;
Now, for a Moment, bright, serene, and clear,
Then, on a sudden, clouded with Despair:
The unsuccessful and successful Card,
Alternate kiss'd and torn as a Reward
Of Fortune's Caprice, whence this thirst of Gain?
'Twas Hell-ordained for human Nature's Bane:
How vast a diff'rence 'twixt thy ZILIA's Soul,
And these whom Wealth and Want alone controul;
From thee, dear AZA, spring my Care and Grief,
From thee I hope kind Comfort and Relief,
From Pride, from Av'rice, from Ambition free,
I only ask—for Liberty and Thee.

LETTER VII

[*Zilia visits a church, where the images of Christ crucified and of the Madonna leave her perplexed*]

The Thought of Worship doubtless first was giv'n
To bless Mankind, the Boon of gracious Heav'n;
But sure these Wretches have that Gift misus'd,
Or by degen'rate Priests have been abus'd,
Or some dark Angel studious to betray,
Has led their Souls, maliciously astray.
Not so thy INCAS watch the sacred Fire;
Not so thy Virgins hail their rising Sire,
Not so thy Youths pollute the Temple Floor,
Or dare to trifle with Almighty Pow'r:
Alas! my AZA, may some pitying God,
Reclaim their Steps from this mistaken Road . . .

[*She goes to the theatre, and criticizes French taste*]

Can ZILIA hope for Pity, in an Age,
Where her Misfortunes may adorn the Stage,
Where *Cuzco's* Fate, in time, may entertain,

With Virgins, *Incas*, rev'rend *Mama's* slain
And the Sun's Temple be prophan'd again.
Oh! could they add, how providential Fate,
Reliev'd the Suff'rers from their slavish State,
How grateful Subjects hail'd their bounteous Lord,
For Peace, Religion, Liberty restor'd;
How royal AZA from his Bondage free,
Releas'd his ZILIA from Captivity;
How by their Virtues, the *Peruvian* Throne,
In them restor'd, with double Lustre shone:
Oh flatt'ring Hopes! how soon do ye subside,
How fade the Prospects of such airy Pride;
Perhaps my Fate has no such Joys in store,
Perhaps, my AZA doats on me no more . . .

LETTER VIII

[*Zilia learns of Aza's conversion to Christianity, and of his engagement to a Spanish lady*]

Cans't thou presume unpunish'd, to begin
Thy new Belief with such a flagrant Sin?
Can'st thou, with all thy Crimes upon thy Head,
Approach the new-sought Shrine without a Dread?
Can *Christian* Gods of perjur'd Vows approve;
Can Vows once perjur'd charm a Maid to Love?
The specious Sophistry of Priests has drawn
Thy wavr'ing Heart, from me and from the Sun,
Their barren Promises such Hopes have giv'n,
Of present Freedom, and a future Heav'n,
If to their Notions, willing you subscribe,
Thy Soul is dazzled with the mighty Bribe . . .
Go boast your Freedom, foolish Man, but still
You breath dependant on your Tyrant's Will;
Can you, unconscious of a Blush, behold
The *Spaniard* shine in thy once-subject Gold?
Or from his Hands contentedly receive
The scanty Portion, which he deigns to give?
Then for those Scenes that crafty Priests devise,
The least Reflection shames the thin Disguise,
Not thy Hereafter, but their own Applause

For thy Conversion, is the real Cause;
In thee reform'd, their Excellence is shewn,
They grant you Merit, to enhance their own;
Has gracious Providence its Pow'r consign'd,
To these pale Wretches over human Kind?
Who can believe that Men of mortal Mould,
Can grant, refuse, or barter Heav'n for Gold?
These will absolve you from your sacred Vow,
That once you swore, but oh! abjur'd it now;
They'll call it Virtue, Piety to break
A *Pagan* Vow for their Religion's sake;
Nor will suffice this Circumstance alone,
A *Christian* Wife confirms you all their own . . .

Mays't thou most happy with my Rival live,
In all the Bliss propitious Heav'n can give,
May both with Pleasure tread this mortal Stage,
And drop together in a calm old Age;
May blessed Angels waft your Souls to Bliss,
In some new World on your release from this;
Be all your Errors in the Grave forgiv'n,
And all your Virtues rise with you to Heav'n;
Now hold my Heart—Adieu thou dear lov'd Lord,
How my Hand trembles at that fatal Word;
Conceive the poignant Horror that I feel,
I faint—I die—Eternally Farewell.

FINIS

2. *The Peruvian Letters, Translated from the French, with an additional Volume, by R. Roberts* . . . (London: T. Cadell, 1774)

Mrs R. Roberts translated several moral tales of Marmontel, and was the author of *Sermons by a Lady*. Her continuation of the *Letters* re-situates Graffigny's novel firmly in a tradition of texts designed for the reader's moral improvement.

PREFACE

I read the first volume of the Peruvian Letters many years since, and found an elegant simplicity, in the manner in which the story was told, in the language in which it was originally written, that I much admired, and could not help thinking the Peruvian character pleasingly delineated.

I was not indeed altogether satisfied with the conclusion, being desirous the Indian Princess should become a convert to Christianity, through conviction; and that so generous a friend as Deterville might be as happy as his virtues deserved. This thought determined me to add a second volume.

I was, I must confess, a little afraid of engaging in the novel kind of writing, being fearful of deviating in the least from that strict delicacy which ought to be always observed by a woman's pen. I hope I have written nothing which can at all hurt the young female mind; but if I have in any degree been beneficial to it, that thought will be among those which will afford me comfort in that dread hour when all the transitory pleasures of this life shall be able to give none, by the reflection of not having lived in vain . . .

[*Roberts translates the 1747 text (I–XXXVIII), adding the seven letters of the anonymous Sequel (XXXIX–XLV). The translator's new letters begin with letter XLVI. Deterville returns to Paris. Writing to his friend and confidant on Malta, the Chevalier Dubois, he recounts a conversation with Zilia, in which she has confessed that she cannot forget Aza; Deterville has reaffirmed his own love.*]

LETTER XLIX

To the Chevalier DUBOIS, at Malta

[*Zilia discovers the beauties of nature with Deterville*]

After our repast, we strolled through a winding path, which gradually opened to the banks of a river; here we seated ourselves in an arbour, composed of jessamine and woodbines. The prospect on the other side was delightfully romantic; the green sloping hills, which descended to the water, were shaded round with woods and vineyards: and it being the time of the vintage, nothing could appear more luxuriant.

What added to the beauty of the scene, was a small rock which stood opposite to us, at the top of which rose a brook that ran down its craggy sides, till it was lost in the current of the river. The sweetness of the air, the soft melody of the birds, the continual murmur of the water, and the sublimity of the prospect, all concurred to give our minds a turn to something serious and solemn.

We began by admiring the fineness of the evening, and the charming diversity of scenes which surrounded us: we looked up to the cloudless sky, and were delighted with the blue ether which composed it. This naturally led us to contemplate the great first mover, and to express our grateful adoration in terms suited to hearts at that time warmed by his blessings.

We observed that devotion was implanted in the heart of man; since there was no nation under heaven, however rude and barbarous, that did not worship a Deity.

Zilia hearkened with silent attention to all that was said; then resuming the subject, As I can no longer, says she, look on the Sun as God, but as a striking proof, among many others, of the wisdom and goodness of some all-powerful being, I wish to know as much of this revered Deity as possible; for this end, I have long secretly desired to be instructed in the tenets of your religion, but have yet never had it in my power. The priest, who formerly, in the Convent, pretended to enlighten my mind, though there appeared the marks of divinity in what he attempted to teach, yet he so obscured and puzzled it by his manner, that I could by no means reconcile it to my understanding.

It may be, says I, that you was at that time less inclinable to attend to any arguments in its favour than you are now; however, as your mind is disposed, it is certainly worth a second enquiry. The great book of nature is before you, study it, an intelligent being must, in every page, behold the traces of its almighty Author. This will naturally lead you to wish a more perfect knowledge of him; which is only to be gained by reading, without prejudice, those books wherein he has revealed His will.

That is, returned she, what I wish to do, and in which you must assist me: let me not bewilder myself, in reasoning on what is difficult to be understood, but do you clear the way before me, remove error from my sight, and teach me to distinguish truth from falsehood.

Since that time our mornings have been devoted to this sacred employment: I look on myself as a missionary sent by heaven, to convert my Zilia. I have put into her hands those books which treat of the life and miracles of our Saviour; it opens to her a daily scene of wonders; she reads, she admires, she comments; she makes her objections, I endeavour to obviate them; she seems pleased to be convinced . . .

LETTER LXVI

To the Chevalier DUBOIS, *at Malta*

[*Deterville has returned to Paris, and Zilia has confessed her love for him*]

My suit is granted, my dear Dubois; I am free from my vows, and again with my Zilia. Oh, my friend, how changed my situation! I fear giving way to the transports of my soul, lest some envious stroke of fortune should dash the cup of joy from my lips. At present, indeed, all is smiling: my lovely Indian received me with all the expressions of the most lively friendship, mixed with a soft confusion, which indicated something more.

As soon as we were alone together, I may now, my dearest girl, says I, without offence, venture to mention that passion which I once scarcely dared breathe even in secret. Zilia blushed. All the pleasure you can derive from that liberty, replied she, will be ever yours, if that will make you amends for the pains I have given you. I pressed her hand, with excess of joy; and whilst I still held it trembling within mine, Such a permission, my dearest Zilia, makes me ample amends for all the past evils of my life: I shall now daily have it in my power to remind you of a lover who is no longer disagreeable to you. She recovered herself, and with a sweet smile replied, You will certainly have opportunities enough; but at present it is proper you should pay what you owe to friendship, and not deprive those too long of your company who are so fond of it.

I was ravished with her words; and pressing her hand, which I still held in mine, to my lips, kissed it with rapture. Let them wait, says I, however, whilst I first pay what is due to love. Whilst I thus express my thanks for this extreme kindness, Oh! teach me, Zilia, how to return such mighty obligations. Mention not obligations, added she; I owe you already more than I can ever pay: but all I have to give is yours, my hand, and my heart. Your hand, your heart, my love, what can the world bestow of half their value? May I give credit to words so full of sweetness! Yet why should I doubt, when they fall from lips which never knew deceit! Will this fair form then give itself to me, and receive a heart over-flowing with tenderness in exchange?

Henceforth, returned she, you may dispose of mine; it was yours long before I was myself sensible of it. My loved, my adorable girl, says I, what words shall I find to express the feelings of my soul on this occasion, but the constant uniform tenor of my life will be to make myself worthy of this excess of goodness. You daily, replied she, merit every return, both of affection and gratitude, which I can ever make: but our friends wait us, in that favourite room of yours, which fronts the garden, and commands a view of the fountain . . .

APPENDIX 4

THE EDUCATION OF YOUNG WOMEN

Marquise de Lambert. *Advice from a Mother to her Son and Daughter. Written originally in French by the Marchioness de Lambert . . . Done into English by a gentleman.* London, 1729.

Anne Thérèse de Marguenat de Courcelles, marquise de Lambert (1647–1733), was the author of several works of moral reflection; her *Advice from a Mother to her Daughter* was published in 1728. Noted for her learning and refined taste, her celebrated salon attracted members of the aristocracy and the literary world in the early decades of the eighteenth century.

[The inadequacies of the education of young women are outlined]

The Education of our Sex has, in all Ages, been neglected; that of Man seems to engross the whole Care and Attention, while Women, as if a Species apart, are left helpless to themselves. They don't consider we compose one half of the World; that it is necessary for them to be united to us, by the most tender Alliances; that we make their Happiness or Misfortune, according as we are capable of using our Reason; that it is by us Families are supported or extinguished; and that the bringing up of Children is entrusted to our Care, at a time when their Minds are capable of receiving the most lasting Impressions. What can they hope we should inspire them with, since we ourselves were left, in our Infancy, to the Care of Governesses, who being ordinarily chosen from the Commonalty of the People, instil mean Notions into us, awake all the timid Passions, and infuse Superstition instead of Religion? It would be much better to think of rendering hereditary certain Virtues, which might descend from Mother to Daughter, than, by saving the Expense of it, to breed them up in Ignorance. Nothing therefore is so ill managed as the Education of young People; their Study is to make them be thought agreeable in their Persons; they fortify their Self-love, they yield them up to Idleness, the World, and the false Opinions of it, but never give them Lessons of Virtue and Reason. Is it not then an Injustice, or rather a Folly to expect such an Education should prove advantageous to them?

[*Intellectual pursuits are recommended*]

Let not Curiosity be totally extinguished in you, but direct it, with Discretion, to a good Object. Curiosity is an Inlet to Knowledge, and the more you extend it, the nearer you approach Sublimity: 'tis a Promptitude of Nature, which prepares the Way for Instruction, and ought not to be interrupted by Indifference or Sloth.

Nothing is more commendable for young People, than to employ their Time in solid Studies: The *Greek* and *Roman* Histories elevate the Soul, and give fresh Vigour to the Courage, by the great Actions contained in them; neither ought we to be unacquainted with the Annals of our own Country. I should also approve of a little Philosophy, if one were capable of it: it forms the Judgement, distinguishes your Ideas, and teaches you to think justly on the Nature of things. As for Morality, by reading *Pliny*, *Cicero*, and the rest, your Inclination for Virtue will be improved, and an agreeable Impression left on the Mind. The Habit of Vice corrects itself by the Example of so many Virtues, and rarely do you find those naturally prone to Ill, have any taste for this sort of Entertainment: they choose not to examine what accuses, and never fails to condemn them.

Concerning the Languages, though a Woman ought to content herself with speaking that of her own Country, yet I cannot oppose the Inclination one may have to learn *Latin*: 'tis the Language of the Church; it opens a way to all the Sciences; and makes you conversant with the best Authors of all Ages. Women willingly learn *Italian*, which appears to me a dangerous Study: 'tis the Language of Love; the Authors of that Country seem to have little Chastity; there reigns thro' all their Works a certain Play of Words; and an Imagination without Rule, quite opposite to a just Understanding.

Poetry may have its Inconveniences; though I should be very unwilling to oppose the reading of the fine Tragedies of *Corneille*; but often the best of them give you Lessons of *Virtue*, and leave behind the Impressions of *Vice*.

The reading of Romances is still far more pernicious: I would not wish you to make any great use of them; they very much corrupt the Mind. Romances being never founded on Truth, fire the Imagination, weaken Modesty, disorder the whole Heart, and how little soever a young Person is disposed to Tenderness, hasten and precipitate her Inclination. We must not augment the Charms, nor the Delusions of Love: the more it is softened in the Expression, the more dangerous it proves in the Consequence. I don't however forbid you this Amusement;

all Prohibitions wound Liberty, and increase the desire of it; but I advise you, as much as possible, to accustom yourself to solid Reading, which only can adorn the Mind and fortify the Heart: one cannot too much avoid that, which leaves Impressions difficult to be erased.

[*Self-reliance and independence of thought should be sought above all*]

Accustom yourself to exercise your Wit, and make more use of it, than of your Memory. We fill our Heads with other People's Ideas, and draw nothing from our own Fund. We think we have made a great Progress, in charging our Memories with various Passages of History; but that little contributes to the Perfection of Wit. You must often enter into Reflection: Wit extends and augments itself, by comparing the Difference of Ideas; but few Persons put this Maxim into practice.

To know how to think, is a Talent that's lasting within us. Neither Historical Passages, nor the Opinions of Philosophers will be able to defend you from a sudden Misfortune: you will not find yourself the more strengthened by them. Should any Affliction befall you, and you have recourse to *Seneca* and *Epictetus*, is it in the power of their Reason to afford you Consolation? Is it not rather the proper Function of your own? Be, therefore, your own Assistant: make provision in time of Tranquillity, against the Troubles you must expect to meet with; you'll be much better supported by your own Arguments, than by those of others.

If you could regulate your Imagination, and render it submissive to Truth and Reason, you would go a great way towards Perfection and Happiness. Women are commonly governed by their Imaginations, and as they are employed in nothing solid, nor burdened with the Care of their Fortune, or the Conduct of their Affairs, they deliver themselves up wholly to Pleasures. Shows, Dresses, Romances, and trifling Sentiments engross the Empire of their Minds. I know that to regulate the Fancy, you must take from the Pleasures: 'tis she is the source of them, and gives those Charms and Illusions which compose their Delight; but what Ills attend not such Pleasures? Fancy stands always between Truth and you: Reason dares not appear where she commands. We see not but as she pleases: the People she governs, are fully sensible of her power. It would be a happy Agreement, to render back her Pleasures, on condition, we might feel none of her Pains. To conclude, nothing is more opposite to Tranquillity, than a roving and too fiery Imagination.

Form within yourself a true Idea of things: judge not with the Multitude: be not biased by Opinion: extricate yourself from the Prejudices of Infancy. When you are involved in any Trouble, have recourse to the following Method; I have found consolation in it. Examine well the Motives of your Grief; separate the real from the imaginary Cause, and you'll often find little of the former remaining. Esteem things but as they are: We have more reason to complain of our own false Opinions, than of Fortune: they wound us more than the Accidents themselves.

Happiness consists in thinking well. We ought to pay a great Respect to common Opinion, when it regards Religion; but we should not comply with the Vulgar, on that which is called Morality, and the good Fortune of Life. I call Vulgar, all those who think meanly: the Court is full of them; the World speaks of nothing but Riches and Credit: we hear nothing but, *pursue your Designs; hasten to advance yourself.* And Wisdom says, *humble your Vanity for great things: make choice of an obscure, but tranquil Life: snatch yourself from Tumult: fly Hurry and Confusion.* The Recompense of Virtue is not in Fame, but in the Testimony of your own Conscience. Great Virtue can well dispense with the loss of a little Glory.

Take notice, that the greatest Art is to know how to find every thing in yourself. *I have learnt,* said an Ancient, *to be my Friend; so I shall never be alone.* You must reserve internal Remedies against the Troubles of Life, and Equivalents for the Good you depended on. Let your Retreat and Asylum be in your self: there you can always go and find reception. The World being thus become less necessary to you, your Inclinations for it will diminish in proportion. If you have not Solidity enough to depend on your self, you must depend on every body.

EXPLANATORY NOTES

3 *How can someone be Persian?*: in Montesquieu's *Persian Letters*, 28, Rica, a Persian travelling in France, comments on the French reaction of almost disbelieving astonishment at his exotic appearance: 'if someone in the circle happened to mention that I was Persian, I'd immediately hear a buzzing around me: "Oh! Oh! Monsieur is Persian? That's most extraordinary! How can someone be Persian?"' (All references to me *Persian Letters* are to the translation by Margaret Mauldon in the Oxford World's Classics edition.)

the soundness of their philosophy: Garcilaso de la Vega's *Royal Commentaries of the Incas* were translated into French by J. Baudoin in 1633, and often reprinted during the eighteenth century. A second translation, by T.-F. Dalibard, which was freer and gave a more thematic structure to Garcilaso's text, was published in 1744. Graffigny clearly read both of these versions.

to make them better known: Voltaire's *Alzire, or the Americans* was first performed in 1736. Set in Lima, it depicts the victory of two Inca lovers, Zamore and Alzire, over Gusman, a cruel Spanish governor. It ends, though, with the prospect of Zamore's conversion to Christianity.

4 *if the same hand had not rewritten them in our language*: Graffigny's decision to make her heroine the translator of her own *quipus* not only increases the plausibility of her narrative, but it also creates considerable thematic potential for her text. See note to p. 16.

the spirit of innocence which predominates in this work: this kind of observation is common in pseudo-translations of exotic works. Translation often took the form of 'domestication', in order to bridge the gap between the foreign (and, by implication, unrefined) text and the cultivated reader. Cf. the translator's preface to Montesquieu's *Persian Letters*: 'I have relieved the reader of as much of the Asian style as I could, and have saved him from a vast number of high-flown expressions, which would have bored him to tears.' Similar comments were made, too, with reference to the writings of women, whose apparent stylistic irregularities were often remarked on.

5 *would invade their kingdom and destroy their religion*: Graffigny follows Garcilaso quite closely here.

6 *the most humiliating worship*: Graffigny interprets the evidence differently from her source. In Garcilaso, stress falls on the political reasons for the Incas' reaction: subjugated by Atahualpa, violent usurper of the throne, they saw the Spanish at first as political liberators. Graffigny, however, focuses on their naivety.

7 *to such wretched disasters*: Montaigne's essay 'On Carriages' ('Des coches')
was first published in the second, expanded edition of his *Essays* in 1588.
A cultural relativist, he was fiercely critical of the Spanish conquest of the
New World.

fashioned with a skill unknown in Europe!: Garcilaso gives a detailed
account of Inca craftsmanship. See Appendix 1.

with displays of the utmost awe: Garcilaso gives this account of the veneration with which the name is held: 'Besides the Sun, whom they worshipped for the visible God, to whom they offered Sacrifice, and kept
Festivals . . . the *Incas*, who were Kings, and the *Amautas*, who were
Philosophers, proceeded by the mere light of Nature, to the knowledge of
the True Almighty God our Lord, Maker of Heaven and Earth, . . . which
they called by the Name of *Pachacamac*, and is a word compounded of
Pacha, which is the Universe, and *Camac*, which is the Soul; and is as
much as he that animates the World. . . . They never took this name into
their Mouths, but seldom, and when they did, it was with great Veneration,
bowing their Heads and Bodies, casting up their Eyes to Heaven, and then
down to the Earth, lifting their hands open as high as their Shoulders, and
kissing the Air, which were the common manifestations of Reverence and
Adorations, which were in use amongst the *Incas* and his People; these,
and such like demonstrations of Honour they used when they were forced
to pronounce the word *Pachacamac*' (Book II, ch. 2).

falling to the earth and destroying it by her fall: Garcilaso comments on the
Inca fear of eclipses, which they associate with the end of the world:
'When they observed the Moon begin to grow dark in her Eclipse, they
said, she was sick; and when she was totally obscured, that she was dead;
and then they feared, lest she should fall from Heaven, and overwhelm,
and kill them, and that the World should be entirely dissolved. With these
apprehensions, so soon as the Moon entered into Eclipse, they sounded
their Trumpets and Cornets, beat their Kettles, Cymbals, and all the
Instruments which could make noise and sound; they tied their Dogs in
Strings, and beat them till they cried and howled; saying that with their
Voices they called upon the Moon; who having received certain Services
from them, was very inclinable to hearken to their call; and that all these
varieties of Sounds together served to rouse and awaken her, being fallen
into a drowsiness and slumber, which her sickness had caused, and then
they made their Children cry and call *Mama Quilla*, or Mother-Moon,
Do not die, lest we all perish' (Book II, ch. 11).

8 *whose firearms they took to be instruments of thunder*: Garcilaso describes the
Inca respect for thunder in these terms: 'Thunder, and Lightning, and
Thunder-bolts they judged to be Servants of the Sun . . .; and in that
place or field where a Thunder-bolt happens to fall, they say that their
Father the Sun hath marked out that place as unfortunate, and accursed
to common use, and for that Reason they cover it with heaps of Stones,
that none may tread or trample on it . . . And whereas the Historians say,

that they esteemed Thunder and Lightning for Gods, it is a mistake; for they did indeed account those places for sacred, saying that their Gods had by Thunder, and Thunder-bolts, and Lightning marked out those places for their Worship . . . To these three they gave the common Name of *Yllapa;* and for the similitude hereunto they called all Fire-arms by the same word' (Book II, ch. 1).

who was a Virgin of the Sun: Graffigny is here edulcorating her source. Garcilaso notes that some Virgins of the Sun were raised to become the king's mistresses.

9 *halted the growth of incipient passions*: this is an accurate reference to J.-F. Bernard, A.-A. Bruzon de La Martinière, *et al.*, *Ceremonies and Religious Customs of Idolatrous Peoples*, 9 vols. (Amsterdam, 1723–43). One of the most fascinating anthologies of the early Enlightenment, the *Ceremonies* were an early attempt at the study of comparative religion.

as easily with Quipos as they could have been using writing: this is the view of Garcilaso. (See Appendix 1.) Other accounts attribute to *quipus* more sophisticated potential for communication, which is clearly at the heart of Graffigny's vision. Cf. the *Ceremonies and Religious Customs*, vi: 19, p. 73: 'with these cords, cordlets, knots and colours, they created as many different combinations as we have with the twenty three [*sic*] letters of our alphabet'. The exact expressive potential of the *quipus* was a matter of debate after the publication of this novel.

days devoted to such work were days of rejoicing: Garcilaso gives a detailed account of the devotion and community spirit of the Incas: 'The last Lands to be tilled were those of the King, to which, and to those of the Sun, the People in general applied themselves with great alacrity and rejoicing; they then at that work appeared in their best Cloths, full of Gold and Silver plates, and feathers on their Heads, in the same manner as they were dressed on their festival days. When they ploughed, which seemed the more pleasant work, they sung the Sonnets made in praise of their *Incas,* with which the time passed so easily, that their Labour seemed a Recreation, so great was their Devotion towards their God and their King' (Book V, ch. 2).

10 *that few nations can claim to have bettered them in this respect*: Graffigny's reference here is, for once, inaccurate. The *Introduction to the General and Political History of the Universe* by Samuel, Freiherr von Pufendorf, deals only with Europe. Bruzen de La Martinière wrote on the Americas in a continuation added to the seven-volume edition of 1738; this reference, however, is to be found in Garcilaso.

13 *the cries of your loving Zilia*: Aza is the only character in the novel addressed by Zilia in the familiar form of *tutoiement*. This particularity is inevitably lost in modern translation. Note, however, the extract from the eighteenth-century translation of the *Letters of Aza* in Appendix 2, which differentiates between 'thou' and 'you' to suggest fluctuating levels of intimacy.

15 *the panels of gold which adorned the walls*: Garcilaso gives a
detailed account of the rich decorations in the Temples of the Sun. See
Appendix 1.

dared to lay their sacrilegious hands on a daughter of the Sun: Zilia will be
subjected to an equivalent act of sacrilege in the apparently more civilized
context of a Paris drawing room (letter 14).

only meant to cross in the trappings of Royalty: Garcilaso does not specify
that the Virgins are destined for marriage with the Inca, and adopts a
more measured approach: 'It was likewise ordained, that a House should
be built for Virgins dedicated to the Sun, and that the same should be
possessed by none, but such as were of the Royal Blood and Family, and
supplied from thence, so soon as the number of the Royal Race was sufficiently increased. All which he ordained and appointed to his People, that
they should inviolably observe in grateful acknowledgment of the benefits
received; promising on the other side, that in reward thereof they might
expect perpetual additions of good to them from the blessings of the Sun
who had revealed these secrets, and sent his Messengers to the *Indians* to
instruct and guide them in the ways of Wisdom: all which matters, and
much more, the poor *Indians* believed, and by tradition have conserved to
these our days; it being the main point of their belief, that the *Inca* was a
Child of the Sun; of which and of such like fables they greatly boast'
(Book I, ch. 12).

16 *when they are retied in your hands*: Zilia's first *quipu* will be retied to form
Aza's reply, announced in the next letter. Following the logic of the narrative, this first letter must therefore be Zilia's later reconstruction of
events, and not the translation of an existing *quipu*.

17 *the humiliating honour of giving life to your descendants*: Zilia's sharp and
outspoken criticism of the subordinate role ascribed to married women
and mothers contrasts with Garcilaso's evocation of shared domestic
responsibility: 'The married Women always employed themselves at
home in spinning and weaving Wool in the cold Countries, and of Cottons
in the hot, every one spinning and making Cloths for themselves, their
Husbands, and Children; sewing was the least of their work, either for
Men or Women, for their thread was bad, and their needles worse . . .
Their Women took care of their Houses and Clothing, only the Men were
to provide the Hose, or Stockings, and Arms; . . . but as to the Labours
of the field both Men and Women, did jointly concur in their assistance
one of the other' (Book IV, ch. 13).

20 *I was your closest female relative*: the nature of Zilia's kinship with Aza was
of the utmost importance. Graffigny was very careful to keep the issue
blurred, as she notes in a letter to Devaux, 30 June 1747: 'Could I make
Aza the brother of Zilia without seeming to promote incest, and to promote it enthusiastically at that. . . . But what a crime that would be! I
would be cast out with the rubbish. I had to avoid that at all costs. I have
said nothing specific about it, readers can infer what they wish.'

I knew nothing of the laws of your empire: Garcilaso explains the custom thus: 'it was the most ancient Custom, and fundamental Law of those Kings, that the Prince, who was Heir, should marry with her that was his own Sister by Father and Mother, and she only was capable of being his Legitimate Wife, whom they called *Coya*, which is as much as Queen, or Empress; and the Eldest Son of these two was allowed for the true and lawful Heir of the Kingdom.

The Original of this Law and Custom was derived from the first *Inca, Manco Capac*, and his Wife, *Mama Occlo Huaco*, who feigning themselves to be the Children and descended from the Sun, and to be Brother and Sister, it was therefore concluded by all the *Indians*, (who perfectly believed this Story) that by the example of these two, the same Rule was to be observed in the succession of all future Ages; and this they confirmed by another Example of the Sun and Moon themselves, who being Brother and Sister, were joined in Marriage; and therefore this served for an undeniable Authority and Argument to prove the Legality of such a Marriage, by an instance so convincing, as that of these Deities: Yet for want of such Issue female, the Prince might then marry with the nearest of Kindred, such as his Cousin-German, or Aunt, who, for want of Heirs male, were capable of inheriting the Crown. . . . For want of Heirs male by the first Sister, the Prince might marry with the second, or third, and so on, until he met with one that produced such issue: and this Rite was punctually observed, and maintained to be legal, from the example of the Sun and Moon, and of the first *Inca* and his Sister, and from that Rule which enjoined them to keep the Streams of Royal Blood pure and unmixed, lest they should incur the impiety of mixing Divine Blood with Human Race' (Book IV, ch. 9).

24 *everything stirs my curiosity, and nothing can satisfy it*: Zilia is already showing signs of that intellectual curiosity which anticipates her critical role later in the novel. It is a quality promoted by Mme de Lambert in her *Advice from a Mother to her Daughter*. See Appendix 4.

25 *whom I take to be the Cacique, judging by his noble air*: Garcilaso points out the superior moral qualities of these leaders: 'Over every one of these Colonies he ordained a Chief, which they called *Curaca*, and is the same which *Cacique* signifies in the Language of *Cuba*, and *Sancto Domingo*, which is as much as a Ruler over Subjects: and these were chosen for their merits; for when any one was more gentle, affable, pious, ingenious and more zealous for the public good than others, he was presently advanced to Government, and to be an Instructor of the ignorant *Indians*, who obeyed him with as much reverence, as Children do their Parents' (Book I, ch. 12).

27 *he seems lost in deep contemplation*: Garcilaso's account of the feast of the Raymi draws attention to this moment of silent adoration: 'All things being well prepared, and disposed, on the Eve, the Feast being come, the *Inca*, accompanied with his Brethren, and every one ranked in his place and

order, according to his Quality and Age, went in procession by break of day into the Market-place of the City, which they call *Haucaypata,* where remaining bare-foot, they looked attentively toward the East in expectation of the Sun's Rising; when so soon as they saw him appear, they all immediately, casting themselves down on their breeches, (which is as much as with us on our knees) adored and worshipped him, and with open Arms and Hands lifted up, putting them before their Mouths, threw empty Kisses into the Air, and so worshipped with profound reverence, acknowledging the Sun for their God, and their natural Father' (Book VI, ch. 21). Graffigny clearly invites the reader, though, to see naivety in the heroine, who mistakes the early signs of Déterville's love for marks of religious devotion.

32 *we are no more aware of the passage of time than we are of the air which fills space*: some critics of the time were particularly scathing about this opening, scorning its 'metaphysical' quality. Fréron would comment, tartly: 'I have been told that there are but two men in France, whose superior intelligence has penetrated these mysterious veils.'

35 *see a human figure moving about in the most extensive space!*: according to Garcilaso, Incas did have a form of mirror, although not made of glass: 'The Looking-glasses which the Ladies of Quality used, were made of Burnished Copper; but the Men never used any, for that being esteemed a part of effeminacy, was also a disgrace, if not ignominy, to them' (Book II, ch. 16). Graffigny manipulates the historical evidence to permit this striking, allegorical moment.

   they have never been to Cuzco: Garcilaso draws attention to the geographical and cultural centrality of this city: 'The City of *Cozco* they esteemed the Point and Centre of all, and in the *Indian* Language is as much as the Navel of the Earth, for the Country of *Peru* being long and narrow, in fashion of a Man's body, and that City in the middle, it may aptly be termed the Navel of that Empire' (Book II, ch. 5).

39 *the object of tiresome looks wherever I went*: Graffigny rewrites an incident in Montesquieu's *Persian Letters,* 28, in which one of the Persian travellers, Rica, laments that he is totally ignored as soon as he abandons his national dress for French clothing; for Zilia, the attention of others is much more intrusive and unsettling.

41 *a paler star rises . . . when compared with the works of nature*: this passage is added by Graffigny to the edition of 1752.

43 *the wonders I was told of Quitu*: Garcilaso evokes the wonders of Quito, due to the inspired liberality of the Inca, Huayna-Capac: 'to oblige all that whole Country in general, so soon as the War was ended, he not only made them Aqueducts to refresh, and make fruitful their Soil; but also built a Temple there for the Sun, and a House for the Select Virgins, adorned with Riches, and other Embellishments agreeable to the quality of those Edifices: In performance of which, those *Indians* had great advantage, for their Country yielded much Gold, which they had digged for the

service of their own King, and much more afterwards for the use of the Prince *Huayna Capac*, because they found that they very much gratified his humour by Presents of that Metal' (Book VIII, ch. 7).

44 *it was not one of the least distressing*: this is a rare explicit indication of Zilia's retrospective look over her past.

48 *it is all most entertaining*: Garcilaso draws attention to the particular appeal of these items for the Incas: 'they had not yet arrived to the invention of Scissors, but with a sharp flint cut the Hair, as well as they were able; whence it was, that a certain young *Inca* said to one of my Schoolfellows, with whom he was taught to write and read, that *Had the* Spaniards *introduced no other invention amongst us than the use of Scissors, Looking-Glasses and Combs, they had deserved all that Gold and Silver which our Country produces*' (Book I, ch. 13).

51 *crimes which once disgraced, or oppressed, their fellow man*: in the *Persian Letters*, 26, Rica's account of a visit to the theatre gives prominence to the social games played out among the members of the audience. For Zilia, though, it is the moral attitudes of the nation, reflected in what is performed on stage, which are of more interest.

we require only models of virtue to make us virtuous: Garcilaso gives this account of plays written and performed by the Incas: 'The *Amautas*, who were Men of the best ingenuity amongst them, invented Comedies and Tragedies, which on their solemn Festivals they represented before their King, and the Lords of his Court. . . . The plot or argument of their Tragedies was to represent their military Exploits, and the Triumphs, Victories and Heroic Actions of their renowned Men; and the subject or design of their Comedies was to demonstrate the manner of good Husbandry in cultivating and manuring their Fields, and to show the management of domestic Affairs, with other familiar matters. So soon as the Comedy was ended, the Actors took their places according to their degrees and qualities. These Plays were not made up with interludes of obscene and dishonest farces, but such as were of serious entertainment, composed of grave and acute sentences, fitted to the place and auditory, by whom the Actors were commonly rewarded with Jewels and other Presents, according to their merit' (Book II, ch. 15).

53 *Céline showed the Cacique the paper she had received*: near the very end of this last letter composed originally in *quipus*, Zilia uses for the last time the Inca term *cacique* to refer to Déterville. His identity as a Frenchman, and her control of French, are henceforth implied.

56 *Their worship . . . leads me to think so*: this paragraph was quoted by Jaucourt in his *Encyclopédie* article *Nun (Religieuse)*.

so that her eldest son can become richer: the principle of primogeniture was widely criticized in writings of the time. The *Encyclopédie* contains a short but openly hostile article on the subject, referring to this comment of Montesquieu in the *Persian Letters*, 115: 'It is a spirit of vanity that led

Europeans to establish the unjust law of primogeniture, which is so det-
rimental to procreation in that it focuses the attentions of the father upon
a single child and turns his eyes away from all the others; this law forces
the father, in order to assure the fortune of one child, to oppose the estab-
lishment of several; in short, it does away with the equality of citizens,
which constitutes their greatest wealth.'

58 *needs which have not been adequately satisfied*: the contrast with Inca culture is at its most marked here. Garcilaso stresses the principle of benev-
olence which underlies the Inca's relationship with his subjects: 'The *Inca*
gave the third part of the Lands to the People; but it is not certain
whether this third part was so exactly measured, as to answer an equality
with that of the *Inca*: But this is sure, that great care was taken to render
unto every one a sufficient proportion of Land for his maintenance and
support. In this third part no particular person had such a right, as to be
able to give it away, or sell, or by any ways alienate it to another, because
the *Inca* was the sole Lord of the Fee; and the Original right was in him.
Of these Lands, new Divisions were made every year, according to the
increase or diminution of Families; so that the proportions of Lands were
in general ascertained, and the Divisions already laid out, that there
needed no great trouble farther therein' (Book V, ch. 5).

these unfortunates scarcely have enough to keep themselves alive: the absence
of beggars in Peru was also remarked on by Garcilaso: 'In the Year 1560,
when I departed from *Peru*, it was not the custom for any to beg,
or ask Alms; for where-ever I travelled in that Country, I never observed
any Man or Woman to beg' (Book V, ch. 9). Beggars were frequently
seen as one of the defining characteristics of Christian countries, to their
shame. The *Encyclopédie* article 'Indigent' contains this damning social
criticism: 'INDIGENT, adj. (*Gram.*) man who lacks the essentials in life,
living among his fellow creatures who enjoy all possible luxuries with a
display which is insulting to him. One of the most distressing consequences of bad administration is that it divides society into two classes of
people, those who live in affluence, and those who live in penury.
Indigence is not a vice, it is worse than that. The wicked man is accom-
modated; the indigent man is shunned. He is only to be seen with his
hand open and outstretched. There is not a single indigent man in
uncivilized nations.'

60 *to urge me to embrace it*: the desire to convert others to Christianity would
be satirized in the *Persian Letters*, 59, through the mouth of a priest: 'In
addition, a certain desire to persuade others to share our beliefs torments
us constantly and is, so to speak, integral to our profession. That is as
ridiculous as if Europeans were to labour, on behalf of mankind, to whiten
the faces of Africans.'

*any more incredible than the story of Mancocapa, and of the lake
Tisicaca*: Garcilaso evokes this story in his *Royal Commentaries*. See
Appendix 1.

61 *having taken several Vessels from the Spaniards*: in his review of the novel, Fréron would draw attention to the historical inaccuracy of this statement: Spain and France were not at war at the time of the Conquest of the Indies.

62 *my love for you could only ever be a crime*: this is one of the most striking contrasts of Inca and Christian culture; Graffigny uses the Inca perspective to bring out the moral fragility of Christianity, criticizing the very principles which it might see to be its strength. On the issue of incest, see notes to p. 20 above.

71 *let it be revered by peoples who worship virtue*: it is the possibility of a return to Peru with Aza which is sketched out by Lamarche-Courmont in his rewriting of the novel, *Letters of Aza*. See Appendix 2.

84 *Letter Twenty-Nine*: this was the first of the two letters added by Graffigny to the revised edition of 1752.

85 *all work in the service of extravagant display*: Graffigny echoes Rousseau's attack on luxury in his *Discourse on the Sciences and the Arts*, published in 1750: 'The abuse of time is a great evil, and yet much greater attend letters and arts, such as luxury descending like them from idleness and vanity. Luxury is seldom, very seldom seen, but in company with arts and sciences; but arts and sciences are never met without their constant attendant luxury. I know well enough that our philosophy, always fruitful in singular inventions, will maintain, against the experience of all ages, that luxury forms the splendour of states: but if we pass by the necessity of sumptuary laws, will that philosophy dare affirm that good manners are not essential to the duration of empires, and that luxury is not diametrically opposite to good manners? Let luxury be the certain sign of riches, let it also, if you will, be a means to multiply them: what can be concluded from this paradox so worthy of our days? And what shall become of virtue when we are encouraged to grow rich at any rate? Ancient politicians always conversed on manners and virtue, the moderns only of commerce and money . . . mankind are appraised, like a herd of cattle, according to them a man is worth no more than what he consumes in his commonwealth.'

87 *concern without affection*: the emptiness of polite social exchange is the object of much criticism in the mid-eighteenth century, not least by Rousseau in his *Discourse on the Sciences and the Arts*: 'Friendships are insincere, esteem is not real, and confidence is ill founded; suspicions, jealousies, fears, coolnesses, reserve, hatred, and treasons, are hid under the uniform veil of perfidious politeness, under that boasted civility which we owe to the vast discoveries of our age.'

88 *the feelings behind them are nowhere to be seen*: Zilia demonstrates here the kind of perceptiveness which Rousseau thought would be absent from a stranger visiting France in the present day. Cf. his *Discourse on the Sciences and the Arts*: 'if the inhabitant of some far distant region would

form an idea of our European manners on the condition in which the sciences are amongst us, on the perfection of our arts, on the decency of our public diversions, on the politeness of our behaviour, on the affability of our conversations, on our perpetual demonstration of good will to each other, and on that tumultuous concourse of men of all ages, of all conditions, who, from sun rise to sun set, seem eternally employed in obliging one another; would not this stranger conclude our manners to be the exact reverse of what they really are? Where we see no effect, 'tis vain to seek for a cause; but here the effect is visible, the depravation palpable; our minds have been corrupted in proportion as our arts and sciences have made advances toward their perfection.'

88 *concealing reason, whenever one is obliged to pronounce it*: significantly, this is the only footnote reference to a contemporary text; Duclos's *Considerations* were published in 1751. The reference implies the identity of Zilia as a modern and cultivated French heroine. In most printings of the novel, though, the footnote was removed.

94 *never for the qualities of one's soul*: in Peru, tributes were much more substantial and associated with common endeavour; the contrast with the emptiness of French social display could not be more striking. Cf. Garcilaso: 'The chiefest part of their Tribute did consist in their labour, which was to cultivate and manure the Lands belonging to the Sun, and to the *Inca*, and also to gather and reap the Fruits, and lay them up in the King's Barns . . . Besides this Tribute of Labour which the *Indians* bestowed on the Lands of the Sun, and the *Inca*, and of the gathering in their Fruit; the second Tribute required was a contribution towards the Clothing, Shoes and Arms of the Soldiery, as also for the poor and needy, who by reason of Age, or want of Health, were not able to labour and provide for themselves' (Book V, chs. 5 and 6).

97 *if he refuses to take such cruel vengeance*: Montesquieu's ironic attack on duels in the *Persian Letters*, 88, focuses on the lack of a necessary correlation between skill in fighting and moral authority: 'This fashion of settling differences was rather ill conceived; for it does not follow, because one man is more adroit or stronger than another, that his reasons are the best.'

Letter Thirty-Four: this was the second of the two letters added by Graffigny to the revised edition of 1752. By focusing on the inadequate education offered to girls and the plight of women in society, it underlines the critical dimension of the novel, read by many as a (mere) tale of exotic love.

98 *certain barbarous nations who do not even credit them with one*: in the *Persian Letters*, 135, Zuléma comments on a similar attitude among the Jews: 'there is nothing that has not been done to degrade our sex; there is even a people you can find spread throughout Persia which claims, on the authority of its sacred writings, that we have no soul. These pernicious opinions have no basis other than the pride of men, who wish to extend their superiority beyond their life.'

100 *more knowledgeable than they are in this respect*: Graffigny brings together the two underlying themes of her novel: a woman in society experiences the same sense of alienation as the Peruvian in a foreign land; neither has the means to communicate adequately, neither is taken seriously. Zilia both observes and embodies this double estrangement.

102 *it is wives alone who are bound by them*: we might detect echoes here of the author's own wretched marriage to a profligate and violent husband.

103 *desolation to which she is subjected in all sorts of forms?*: Montesquieu discusses the same subject in his *Persian Letters*, 112, commenting particularly on the cost to society of loveless (and childless) marriages: 'all they see, in the disadvantages of marriage, is their duration for, as it were, eternity; from this come dislike, discord, and contempt, and posterity suffers. Couples married for barely three years will already be neglecting the essential, and spend the next thirty at arm's length from one another.' Graffigny focuses more clearly on the plight of women.

the mistress of the house and her servants were all invisible: Céline's taste in reading is clearly indicated here; she prefers this kind of entertaining tale to the commentaries on contemporary manners which Zilia reads and takes inspiration from.

	Eirik the Red and Other Icelandic Sagas
	The Kalevala
	The Poetic Edda
LUDOVICO ARIOSTO	Orlando Furioso
GIOVANNI BOCCACCIO	The Decameron
GEORG BÜCHNER	Danton's Death, Leonce and Lena, and Woyzeck
LUIS VAZ DE CAMÕES	The Lusiads
MIGUEL DE CERVANTES	Don Quixote Exemplary Stories
CARLO COLLODI	The Adventures of Pinocchio
DANTE ALIGHIERI	The Divine Comedy Vita Nuova
LOPE DE VEGA	Three Major Plays
J. W. VON GOETHE	Elective Affinities Erotic Poems Faust: Part One and Part Two The Flight to Italy
JACOB and WILHELM GRIMM	Selected Tales
E. T. A. HOFFMANN	The Golden Pot and Other Tales
HENRIK IBSEN	An Enemy of the People, The Wild Duck, Rosmersholm Four Major Plays Peer Gynt
LEONARDO DA VINCI	Selections from the Notebooks
FEDERICO GARCIA LORCA	Four Major Plays
MICHELANGELO BUONARROTI	Life, Letters, and Poetry

	Late Victorian Gothic Tales
JANE AUSTEN	Emma
	Mansfield Park
	Persuasion
	Pride and Prejudice
	Selected Letters
	Sense and Sensibility
MRS BEETON	Book of Household Management
MARY ELIZABETH BRADDON	Lady Audley's Secret
ANNE BRONTË	The Tenant of Wildfell Hall
CHARLOTTE BRONTË	Jane Eyre
	Shirley
	Villette
EMILY BRONTË	Wuthering Heights
ROBERT BROWNING	The Major Works
JOHN CLARE	The Major Works
SAMUEL TAYLOR COLERIDGE	The Major Works
WILKIE COLLINS	The Moonstone
	No Name
	The Woman in White
CHARLES DARWIN	The Origin of Species
THOMAS DE QUINCEY	The Confessions of an English Opium-Eater
	On Murder
CHARLES DICKENS	The Adventures of Oliver Twist
	Barnaby Rudge
	Bleak House
	David Copperfield
	Great Expectations
	Nicholas Nickleby
	The Old Curiosity Shop
	Our Mutual Friend
	The Pickwick Papers

Travel Writing 1700–1830

Women's Writing 1778–1838

WILLIAM BECKFORD — Vathek

JAMES BOSWELL — Life of Johnson

FRANCES BURNEY — Camilla
Cecilia
Evelina
The Wanderer

LORD CHESTERFIELD — Lord Chesterfield's Letters

JOHN CLELAND — Memoirs of a Woman of Pleasure

DANIEL DEFOE — A Journal of the Plague Year
Moll Flanders
Robinson Crusoe
Roxana

HENRY FIELDING — Jonathan Wild
Joseph Andrews and Shamela
Tom Jones

WILLIAM GODWIN — Caleb Williams

OLIVER GOLDSMITH — The Vicar of Wakefield

MARY HAYS — Memoirs of Emma Courtney

ELIZABETH INCHBALD — A Simple Story

SAMUEL JOHNSON — The History of Rasselas
The Major Works

CHARLOTTE LENNOX — The Female Quixote

MATTHEW LEWIS — Journal of a West India Proprietor
The Monk

HENRY MACKENZIE — The Man of Feeling